SPRINGFIELD THE NOVEL

SPRINGFIELD

the novel

■

WILLIAM MORRIS

Westphalia Press
An Imprint of the Policy Studies Organization
Washington, DC
2016

Westphalia Press
An imprint of Policy Studies Organization
1527 New Hampshire Ave., NW
Washington, D.C. 20036
info@ipsonet.org

ISBN-10: 1-63391-385-6
ISBN-13: 978-1-63391-385-1

Cover and interior design by Jeffrey Barnes
jbarnesbook.design

Daniel Gutierrez-Sandoval, Executive Director
PSO and Westphalia Press

Updated material and comments on this edition
can be found at the Westphalia Press website:
www.westphaliapress.org

Dedication to:

Ambassador Mark G Hambley, a good friend whose generosity is legendary and indeed whose kindness knows no bounds

PRESCRIPT

Springfield, Massachusetts: A gem of a small city, population around 150,000, nestled on a sweep of the Connecticut River in the heart of the Pioneer Valley. Often called "The City of Firsts," it is the first Springfield of America, settled in 1636 by Pilgrims from England and so named by one of them for his hometown in County Essex in the "old country."

This is the first Springfield of the 41 listed by the U.S. Post Office as the most common place name for a city, town, township or borough in the country, including other well-known ones in Illinois, Virginia, and Missouri.

After an increasing inflow of English Protestants gradually displaced indigenous Agawam, Nipmuc, and Mohawk Indians through conflict and smallpox during the seventeenth century, the population of the Pioneer Valley was boosted, first, by successive waves of French Canadian, Irish, Italian, and Polish Catholics and, later, by other European immigrants, African-Americans, and Latinos of every stripe who provided the skilled work-force who industrialized the city.

The city is now home to small but vibrant communities of Vietnamese, Russians, and pockets of refugees from wars and trauma in Somalia, Haiti, and the Middle East. A city where every neighborhood has its requisite Roman Catholic Church and where Greeks, Russians, Poles, Lebanese Maronite Catholics, and Armenians—not to mention protestant congregations of every variety—populated churches, synagogues, and mosques every week, thereby completing the religious mosaic which represents the Springfield and the America of today.

It was here in 1777 that George Washington lobbed an artillery shell from a barge moored on the Connecticut River up over the town and founded the nation's first armory some 100 yards beyond its reach in the heights above. An armory which made the city famous for its famous Springfield rifles, its introduction of exchangeable parts manufacturing, of the assembly line, and of the hourly wage.

It was in Springfield where one Thomas Jefferson is alleged to have conducted a dig for Indian artifacts on the very bluff on Long Hill wherein much of our story takes place. It is a city visited by the good and the great of years past, including both Roosevelts and both Tafts, plus JFK, Martin Luther King, and a long list of the literati, social, and political figures of the day.

Springfield was a city of craftsmen and inventors who manufactured Smith and Wesson handguns, buggies, cars, trolleys, and other forms of transport from the first gasoline-powered automobile made in the U.S., the Duryea; to the earliest motorcycle, the revered Indian; to the exquisitely fashioned, left-hand drive Rolls Royce automobiles, all of which were assembled in Springfield during the halcyon years of the 1920s.

It was also the home of the Wasson Manufacturing Company which made railway passenger coaches and streetcars, including the one which carried the body of President Abraham Lincoln on its sad progress from Washington, D.C. to Springfield, Illinois, in 1865 and the first coaches for the Transcontinental Railway in 1867.

A city of sports and recreation, from the invention of basketball by a teacher at Springfield College to the first formally endorsed set of golf clubs designed by the one and only Bobby Jones in the midst of the Great Depression of the 1930s. A city whose proud exploits are recorded in brilliant detail in the Lyman and Merrie Wood Museum of Springfield History, one of five thriving museums in the Quadrangle which are the envy of cities thrice its size.

A city whose name has become associated, in popular culture, with the Simpsons cartoon series, but whose streets, factories, parks, and houses are better remembered in the books of Theodor Seuss Geisel, a native son, who, writing under the pseudonym of Dr. Seuss, crafted a series of children's books whose Horton, Grinch, Lorax, and Cat-in-the-Hat characters are memorialized in a National Sculpture Garden and museum likewise located at the Quadrangle.

Springfield has also earned a second nickname as "The City of Homes." From the industry which made it the workshop of America through much of its lifetime, neighborhoods grew up to house both the proprietors and their workers. Although the passage of time has destroyed many of the older commercial buildings, houses, and mansions, a total of 16 areas of the city have been designated historic districts, most by virtue of the Victorian, Queen Anne, Tudor, Gothic, Federal, and Italianate styles of housing and commercial stock retained within each.

One such neighborhood is Forest Park Heights wherein much of our story takes place. Forest Park takes its name from the marvelous 750-acre expanse of gardens and wooded park land designed by Frederick Law Olmsted's company, which borders a particularly attractive collection of Victorian-era houses and stately homes that line the length of Longhill Street overlooking both the Connecticut River and the Pioneer Valley below.

The people described in this story are all imaginary. Any events or happenings recorded are merely figments of a fertile imagination. Many of the streets and some of the places depicted are real but only for the purposes of telling a story, for unraveling a tale of life, of murder, of deceit and of love, both requited and not.

7

PART ONE

in the beginning

CHAPTER ONE: AUGUST

May the words of my mouth and the meditations of my heart be acceptable in Your sight, O Lord, my strength and my Redeemer.

Psalm 19:14

Saturday 11th August: It was a more than beautiful day. Bright warming sunlight glinted through the stained glass windows that loomed large behind the altar of the Church of Our Lady of Perpetual Help in Sumner, Springfield, Mass. This great hall of a church always lifted his spirits. He looked at the altar, pristine and unadorned, whilst Christ crucified, a celebration of love, hung from the rafters at the East end of the Church, as if suspended in space. He felt as though resurrected himself, just through being here. This church was a basilica, one of just six in America, which, in Catholic terminology, meant it had been dedicated by a Pope. The great slab of an altar was cut from marble and sentinelled by four massive candles. Directly behind was an organ, built modern style, its pipes stretched wide against the wall flanked to the right by brilliant red-blue stained glass bearing a huge Alpha–Omega inscription, and to the left by gleaming yellow-blue glass and a True Vine inscription. Quite magnificent. The confessionals were at the back.

Seb made his way to the back of the church where a few souls waited, his responsibility this day. Then his mood jarred, awkward, unbidden.

Poor Angie. Like one of Pavlov's dogs, his response was automatic. The thought of her again summoned anger. He saw her now, the slight curve of her smile ephemeral in his mind's eye, bettering a da Vinci. She had a nose which was a little large, the product of an Italian bloodline but not unattractive. And he liked her hands. Hands fit for the Queen of Heaven. Hands to pray with. They were ivory in his remembrance, like something from a long gone era, ivory and small but long-fingered, hands worthy of a violinist.

Father Sebastian grunted softly and narrowed his dark brown eyes. Sweet Mary Mother of God; why was this problem affecting him so? He felt a sense of shame. Not guilt. Like most men, Father David Sebastian had little understanding of guilt. He regarded guilt as a uniquely female emotion. That revisiting and dwelling on sin was something Father Sebastian understood, as a man understands what it is to walk on the moon. He observed it, even marveled at it, but it was not part of his personal universe.

What Father Sebastian was feeling was profoundly different. Shame. Abiding shame is a thing of now. Hideously real whilst it stays with you. But sooner or later it goes and for men guilt, that tangible revisiting of shame, is unusual. Father Sebastian felt shame at his anger and, though he scarce dared confess it, shame at the way he was allowing himself to think of poor Angie.

Priests had their ways of dealing with these things of course. Thinking of women as objects, dehumanizing them, was effective but inevitably disabling. Father Sebastian had tried and rejected that path. The imitation of Christ was a better way, becoming like Jesus as best you could, filling your mind with prayer and selfless love. But even that path was imperfect, for Christ himself was tempted as other men. Fully, else his trial in the wilderness had been mere sham. No, Jesus was tempted indeed but dealt with it as only the God-man could. How tempted? More so, no doubt, than mortal man, when He, God incarnate, walked with the Magdalene. But He mastered sin and rejected it. Father Sebastian recognized that he himself was

4

built of frailer stuff. And with that recognition came shame. But not too much of it. He too was as God made him and he had his own remedy, which was to avoid being alone with a woman except in the sacred space that was the confessional.

So why this shame over Angie? Was she his Magdalene? The corner of his mouth curled into the beginnings of a smile as he set aside the thought like an unwanted supper. He had heard the scrape of the curtain rings on the rail. Another soul in need of comfort. At the sound of the formulaic words he shook himself gratefully, like a dog doused in water on a hot day, and turned to listen, his eyes narrow again, alert. "Forgive me Father, for I have sinned ..."

Father Sebastian's chin twitched and his face became gloomy. He sighed inwardly. Mary Young. He knew that urgent, pleading voice.

He knew most of his parishioners by voice but Mrs Mary Young of the big house, 200 Longhill, she he knew all too well. He was fond of her in his way. Did Mary Young know what it was to sin? To really sin? Father Sebastian had his doubts.

Practically perfect, like a latter-day Mary Poppins, she was an exemplar to the youth of the parish. She actually reminded him of Julie Andrews. She even looked a little like Maria from the Sound of Music. Was Julie Andrews subject to the corruption that was, in his experience, the norm amongst the women that dragged the curtain aside to talk to him of their dark secrets— of the desires that they had shaped and woven into the fabric of their reality? No not Julie Andrews, not the Blessed Mary ever Virgin, and most certainly not Mrs Mary Young with her china-blue eyes and round, fair face. Yet here she was, back again, to confess once more, as she did each month that passed—to confess to trivia—to yet again confess to nothing—whereas those genuine reprobates more worthy of absolution he was likely to see once a year at best.

What was she going to confess to now? Had she said "shit" when she dropped the pasta? Or failed to remember her evening prayers last Thursday week? Father Sebastian slapped himself on the wrist, or rather he did the mental equivalent, in virtual semblance of self-reproach and allowed himself a wry smile, then settled in to listen. It was what he was there for, after all.

2.

Surely goodness and mercy shall follow me all the days of my life; and I shall dwell in the house of the Lord forever.

Psalm 23:6

Monday 13th August: Father Sebastian was strolling with his hands in his pockets along the section of bike path between Springfield's landmark Basketball Hall of Fame and the Julia Buxton Bridge. Not that it was called that. Locals had long forgotten the first female President of the Chamber of Commerce after whom the bridge was named. To them it was just "South End Bridge," named for its geography and nothing more. He was listening as he walked the recently anointed bike path at the edge of the mighty Connecticut River, a river that runs some 450 miles from the Canadian border down to Long Island Sound.

And hereabouts there was plenty to hear. This was no quiet space. Close by, the Amtrak train for New York bellowed the way trains do in America, its whistle an exercise in throaty harmony. A cacophony surrounded him. The thrum of the cicada competed with the hum of the traffic heading toward the bridge for Agawam, Southwick, and all points West. From here had he looked he could have seen the sweep of the water as it curled under the green crisscross of boxed metalwork that supported each section of the massive bridge, laid pier to pier like pieces from a giant children's toy. But he was looking at none of that.

Angie had asked to meet him here, indeed had said it was important that they meet alone. And he had agreed. Somehow she had threaded her way down through the undergrowth from her house up at 185 Longhill. Not easy. Ash jostled with oak, sumac, birch, and the occasional maple, cluttering the escarpment above the broad sweep of the Connecticut. The pathway was ill-kept and blocked here and there by insurgent grasses, fallen rock, and broken boughs. And then was the culvert under the highway and the railroad tracks to be navigated.

Of course, it wasn't always like this, Father Sebastian mused. In the glory days of Springfield between 1875 and 1930, the long line of large homes on Longhill Street, overlooking the Connecticut River or Pioneer Valley as some would prefer, had lawns and terraced gardens which stretched from the heights above down to Columbus Avenue and the riverfront. The great burghers of the city had lived in these magnificent houses—the Dickinsons, the Chapins, the Lewises, the Gilberts, the Kilroys, and the Bugbees—and now successor entrepreneurs, politicians, and even a diplomat found themselves ensconced in their place.

The rights of eminent domain had first taken some of the land for the railroad and then another large swathe for the highway. Many of the terraced gardens had gone to seed with the omni-present knotweed giving birth to sumac and other "junk" trees fighting the creeper-laden native oak, ash, beech, and maple for places on the hillside.

Still, some of the recent owners—Angie and her husband Baxter among them—had maintained small, private tea houses on lower terraces and pathways down to the river front to the ill-used but nonetheless attractive bike path which squeezed itself between the railroad tracks and the mighty river.

It was here where Angie, with her dog, Titus, a huge golden retriever with more than a little mongrel in him and the build of a Great Dane, pacing at her side, found Father Sebastian waiting patiently for her arrival.

There was something of that lush, full summer smell about that rich green, dark, delicious smell. And the sky was blue and the sun was up. There was a balmy soft breeze. It was a pretty day. The kind of day only God could have made.

And the whites of Angie's slate-blue eyes were red from cry-

8

ing. But she wasn't crying now. Father Sebastian stared at the ground as she spoke to him. They were walking abreast, he and her, the dog between them an unwitting but effective chaperon.

They were dodging the subject of course. Angie needed that; to talk about other things; to prepare herself; and Seb didn't mind.

They'd been talking at a tangent—about Afghanistan. "Seems to me," she was saying, "That this world will never get better. We just go on and on killing one another, hunting one another, hating one another. What we need is for global warming to spiral so severely out of control that the whole species nearly dies out. Then, perhaps at last we may just maybe learn to love." She bit her lower lip waiting nervously lest he want to say something.

Seb glanced sideways at her but didn't respond. He knew when to listen. They continued to walk side by side, the dog no longer between them but sniffing at the bushes and fallen logs as he lollopped along ahead.

"Why is it Seb?" She presumed to shorten his name, a familiarity that he'd encouraged not just in her but in many of his closer parishioners. He favored the West European practice by which priests used their Christian names, thus Father Larry, Padre Pio, Mother Teresa. His colleagues favored the Germanic, Irish-American approach whereby surnames were used as with Father Brown or Pastor Niemoler. Father David Sebastian's pragmatic preference was the clumsy but endearing compromise by which some were asked to call him Seb.

"In High School they'd have called him Father What-a-Waste," Angie thought in irreverent acknowledgment of the fact that he was handsome.

Angie continued, "Why is it that Jesus says to turn the other cheek? Why? Are we supposed to endure? Is that approach seriously expected to bring peace on earth?"

"Changing tack in mid-stream as only a woman can," thought Seb, quite unconscious of the fact that the thought itself betrayed a chauvinist streak. The church gossip was that her husband beat her. Seb wondered if that was where this was leading. He glanced again at this forty-year-old woman, five years his junior. Her lush, golden hair bobbed in the soft balmy breeze of this August afternoon. It was a hot day but not as hot as it might have been. The sky was a heavy pastel blue. A hot day but not oppressive. Sleep naked with just a sheet sort of hot. And this was afternoon. Late afternoon with clouds adrift like battleships, but not so many there wasn't sky aplenty. That liquid blue sky that speaks of the best side of eternity, reaching out earthward like a hoped for embrace. The ancients believed that night was when the sky reached down and wrapped its arms around the earth leaving no space for the sun. In Pharaonic Egypt the sky was the woman and the earth the man. But in the Western world, vice versa, the earth ever feminine. And here in Springfield out beyond Agawam, the sky touches the earth at the horizon and holds fast, and there's comfort in that certainty, as the balm of the breeze softens away the hum of the traffic and reminds you of a time when things might have been simpler but in reality probably weren't. And it was hot. Hot enough to wear a hat. Hot so you'd enjoy sitting in the garden if you sat in the shade. The kind of heat to bathe in, not to resent. That kind of hot. Seb turned back to the path, eyes down, cutting Angie's disturbing image from his field of vision, and answered her, and in so doing tried to address her hidden agenda. "Angela. Christ told us to turn the other cheek but he did not mean by that that we should seek out violence by remaining in the path of aggression. We are to avoid violence if we can. Christ did not seek the cross. He accepted it because it became inevitable ..." He realized that he sounded hollow, pompous even.

Angie looked up at him, studying his averted face and managing a smile; but there was a feint note of irritation in her voice. "And should I therefore draw the inference that you are suggesting that I should divorce Baxter?"

Baxter Merrill, proprietor of Merrill Manufacturing, was one of the great and good of Springfield's Catholic establishment.

They had stopped walking. Seb moved uncomfortably. "No Angela. That's not what I meant. I know you've been having trouble. Maybe counseling would help. We could arrange for both of you to meet the Catholic Marriage Guidance Council. Doing nothing is not an option."

Angie scowled. "Damned right it's not Father Seb ..." For emphasis Angie pulled her shirt from her slacks and started to lift it towards her neck.

Father Sebastian reached out a hand, stopping her. He could see the red–blue–black of the wheals on her side below the ribs. He was stunned. "Have you thought of a separation Angie, of leaving him for a time?"

But now it was Angie's turn to be contrary. "I can't Seb. You don't know what it would do to him. He's under pressure at work. It's me that drives him over the edge. Anyway I love him really. I can't leave him."

Sebastian sighed, frustrated by her stereotypical response. "We'll work this out Angela," he said. And as he said that he realized he was doing what a priest never should—taking sides. It was impossible not to sometimes, especially in circumstances like these. He watched the tears well back into Angie's eyes and, despite himself, he compounded his error, reaching out a hand to comfort her. And he said, "Really Angie, I promise, we will work this out."

For answer Angie stooped to stroke Titus, the tears at last spilling from her eyes. But she didn't brush them away. As if in pride she allowed them to run free onto her wan cheeks as she bent her knees and crouched there a while, continuing to stroke the dog, then finally she looked up at Father Sebastian. "We'd better Seb. Or else—even though I love Baxter with all my heart—I'll kill him someday soon. I will Seb. I swear."

3.

The soul who sins shall die. The son shall not bear the guilt of the father, nor the father bear the guilt of the son. The righteousness of the righteous shall be upon himself, and the wickedness of the wicked shall be upon himself.

Ezekiel 18:20

Monday 13th August: Mrs Mary Young, wife of Schools Superintendant Mr Robert Young of 200 Longhill, Springfield, Massachusetts, looked back at her white boarded mansion. The huge house rode the bluff like a great ocean liner cutting a swathe through the enfolding green. It was a grand home to have, like something from a Southern state, ripped out of place and time. Six white and proud two-story columns supported a bow-shaped porch worthy of a plantation, above which fluttered the ever-present Stars and Stripes. She rounded her home and stepped out onto the sidewalk at 5:45 p.m. shortly before her husband was due back. She was wearing a white sundress, the kind of thing Marilyn Monroe wore when she sang to Kennedy; that plus a broad-brimmed white hat. She looked a picture. Like some latter day Scarlet O'Hara stepping out from Tara, she strolled almost wistfully down Longhill.

She crossed the road and walked on past the exit to Forest Park, bequeathed to the good citizens of Springfield by Everett H. Barney, the inventor of the modern ice skate, who has his mausoleum therein.

It was a glorious afternoon. The liquid sun was just easing that little bit lower in the sky but it was still well warm. The vestige of the day was the hottest part here in Springfield's summers, and the cool crept in late from whatever dark place it was hiding in some other but not here slice of the globe. Here the warmth still eased into Mary Young's flesh, melting away the aches that the day had compounded on her weary frame but failing, this time, to do the same for her much broken mind. Somewhere a bird chirped. As ever the traffic thrummed along with the cicada. It was summer in full pelt with no hint yet of fall. The earth still kept her spring fresh tresses, lush redolent of youth and hope and better days to come—but not for Mary. All that and a sky soft pastel painted by a gentle hand, deep and wide enough to lose your heart in.

She hung her head but on she ambled, crossing back again to join the slip road where Longhill met Columbus Avenue, where it led down to Interstate 91, that great highway that runs from New Haven all the way up to the little town of Stanstead in Eastern Quebec. The I-91 should by rights be on the other side of the river. It was as far as Suffield, Connecticut, where it crossed to the Springfield side because the Republican Mayor of Suffield had appealed to a Republican President to move the highway to the East Bank of the river and avoid blighting his home town. Springfield, as a consequence, was blighted instead.

But none of that much concerned Mary Young at the moment. She just kept walking. Here there was no sidewalk and the cars whipped past her, some honking angrily. No one stopped.

Had someone stopped, things could have been different. But they were heading home. A few wound their windows down to shout, "Hey Lady, get the hell out of here," or slightly more colorful words to that effect. But no one stopped.

And, like Tennyson's mirror doomed mad woman of Shallot, on she wandered, up the ramp to the South End Bridge and past the plaque in memory of the long forgotten Julia B Buxton in whose honor the bridge had been dedicated in 1979, a full quarter-century after its construction. Here there was sidewalk again. Here she was less remarkable.

The traffic thrums its way over South End Bridge in an un-ending stream with a sound which, from a distance, is like the buzzing of many bees. Close up it's just a roar.

On the Agawam side the evergreens are rare, and the gentler pastels of the deciduous trees soften the vista so much that the brightest green was in the highway signs flagging routes "5" and "57" to places too far distant to matter.

It was from Agawam that the Indians had come who'd swooped down the hill and burned the City of Springfield in 1637. Mary had been in Agawam earlier. She liked shopping there. People were polite. It was already mid-August but she'd noticed the 4th of July flags were still up. They'd been up since 30th May for Memorial Day. Time they took them down, she'd thought. It offended her sense of order. She liked things to be tidy. She looked over toward Agawam as she stepped onto the bridge. Close in by the river a clutter of little houses in pastel shades of white and yellow arrayed themselves untidily. Closer in still there was a clutter of scrap and boats and timber and the like that betrayed both activity and neglect.

The Connecticut is clean enough to swim in now, so they say. It used not to be but Springfield's mayor has signed up with the environmentalists because he's been told he should.

Mary had been saving sleeping pills, Halcion. She had fourteen of them set aside. Enough. And now they'd be wasted. But she didn't really trust sleeping pills. All her friends took them. She knew all the names. Lunesta, Rozerem, Sonata or Ambien, the last of which seemed to be the most popular. They took prescription orders of 14 or 30 or 60 pills at a time. Trouble is, take too many and you might be sick; too few, and you might wake up. And she had responsibilities that would not be well served by a failed suicide attempt.

She thought of the children, but she'd seen the last through university. Jenny, the oldest, had graduated in May and was already engaged to a promising medical student from Boston. Robert, Jr. was busy with his new career and had moved to New York. Both kids were launched on new paths. They didn't need her now.

14

Her beautiful china-blue eyes were moist. She looked down at the swirling waters of the Connecticut. It wasn't very deep. It occurred to her that the Memorial Bridge upstream a bit would have been better, more dignified. But that was too long a walk.

She jerked her head up to look at the horizon. The sun was just beginning to set and the sky was streaked an exquisite rose red. Normally she'd be mixing a martini about now for Bob, and a smaller one for herself, and they'd share them in the garden this time of year. Not today though. "Poor Bob," she thought. She had left no note. She so wanted to but couldn't. Not with the children. A note provided too much certainty. The children would need the ambiguity, or so she reasoned, of a death by misadventure. Not a confirmed suicide. No, that would not do. It was another reason she had not chosen the pills.

She thought that could she but never have been born she'd have been happier. The inconsistency escaped her. The thought made her feel a traitor to life and saddened her a little. It hadn't all been bad though. There had been astounding moments of love, even in times of catastrophe. It must always be a little difficult to die, she thought, whether young or old. The end is no less just for a long life than a short one. The appalling cruelty of life at times horrified her. But death wasn't really cruel. Stop the world a moment. There you have it. That is death. And the rest is an experiment. There is no cruelty in it. Not in death. She was unafraid of death. To rest though. That was inviting. So very beautiful to think on. She wasn't set on heaven. She was not even sure she believed in God. Oblivion would be enough for her. Just for it all to end. To be able to rest. Better that way. She had spent too much time working to resolve her own problems—only to accept answers that she had not hoped for. That was what was really sad.

She wanted to cross to the downstream side of the bridge. The view was prettier. But the traffic was heavy and she didn't want the indignity of trying to dodge the cars so she stayed on the

15

upstream side. Here she could see the little wooded creek where the Agawam River had its confluence with the Connecticut. There had been a ferry there from Pynchon Point before ever there was a bridge. They had changed the name of the Agawam now. Called it the Westfield. Why had they done that she wondered?

Despite the constant buzz of traffic, no one noticed Mary hitch her skirt up and climb to the far side of the railing. She wasn't thinking clearly. Here at South End there were big concrete piers for bridge foundations. They needed avoiding. Even so, she closed her eyes when she jumped, like she had done when Bob had taken her for a ride in the front car of the "Bizarro" Roller Coaster at the nearby Six Flags New England Amusement Park. That had not been kind. He'd known she was scared of heights.

So her eyes were closed as she hit her head at the edge of the concrete pier before her lifeless body slid into the embracing waters of the Connecticut.

The Connecticut hadn't always been good at giving up its dead. It was reluctant this time, too. Mrs Mary Young's corpse was eventually found downstream two days later, on a Holy Day of Obligation, the Feast of the Assumption, which was, were you cynically inclined, more than appropriate.

4.

And many of those who sleep in the dust of the earth shall awake, some to everlasting life, some to shame and everlasting contempt.

Isaiah 12:2

Thursday 30th August: The day started well but clouds moved across, graying the sky and with them a freshening breeze, just enough to lift, unfurl, and rest again the eight by twelve Stars and Stripes outside 195 Longhill.

Mary Young had had a good Catholic funeral. A splendid affair worthy of someone much loved whose death had come as a shock to the community. In the absence of clear evidence of suicide from the medical examiner's office, compounded by the lack of a note, the District Attorney was still considering whether her demise was accidental, suicide, or possibly even murder. That indecision had made things easier for the family—and for the church.

The wake, which in traditional Catholic houses in America still takes place with the coffin present, had traumatized Mary's widowed husband.

Jane Hanlin of 195 Longhill, Mary's neighbor, stepped in when Bob Young felt unable to organize a post-funeral reception for his late wife. Jane had been close to Mary, had indeed thought she knew her, until this had happened. Jane was Episcopalian but she had been as shocked by this death as any of the members of the nearby congregation of Our Lady of Perpetual Help on Sumner.

Jane's husband, Michael, a former State Department diplomat, presided over the elaborate reception. More than four hundred guests came and went through the doors of 195 Longhill that late August day. A fitting place for a funereal tribute. The solid pillars at the end of the circular driveway; the bucolic entry gardens, recognition of Jane's prodigious green thumb; and the imposing entry way into one of the oldest and grandest houses on the street provided an atmosphere both welcoming and respectful for the occasion.

Now most of the guests had melted away. Those still there were in the Hanlin's oak-paneled living room, collapsed in assorted armchairs and sofas under the imperious gaze of an array of bronze coffee pots, mortars, and pestles—keepsakes and artifacts from Michael Hanlin's days posted as an ambassador in the Middle East.

Things were calmer, and the Hanlin's part-time housekeeper, Anna, was mixing apple martinis for the few remaining stalwarts in honor of the fact that apple martini had been Mary's drink of preference, one of the few indulgences she had allowed herself. Smirnoff apple-flavored vodka, shaken over ice with a touch of apple schnapps and a dash of apple cider, poured into a chilled martini glass.

The Bishop was one of those who had lingered behind. Patrick O'Malley, Bishop of Springfield, Massachusetts, whose diocese comprised the Western part of the Commonwealth, was younger than most who achieved these exalted ranks. The rest of the company now numbered twelve in mute resonance with Christ and his apostles: Our hosts, Jane and Michael Hanlin; Father Sebastian; poor hard done by Angela, blue-eyed, battered blonde; her reprobate husband, Baxter Merrill; and the recently married Hartnetts, Sean and Trish. Sean worked as a master carpenter, Trish as an interior designer.

Also present were Richard and Marilyn Bryer who lived across the river in Westfield. Richard had been a spook for the CIA and shared postings with Michael. Time had weathered him. His hair cut short as ever was sparse and blanched snow white. The skin stretched sun dried now on that same sanguine, gentle face he'd worn forty years back as a spy. He'd aged well.

Marilyn, his wife, the pillar of every church potluck and annual fair, could bake up a storm and had provided a pantry-full selection of apple, cherry, and pecan pies, as well as chocolate and angel food cake for this occasion. Then there was Vicky Walters, trainee teacher at the local Sumner Avenue elementary school and latter-day hippie. And last, but not least, young police detective Donna White and her widowed mother Alicia.

Conversation revolved around the Bishop. He had sent Bob Young home in the care of the alternate priest of the parish, Father Davidson, together with Bob's two children, Jenny and Bob, Jr., and was now waxing lyrical. This apple martini was not his first drink of the proceedings, nor was it his beverage of choice, but the Bishop was not one to quibble, especially considering the occasion and the company.

Alicia White had encouraged Bishop O'Malley by asking why there was suffering in the world. The death of her own husband had hit her like a sledgehammer, and she empathized with Bob.

Before the Bishop could reply the ever-loquacious Marilyn Bryer chipped in. She had taught the children of OLPH parish their catechism and had done well at it. An achievement indeed. Teaching a gum-chewing, pubescent twelve-year-old how to tell the rosary is no easy task. Marilyn's success had given her some authority in matters spiritual, a position on which she traded on this occasion.

"Points in heaven," she articulated. "The more you suffer, the more points you earn in heaven. Could save you fifty years in purgatory."

The Bishop raised a quizzical eyebrow at what he regarded as a curious approach to church doctrine but didn't contradict her. This was at least in part spiritually sound. He cleared his throat and raised his hand—a gesture severe enough to still even Marilyn. She widened her eyes in anticipation as the Bishop allowed the silence to build for a second before launching forth.

He stretched out crossed legs and leaned back in his chair. "As I see it," he pronounced, flicking a near invisible speck of dust from his lapel, "When God created the universe, all that existed was made in a state of utter perfection." Bishop O'Malley's bright blue eyes glistened as his audience waited. He enjoyed exercising authority. His eye rested on young Sean Hartnett, who seemed transfixed by the Bishop.

Bishop O'Malley smiled at the young man and addressed the remainder of his conversation to him. It was his way, to pick one member of his audience as a focal point, little by little dominating that one individual with his intellect and thus avoiding the complication of having to empathize with the audience as a whole.

"As the bible tells us," said Bishop O'Malley, brushing aside a strand of boyish black hair that had fallen over his forehead, "God saw that everything was good. And he gave us free will. Both a blessing and a curse."

"Without free will we would be mere automatons. It is present, as the tree is present in Eden. We are not expected to exercise the option for negative choice it represents. We are expected to be perfect."

Father Sebastian surprised himself by interrupting. "But Bishop, we are told that we all fall short of the glory of God."

The Bishop smiled as to an indulgent child and sat up straight in his chair. He subscribed to Albert Einstein's aphorism: Everything should be made as simple as possible, but not simpler. "Yes, quite correct," he said. "But there are moments, for instance when you are engaged in selfless prayer, when you approach perfection—however briefly. God expects us to extend those moments, until we are true expressions of love. In the Sermon on the Mount, Christ commands us to be perfect, despite our frailty."

"Yeah, Bishop, that's great. But none of that explains why God tolerates suffering," said Sean Harnett. "It don't answer the question."

The Bishop's head snapped round like a toad on a gnat. Then he refocused and relaxed. The skin at the corners of Bishop O'Malley's eyes crinkled as his smile broadened. "Come by and discuss it with me over coffee some time," he said to Sean. Then to the assembled company, "I am not dodging the question. There is no way God would intervene in the lives you and I lead unless he's asked."

"And the victims of disease, war; don't they ask?" said Sean.

The Bishop smiled again. Questioning of this kind was often prompted by anxiety and confusion—"The better we know what is in God's mind, the more peaceful we will be in our own mind," he said. "God answers. But not in such a way that it would subvert free will. Remember that for God there is no death. He sees us live for ever. The issues are different from God's perspective."

Sean wasn't ready to be dismissed. "Just sayin' that doesn't make it true. Tsunamis, earthquakes, that sort of thing. God does that. That's the truth, but maybe you don'ow that, or do you just not wanna dare face it? Perhaps God's a traitor to life."

The Bishop ran his tongue over his lower lip. "Pat Robertson, the televangelist, said the Haiti earthquake was God's vengeance against Haitians who'd made a pact with Satan. He was wrong. Though clearly the earthquake tests faith, any earthquake is as much a test of false science that believes in optimism in a utopian universe as it is in the world of faith. You know what I hope," the Bishop mused. "I hope that the earthquake is an example of God's love in action. That He doesn't so much cause these disasters as fail to intervene. It is a straightforward inconsistency, thinking an all powerful, all good God permits suffering. What matters is that suffering gives us the opportunity to help one another. St Paul teaches us in Romans Eight that the whole of creation is alive, aching for redemption. God has set everything in motion, then removed his hand. He has had to."

Sean wasn't giving up. "No average human parent would construct a home which would crush or maim his child. And even if the earthquake is not His fault—all the same, He doesn't care about the world if he does nothing. One thing I don't need is a God who doesn't care."

The Bishop reached across, touching the younger man on the knee, focusing in on him entirely. "There is only one way in which God can intervene, interfere directly I mean. That is in answer to prayer." The Bishop took his hand away from Sean's knee and looked round at the others. "That because your act of prayer is an enabling act of free will. God is responding, not initiating."

"But his response is limited," Sean contended. "He doesn't wanna stop wars and prevent evil."

The Bishop looked steadily at Sean and spoke with slow emphasis. "You think that God should move across the stage of this world leaving quivering nerves and cut tissue?"

"Not exactly how I'd put it but," Sean nodded, "I guess ... Uh huh."

"Wrong. Not that God couldn't do so if He chose. Obviously I acknowledge that it is wrong to place limits on God. But in my experience, God's priorities are not necessarily our priorities. Unfortunately ..."

A silence fell on the assembled company, which embarrassed their Episcopalian host, Michael Hanlin. He stretched, smiled broadly, and climbed to his feet. He had that stooped posture common in the tallest of men. He brushed his sleek still black hair from his eyes and embraced the company with the sweep of his arm. "Anna ... another round of martinis I think."

5.

For wickedness burns as the fire; it shall devour the briars and thorns, and kindle in the thickets of the forest; they shall mount up like rising smoke.

Isaiah 9:18

Friday 31ˢᵗ August: Patricia, "Trish," Hartnett was everyone's idea of a successful woman; starting from the day she'd been crowned homecoming queen at Springfield's Classical High School. Five-foot-three with wide, welcoming, green-gray eyes and rich, auburn hair, she could fill a bathing suit in knock-you-dead fashion, or pour herself into a ball dress like some sort of package from heaven. She was New York born and still retained something of the accent that her first eleven years had given her. Perhaps it was part affectation because she knew men were charmed by the softer lilt of the longer vowels that made New York into "New Yaawk." There were those that regarded Trish Hartnett as the blowzy barmaid type—but mostly they were older and mostly they were women. Trish was as bright as a button with her high-stepping boots and plummeting neckline. She could talk the hind legs off a donkey but she sure knew her stuff. And she knew how to work hard. She hated not to work, she found idleness enervating; she was never drained by work. A high earner with family money to back her up, she had a baby-pink house and swimming pool to match—way before she'd been married to her childhood sweetheart, Sean.

Sean Hartnett was Sean-baby to Tricia. Sean had led a tougher life, kicked, slashed and gouged at the whim of outrageous fortune. For Sean, Trish had been a refuge. Whilst she earned her money through interior design, Sean worked as a master carpenter. Hence the re-encounter. Sean had in turn represented security for Trish after a series of unhappy love affairs. They'd have been married sooner but for the fact the church demanded a year's engagement—not the Catholic Church in general but rather Our Lady of Perpetual Help in particular.

Tonight Sean had come home late. Sean often wasn't home 'till late these days and Trish was about ready to lam into him heavy. She was tired of being taken for granted. The first couple of months of their marriage he'd been late and she'd been angry but sex had been a great healer. She had started by wanting to rip his heart out but he'd smile his boyish smile and she'd find herself wanting to rip his pants off instead. For Trish, as for most women, sex was more than the mere pleasure of the act. Sex represented shared comfort and intimacy, surrender and dominion, freedom and expiation as well as laughter and exquisite relief. She was that type of person incapable of celibacy. And for Trish that meant a need for a man of her own. Not some shallow one-night stand. Nor, like some latter day Saint Teresa, did Trish find religion a substitute for sex. For her, commitment to one partner would be sullied by any secret betrayal, whether the object of your sexual sublimation was a boy in a bar, a vibrator in the bathroom, or Christ crucified. She had one lover and one lover only—and that was Sean. But six months into the marriage the sex wasn't there. Sure she'd make a play for him out of sheer frustration but he'd say he was too tired and she'd sulk. This all in all depressed her because a lifetime's experience had taught her that what men invariably wanted was her body. To be rejected was humiliating. She was being rejected now and she couldn't bear it. She realized this damn rejection was becoming the norm. And she was so tired of feeling like she couldn't stop crying. Of being exhausted by everything, because everything made her cry.

Sean was the love of her life. To begin with she had felt he was truly, the greatest man she had ever met. He had treated her like she was a goddess, like she was the only woman alive. Until she believed for him, she was; Lord, how she longed for that now.

She had not really shown her feelings then. Perhaps that had pushed him away.

And now it was too late. He had decided that he did not need her. That was how it seemed even though he still said she was everything to him; but she could not believe him any more.

That cut her up inside. Her entire life, she had never felt this way about any man. She wanted to have his children, his beautiful, brown-haired, brown-eyed little boys. She had felt like he would always protect her, no matter what. That she could be herself, could break down and be weak because Sean would hold her in his strong arms and do it because he wanted to. Only now he must have another woman. And it hurt her.

Yesterday he had told her, "I'm your man." The words echoed in her head. In the past, when he had touched her, she would tremble. Perhaps he was afraid of her now. There had to be another woman. Nothing else explained it. He must have found someone else, someone who was fucking him so that he no longer needed physical gratification from her. Anyone could do that but could this other woman do what she had? Could she just stand in front of him with her hands on her hips and make him want her? Could she reach into him while he lay on top of her? Did his skin tingle where her fingers touched it? Did she kiss his nose, his eyes, and his heart?

Her sadness turned to venom. "What is it Sean-baby?" She spat out the words. "Can't get it up?"

He raised an eyebrow. Dissatisfaction spread from his eyes to the rest of his face. "Don't be so disgusting," he said. But to stand his ground required an arrogance he didn't have. He turned his back on her and stepped to the huge freezer next to a small, built-in bar, where she kept ice, beer, and bourbon always at the ready. He reached for the bourbon, sloshing it neat into a highball glass over ice like it was tea. Then he sank into a red leather chair.

She spoke with slow emphasis, not even liking herself, but who knows what poisons in the mind can do. "You drink too much

Sean-baby. Maybe that's why you can't get it up." She felt strong but vulnerable. Raw maybe describes it.

But Trish could do nearly anything if the pressure was great enough. Trish walked toward him, fingering the buttons of her blouse. The shakiness of her hands contrasted with the steadiness of her voice. She was breathing through her mouth and tiny beads of sweat pricked the backs of her arms. The muscles in her face tightened. She shivered. She was furious with the man but still hoped to break the tension with sex. She ran her tongue over her lower lip. She was wearing no bra and her nipples were outlined hard against the taut, silk fabric of her blouse. She felt like some star about to go supernova, almost rocking with repressed sexual energy.

It wasn't going to happen. Sean flinched as she reached to touch him. "Cut it out Trish. Give me a breather."

She remained in front of him for a long moment, the fingers of one hand still lingering on the buttons of her blouse. Then she seemed to give up, her hands dropping to her side.

He had turned his face away. He swallowed half of the bourbon that remained in his tumbler then moved his highball glass in a careless arc, dismissing her. "I've had a hard day."

For answer she slapped him hard—hard enough to pink his cheek and slop his whiskey. Then her inner dignity, forged so long ago, took hold and she turned and walked from the room. The tears were bubbling up, filling her pretty green-gray eyes— but she wasn't going to let him see her cry.

CHAPTER TWO: SEPTEMBER

Surely I have cleansed my heart in vain, and washed my hands in innocence.

Psalm 73:13

Saturday 1st September: Father Sebastian had just closed OLPH.

OLPH. was the acronym parishioners preferred when referring to their mother church, Our Lady of Perpetual Help. Father Seb had celebrated evening mass, seen the last few communicants off the premises, closed the doors, and was heading home.

Only the monsignor lived in the Parish House on Sumner. Father Seb was no monsignor nor ever, so he thought, likes to be one. Monsignor was an honorary title granted by His Holiness at the local bishop's request with little rhyme or reason. With becoming modesty, Father Seb failed to think of himself as a man of influence. Father Sebastian lived in a small pale gray house on Cherryvale only a couple of blocks away from OLPH. He was going home to think things out. He had begun to question his calling of late.

It had already grown dark, cloud obscuring the moon. Seb was walking briskly. Then he heard the angry male voice.

"Hey Sebby Boy, you want to talk a minute?"

He recognized the voice but just couldn't bring the speaker's name to mind. Then he had it. Bob Young.

Not the Bob Young that Father Sebastian was used to. This Bob Young had consumed more than a little alcohol – and was looking seriously intent on being disrespectful. His eyes appeared coal dark and angry in the half-light provided by the street lamp. His face seemed eerily white. He was wearing a blue suit that needed pressing. His voice had a metallic thinness with an edge of savagery, a little bit like the monster latent in us all.

"Hold up right there, Sebby Boy."

So Sebastian did just that.

Like with most right-handed men, Bob Young's left hand was stronger. You haul bags with your left whilst the right is for the complicated but less taxing business of writing and such. Unfortunate for Father Sebastian that Bob Young chose to strike southpaw. The fist, when it came, connected savagely. The punch was clumsy but carried Bob's full body weight. Father Sebastian dragged himself up into a sitting position from the ground on which he found himself. "Why?" he asked. He was confused. Limited by not being able to read what was going on in Bob Young's mind.

And Bob Young paused. He knew it wasn't the big thing that still caused him pain. The fact of Mary's death. He could endure that agony, even grow from it. It was the little things that now hurt. The gnawing questions. Why had she done it? Who had she confided in? Why had he not known? He had given a name to his pain and that name was Father David Sebastian. "Why?" he said. "Cause you were with my Mary the night she died. Down by the towpath. But you never told a soul. That's why." His voice was sneering, contemptuous, and absolutely cold; his chest moved out and in as his breathing quickened. "She was an angel, the best wife a man could have—and now she's dead."

"I was not with your wife," Seb said cautiously.

Bob Young frowned and leaned down, pushing his face nearer Seb's. His eyes narrowed. "You were seen," he said, his voice shrill like a saw.

Father Sebastian responded wearily. "That was not your wife I was with."

Annoyance brought spots of color into Bob Young's cheeks. Father Seb felt absolutely no surprise at what Bob Young did next. It was, all in all, understandable.

He straddled the priest, then paused before slamming his knee into Father Sebastian's face. "You were seen," he replied a second time.

And this time Father Sebastian remained silent and wondered why he hadn't remained silent in the first place. In this kind of situation Christ would have been silent. Words only provoke.

And the normally gentle Mr Young, cursed in his frustration, turned aside and stalked away, disappearing into the New England night.

2.

The mystery of Christ is among you. Your hope of glory.

Collossians 1:27

Tuesday 4 September: "Forgive me Father for I have sinned ..."

It had been three days since the Bob Young attack and Father Sebastian felt his whole world was subsumed in sin. Whereas a secular man might seek refuge in whisky, Seb had sought refuge in donuts and iced mocha coffee. The solace they provided was both tiresome and temporary. And he was tired. Tired of trying to think himself out of this maze he was in. The confessional should be a refuge. Most priests regard this little box as a safe place, a place where you thought of the troubles of others, where your own failings were of less significance.

Like other men, fear of failure was an issue for Father Sebastian. This uniquely male burden was something he, as a priest, could empathize with. His latest confessant was male. Men confessed less frequently than women. Far less frequently. Men don't listen to what they do not want to hear. He recognized that in himself and noticed it in other men and would often be more patient with the men of the parish. At least their sins were not dull. It took a pretty powerful motive to drive a man to the confessional. Male sins were invariably sexual. This man was no exception.

"I have sinned Father."

"In what way, my son?"

"I have committed a homosexual act Father."

Seb was taken off guard and responded clumsily. "You have had sex with another man?"

There was a pause long enough to boil a kettle. Seb said nothing.

Eventually the disembodied voice responded, "Uh huh," then added, "Yes Father," and after a pause. "Is it a sin, being gay I mean?"

It was Seb's turn to hesitate. "No. Being gay is not a sin. But the homosexual act is most definitely a sin in the eyes of the church. The act itself —not the state of being gay. In the eyes of today's world, on the other hand, homosexuality is not a sin, not these days."

"So I have sinned." It was a statement not a question.

"In the eyes of God? Who can read the mind of God?"

"But you speak for God; so Father, have I sinned?"

Seb wanted to equivocate. But he knew that would help no one. So reluctantly but firmly, he responded, "Yes, you have sinned. However, there is penance indeed in your coming forward. This cannot be easy for you."

There was no response so Father Seb remained quiet, waiting a moment without saying anything else. Then added, "But tell me—are you married?" This was no familiar communicant but Father Sebastian half-thought he recognized the voice, and the half-thought disturbed him. Which was what prompted the question.

"Yes sir," the voice responded. Then added, "Yes Father."

And Seb sighed. "St Paul tells us many things. He tells us that women should cover their heads in church but most modern women here in Springfield do not. Does that make them sinners?"

The disembodied voice took a second to reply. "No Father," he said.

"On the other hand, were one of these same women to enter an adulterous relationship with another person, would they have sinned?"

"Yes Father."

"So it is with you. Promiscuous sex is always wrong. Adulterous sex is doubly wrong for you break a vow before God. You understand that?"

"Yes Father."

"So of all your sins I absolve you, but for your adultery, and for that alone, I expect an act of real contrition and penance?"

"What am I to do?"

And Father Sebastian at last recognized the man's voice, and that recognition saddened him. He paused, wondering how to make the punishment fit the crime, for this man was not long married.

And Sebastian was careful to keep his voice warm and round lest he seem like he was judging the other. Even though that was precisely what he was doing, what he was here to do. But absolution had to be well done, not clouded by emotion, since it was, or so Father Sebastian believed, underwritten by God. To absolve another of their sins was to take on the mantle, the very persona, of Christ. Nothing made a deeper mark in people than sin. Nothing was more cleansing than absolution. "You will set aside a day, at your own time, anytime, but a complete day."

"Yes Father."

"Give that day entirely to God in prayer, and in refection. Commit that day to God. Will you attempt to do that?"

"Uh huh," he said, "I will do it Father."

"Then I absolve you. Go. You are completely forgiven."

And Father Sebastian allowed himself a time of quiet before the next confessant. He needed space to think and to pray. Taking confession drained him, the way other priests were drained by the act of celebrating communion. For in Father Sebastian's view, the act of being confessor was one in which you dispensed more than life, for confession enabled absolution which in turn enabled immortality.

And Father Sebastian listened a moment longer to the silent echoes of the footsteps, as pretty Trish Hartnett's husband, Sean, walked slowly away.

3

Nothing that the world has to offer—the sensual body, the lustful eye, pride in possessions—could ever come from the Father but only from the world.

1 John 1:16

Sunday 9 September: Father Seb enjoyed his reputation as a man of integrity, a man you could talk to. He had earned this reputation, not merely because of his status as a priest, nor really through any series of acts that might be regarded as indicators of high character, but rather through a sort of natural neutralism, born of and nurtured by an almost chronic inability to be judgmental of the other. He believed in the maxim, "Condemn the sin and not the sinner"; and he lived it.

But he dreaded this. She had come up to him after Saturday mass.

Question: Why did so many of his parishioners take mass on Saturday these days?

Answer: To keep Sunday clear for golf.

Or so thought Father Sebastian. That was what he had been mulling on when she'd sought him out to shake his hand and congratulate him on the sermon.

Edging six foot, Father Sebastian was a good height but no giant. Not in modern American terms, where male offspring were bred competitively tall on whole milk, chocolate chip cookies, and hormone-laced steak. Trish Hartnett was short by comparison. Father Sebastian looked dispassionately at the woman in front of him. Five-foot-three maybe but, like in the song, "Oh what those five foot could do." She was dynamite. Pretty as a picture. A little voluptuous for his taste with all that bosom. But shapely in a top heavy sort of way.

All of which was unusual. Springfield was full of women with beautiful faces. But so many of his own congregation were either overweight, pretty faces on tree-trunk legs, or underweight, stick insect model types with cheekbones worthy of a fashion magazine but neo-anorexic bodies. It was just the way it was. You couldn't ask the rain to stop raining or the sun to stop shining—any more than you could ask a Springfield girl to take good care of herself. There were just so few genuine old-style American women the likes of Trish.

There was Angie. He pushed the thought aside.

He knew why Trish had buttonholed him, and it wasn't in order to congratulate him on his sermon. And he had agreed to meet her. In keeping with his policy when it came to anything but the most spinsterly of matrons, he'd chosen Partner's, out cross-river in the town of Agawam. "At 12:45 p.m. tomorrow after the morning 11:00 a.m. mass," he had told her. Her husband was one of the growing numbers who spent their Sundays on the golf course, which for once would be a blessing. Trish Hartnett could speak to Father Sebastian alone and unhindered, in his favorite side table in one of the most crowded places in Western Massachusetts.

Mrs Trish Hartnett was the kind of woman that men always wanted to dominate and possess—but fully realized they never could. Not that she'd be averse to letting them try. Back in college, she'd worn bobby socks like a fifties throwback, along with sneakers and rah-rah skirts; and if it had a reindeer sweater on it, she went out with it. Trish Hartnett with green-gray eyes to drown in, a sensual figure and auburn hair, alone across a small table, over good coffee, hash browns and eggs over-easy. The prospect was pleasing but for the agonizing nature of her situation.

And now she was there before him. He'd found her in the little side room, separated from the main dining area with its dull dark red walls by lacy little curtains on which daisies and poppies danced in confusion. Her smile of welcome was made with her whole face, which of itself made taking a seat opposite her, a heartening experience. Then, like a cloud passing over the face of the sun, her expression changed, crumpling almost. "It's Sean, Father Seb ... " Though she drank her coffee sedately, her voice was small and mean—and desperately earnest.

She paused for them to bring fresh squeezed orange juice and a great steaming mug of coffee before he lent across his arm which rested on the table and nodded, encouraging her to continue. "Poor woman," thought Father Sebastian, for he already knew what her problem was. But he couldn't tell her he knew. They brought their food then. He'd broken with his usual habit and ordered eggs Benedict: English muffin, Canadian bacon, poached eggs, hollandaise sauce, with a side order of shredded home fries (the Massachusetts equivalent of hash browns but better). She'd ordered sweet potato pancakes with two eggs over-easy. Which was "kinda stodgy" he thought as the three enormous pancakes came into view. But maybe she was hungry. He wondered what he would do in her circumstances, if his world had fallen apart and it seemed that the very heavens were merciless in their cruelty. There were many responses available to the person faced with this kind of betrayal. They included anger, stalwart defiance or love. He hoped that, in her shoes, he would have the strength to hold to love. But it wasn't counsel she needed. Not yet anyway. So he listened and he tried to be kind and understanding, and a bit stupid, as expected of him.

Her eyes danced around the room as if taking in the old-fashioned buff yellow and pastel red walls and the large startled chicken crafted out of something resembling terracotta that loomed over the diners. His eyes rested all the while on hers, patiently, as she gathered her thoughts and started to speak. "I love him so much I would gladly die to give him perfect happiness even for a day," she said, more than a little melodramatically, not looking at him, but staring down into the coffee cup she cradled in her hands. And he watched her eyes brim with tears and her pretty cheeks pink to match her ears with a mix of shame and congealed jealousy as she told him what she suspected. "He's having an affair, Father Seb ..."

There's a Russian proverb that goes, "One word of truth outweighs the whole world." It flashed through Seb's mind and he shook his head as if to shake the thought away. And he watched as the telling of this monstrous truth humiliated her, like she wished she'd never lived.

Her confession of what she regarded as her failure silenced them both momentarily, a process fraught with too much anguish. And then she asked the inevitable question.

"What should I do?"

4.

Each one of us, however, has been given his own share of grace, given as Christ allotted it.

Ephesians 4:7

Monday 10th September: It was early evening. The previous morning's awkward encounter at Partner's Diner gone but not forgotten. Father Sebastian was reflecting on the problem in the study of the ground floor of the small house that the diocese had provided as his home. He was reluctant to answer the door when the bell rang. It was after all Monday, the traditional rest day or "weekend" for most clergy. But he mustered his bonhomie with considerable effort and dragged himself to his feet.

"Good to see you, Donna. To what do I owe the honor of this visit?"

Donna White was one of only eight per cent of the 350 sworn officers on the Springfield Force that were female and the only woman on the city's eleven strong homicide squad. There were other specialist squads: The "Narcs" to go after narcotics as well as specialist teams to work with gangs or youth crime or schools, there were 38 in the Schools Squad; but the homicide squad was top of the tree. Donna, like all homicide squad detectives, wore civilian clothes. But the Springfield force was still old fashioned and its homicide squad detectives were called "suits" by the other officers for a reason. The tailored linen business suit Donna was wearing was a snappy pale blue. She wore it with a simple white blouse and looked good; that despite her short stature that came with an Italian heritage that had left her just a little provincially podgy but it was better than scrawny if that were the alternative. "Like a sweet in a blue and white wrapper," thought Seb—then mentally he took two paces back. He was a priest for heaven's sake. But he wasn't that hard on himself. He recognized that the general public regarded celibacy as the spiritual equivalent of castration. Which it is not.

The boss, the Captain of Detectives, had told Donna she had to do this job.

Donna wasn't bothered. She was new to the squad. Not a rooky. Rookies were what they called you when you started out on the force after 16 weeks at the academy. You were a rooky until the next academy class came along or until you proved yourself. You proved yourself when you stopped making rooky mistakes like being overzealous, for instance not assessing a situation before you weighed in. But that was all more than eight years back for Donna. She was thirty years old which was about as young as you could be and be a detective. But she'd always wanted to be a detective so hadn't gone for promotion with the uniforms or she could have made sergeant or lieutenant long ago. She reckoned being a detective was going to be easier on her married life if she'd got married. But at the moment she didn't even have a boyfriend, which, to her way of thinking, was a bum deal.

Making detective was a Chief's assignment. Donna had worked for it. Detective Muse, now her partner, had once told her the recipe back when she was just a rookie. He'd said it was to write clear and concise reports, obey her supervisors, and treat people like you'd like to be treated yourself. She'd tried to do that and it had worked. Getting a run of good arrests had helped of course. That mattered if you wanted to get noticed. "Nice grab" was just about the highest accolade one cop could give another. Plus you needed to impress the D.A.'s office. That was where the good reports came in.

She had pulled the short straw on this down at the station house because, said the Captain of Detectives, this was a "one-man car" job and her partner, Robert Muse, was off sick. The work was computer generated these days, or at least computer categorized. A shooting was a two-man car job. The Springfield homicide squad was divided into five two-man teams plus the boss. One-third of the teams worked days, one-third the 4 p.m. shift and one-third nights. White and Muse were a team.

Muse would have come in regardless with his heavy cold but the Captain had sent him home. With the uniforms the two-man cars were really three-man teams working rotation, four days on two days off. But there were normally always teams of two.

"You know the guy," the Captain had told Donna when Father Seb's name had come up.

Which she did, of course, being Catholic herself. Still, so were a goodly chunk of the boys in the precinct. She'd just been suckered into this, Donna reflected. But she didn't mind. She would rather it were her. She liked Father Sebastian.

"Sorry Father; it's professional, not social."

"Ah," Father Sebastian paused. "Well if this is professional I should call you Officer White."

Donna tilted her head and smiled. "I'm not sure I'd be comfortable with that."

"Very well. But we have to be on equal footing. Call me Seb like your mother does. How is Alicia by the way?"

"My mother's fine. Thank you, Seb," said Donna. Her good-humored eyes crinkled with amusement. It was not so many years back Father Sebastian had been testing her on her catechism, and she'd been quite in awe of him.

"Look Seb, I'm new on the squad. Normally they wouldn't send me out on a call alone like this but for the fact that it's not very important. Still, we have to check things, no matter how trivial. You understand?"

"Sure Donna, I understand. But I thought you were on the homicide squad. This is a murder investigation?"

"The homicide squad covers assault as well as homicide, we may even cover robbery if it's a felony, a felony being anything over

40

$280, under that it's larceny and belongs to the uniforms. Plus the uniforms call the squad to the scene to investigate every suspicious death, even if it's not, on the face of it, homicide. We get called in for suicides for instance."

Seb nodded. He got the drift. "Will you come in and sit down? Can I get you a coffee?"

Donna declined. She wanted to keep this professional and get it done with. She didn't want to make more of this than it was. And what it was was nonsense.

"Thing is, we received an anonymous note down at Pearl Street, telling us you were with Mary Young the night she died. On the river front bike path between the Hall of Fame and the South End Bridge, and that we should ask you what you were doing."

"I was most certainly not with Mrs Young." Father Sebastian grimaced, "I wish I had been with her. I might have been able to help." And he meant it. He felt that the community, all that knew her, bore collective responsibility for Mary Young's death. How could we all have so profoundly failed to understand that woman?

Donna relaxed visibly. "I knew that. I knew you weren't with her. I told the cap'n: 'Just because someone accuses someone doesn't make it true'." Donna moved back toward the door, relieved that she could bring this to swift closure. She had other stuff to do.

Then she hesitated. "So you weren't on the towpath?" asked Donna, almost as an afterthought.

"I didn't say that I wasn't there."

Donna shrugged. It didn't matter. This was just a formality after all. "Alone Father?" she asked.

"No. And please call me Seb. No, I was not alone."

"Well thank the Lord for that. Puts an end to the whole business. Who were you with?"

"I'm sorry. I don't think I should tell you that."

Which he didn't. He was fully aware of the complications that this engendered but Angie had talked with him of her troubles. Confided in him. It was not the confessional, but it amounted to the same thing, besides ... "No. I'm sorry. I can't."

Officer Donna White's heart sank, then her disappointment turned into irritation. What was she doing being so deferential to this man? She was a police officer, a detective, and he was a witness, possibly a suspect. Still she had respected him and now, for some reason, she didn't. Which bothered her. Priests had their rules of confidentiality just like police officers. But it was something about the way he'd replied that disturbed her. The lack of an explanation maybe. Call it woman's intuition but she recognized an element of awkwardness in Seb's reply, embarrassment even. Her response was *sotto voce,* but Father Sebastian heard her none the less as this curious dialogue finally reached its climax and she said, "Aw ... Shit!"

5.

Listen now, House of David: Are you not satisfied with trying the patience of men without trying the patience of my God, too?

Isaiah 7:13

Tuesday 11th September: Bob Young wasn't expected to keep coordinating the Churchwatch group, not with his wife Mary fresh lain in grave. But people quite understood when he'd said he would rather carry on—keep his mind off things.

In any case Bob genuinely felt that everyone had to pull their weight in an environment in which they were closing churches because of law suits on pedophilia and a general lack of priests. Churchwatch was a mechanism whereby members of the parish committed to keeping the church open as near 24/7 as they could manage. In the case of Our Lady of Perpetual Help, the doors were unlocked from 6 a.m. each morning till 9 p.m. at night, which was impressive, even by Catholic standards. Bob kept the roster as well as managing some of the slots, which he was doing now, in partnership with Baxter's wife, Angie Merrill.

Today, more than any day, Churchwatch was important. Bob regarded worship as the doorstep to heaven and Churchwatch as his contribution to keeping the threshold clean. Today was the anniversary of 9/11 and, as such, quite poignant. It was the day Bob had chosen to take up his role. But now the annual memorial service for the dead of the Twin Towers was long over. Angie sat at the back of the church with Bob. And there was no one else. The place was as empty as only a church could be.

Angie was dressed in black, which she thought demur, as appropriate for her Churchwatch duties. But the effect was the reverse. Given her shock of blonde hair and wide slate-blue eyes for contrast, the figure-hugging dress was enchanting, despite its high neckline, provocative even.

None of which Bob appeared to have noticed. They had been talking of Mary and little by little tears had filled his eyes, apparently, or so he told Angie, for the first time since Mary had died. "Since she fell from the South End Bridge," was how he put it.

"She was perfect Angie," Bob was saying, "Perfect like the Blessed Mother. She was named Mary for good reason. She'd never refuse a person in need. She never said 'No'."

Angie realized he needed to think this. It didn't make it true. Perhaps he did not know the truth, or could not face it—whatever the truth was. She smiled again, encouraging him as she would a child. "Yes, that's right. She was like that. And so was the Blessed Mother. That was what was so important about the Mother, her saying 'Yes' to the Archangel Gabriel when he told her she'd bear the Christ child. She could have refused."

"Could she you suppose? Refuse the Archangel Gabriel?" Now Bob Young was smiling, showing her his strong white teeth, "I don't think my Mary could have said 'No' to anyone. You ever said 'No' to Baxter?"

Angie Merrill laughed but there was brittleness in her voice, as she replied, "No. I wish I could but apparently I can't." Not without complications, she was thinking. "Certainly not. I wouldn't dare," she said. She shrugged the darkness back into the recess of her mind from whence it threatened to emerge and, feeling humbled and apologetic inside, she smiled again for Bob, who, thankfully, hadn't grasped what she was talking about. She changed tack abruptly. "I once met a priest, Father Sean Lennon from the Servites of Mary, who told me that our mission in life was to stand at the foot of the cross with Mary in the thousands of places throughout the world where Christ is being crucified today."

Bob Young looked at her and managed to say, "That's beautiful Angie."

Then the tears at last really came, wrenching his body in great gulps as he gasped for air.

6.

"My thoughts," says the Lord, "Are not like yours, and my ways are different from yours. As high as the heavens are above the earth, so high are my ways and thoughts above yours."

Isaiah 55: 8-9

Wednesday 12th September: "Well. It's a little late for coffee. Would you take something stronger?"

Sean Hartnett smiled in answer, hesitated, then said, "Cawffee is fine, Bishop."

Bishop O'Malley raised an eyebrow. "If you are sure, Sean," and turned to his housekeeper issuing the requisite order.

He indicated a chair at right angles to his own, "And call me Patrick."

"Uh huh, Patrick it is," said Sean, surprising himself by the ease with which he mimicked the Bishop's urbane manner.

"I'm glad you accepted this invitation," the Bishop was saying as Molly, the housekeeper, brought a tray. He smiled at Molly, nodding thanks, and turned back to Sean, his entire attention focused on his visitor. "But what made you come to see me?" and as an afterthought, "Sugar?"

Sean shook his head, accepting the cup. "'Cause of that conversation I guess, at Bob Young's wake." He took a sip from the too hot coffee and set it aside on the coaster that Molly had provided.

"Ah, yes. About suffering." The Bishop smiled just a little, more with his eyes than his mouth. He reached across and grasped Sean's arm above the elbow as if to get his full attention. "And you, Sean, are you suffering?"

Sean's answer was soft spoken; the Bishop could barely catch it. "Yeh," he said. "My marriage is not what it was. At first we were attentive to one another's needs, but that's changed," he said, his words almost a whisper. Then he continued in a more normal voice. "Is there a devil, Bishop? A Satan? Who sets out to tempt us? To corrupt us?"

"Patrick, call me Patrick." The words were staccato, almost sharp. Then more gently, "Yes Sean, there is a devil. The cannon of scripture tells us half the story. There are apocryphal writings, including the Muslim Koran, that give us a fuller idea of the ancient myth."

"Which was?"

"Which was that in the beginning, God created all the angels before he made man, that he made them out of light. They serve God but have no free will. Next he created the Spirits or 'Jinn'. These beings have free will and therefore possess souls, and will have to face Judgment Day. They were created from fire, from the very heart of the flame. They exist on earth. The greatest of these was so devoted to God that the creator took him to heaven. The Arabs call him Iblis. He was the creature we call Lucifer. In heaven he became known as 'The Prince of the Angels'." The Bishop paused.

"Then God made man out of clay and mud and called him Adam. And God told the angels to serve man, to bow down and worship him. And the angels did so.

"But Lucifer was not happy. And God said, 'Why did you not prostrate yourself when I commanded you to?'

"And Lucifer said, 'How can I prostrate myself to a mortal created out of clay and black mud? I am made from fire and light. Should I worship him?'

"And God said, 'Yes. You must. You will serve him.' But Lucifer was still reluctant, and said so. And God asked him, 'Why will you not serve him?'

"And Lucifer answered, 'Because I am better than him.'

"And for that answer God said, 'You are cursed.' And God took Lucifer and was about to cast him down from heaven to hell. But Lucifer begged a stay of execution until Judgment Day and was granted his wish.

"And Lucifer told God, 'I will devote myself to corrupting mankind. I shall mislead them all, except those of them who are your chosen servants.'

"In reply, God said, 'Begone! From this day forward you shall be despised and an outcast. As for those of mankind that choose to follow you, I shall fill hell with them.' And so it was that Lucifer was thrown out of Paradise."

The Bishop raised his coffee cup to his lips to punctuate the end of his observation.

Sean Hartnett managed a smile. "A good 'nuff story. But it doesn't gimme' an answer."

"Does it not? Well then there is another idea that the Christian Scientists favor. They believe that evil is a sort of absence of God, essentially that it is error, unreality. But that you can make this evil real with your belief. They call evil, 'mortal mind' as opposed to the omnipotent mind that is God. The personification of this mortal mind is Satan. Does that satisfy you?"

"Maybe," answered Sean who was unfazed by this curious conversation. "Perhaps it does. And does temptation come from God or from Satan?"

"A difficult question, Sean. One on which crystal clarity is hard to find. There are those that favor the belief that God is quintessentially good and that all trials are from Satan; that God uses the trials Satan puts our way to hone us, like silver in the furnace. We fall; we experience the fall; and we learn from that experience as we repent what we have done."

The Bishop reflected for a moment before continuing. "Indeed that view is scripturally sound. God himself tempts no one, or so we are told in the first chapter of James. But the church tends to go with the Saint Paul perspective, on this as on most things. And Saint Paul tends to the opinion that we are indeed tested by God, for our own benefit; and God does indeed interfere for the benefit of the world as a whole. But that disasters such as earthquake, fire and flood, though they may come from God, as with the flood to cleanse the world at the time of Noah, they may equally come from Satan."

"Well that pretty conveniently 'bout lets everyone off the hook; God and Satan can blame each other," said Sean. "I'm not entirely sure if I wanna buy that as an excuse for suffering."

The Bishop smiled, then answered pompously but kindly, "Some say God cannot truly perceive evil. There's an Old Testament book called Habakkuk that has a statement in its first chapter that God's eyes are too holy to even look at evil. And similarly the first letter of John opens with a statement that, 'God is light. There is no darkness in him.' Some early Christians resorted to dualism to accommodate this idea of a perfect God. A dualism whereby Christ was the creator on behalf of God the Father. The early Gnostic Christians took the concept further. They developed the idea of the creation of good and evil each in their own domain, heaven and hell respectively—and humanity torn between the two. Modern science echoes the concept. We believe today that you can't have the creation of matter without the making of its opposite, antimatter.

"But suffering is a relative concept. Relative to your belief in God that is. If there is a caring God and the logical concomitant of that idea is indeed eternal life, then God can put the first last and the last first and suffering thus becomes staggeringly transient when viewed from the perspective of eternity. So ironically suffering is only truly unjust if there is no such thing as a merciful God ready to compensate."

The Bishop, whose hand had fallen from Sean's shoulder, reached across to place his right hand over Sean's. "Now Sean, that drink?"

"Huh." Sean grimaced. "I think after all that, bourbon would be good, on ice."

The Bishop smiled. "There's a great little cocktail: Maker's Mark bourbon, Amaretto, lime juice, one-third each, chilled. You want to try it? It's called a stiletto."

"Sure. Whyn't lemme try it." Sean nodded. "Thank you, Patrick."

The Bishop moved to a small discreet bar in a corner of his study. Sean watched the long-fingered hands of Patrick O'Malley as he mixed the cocktail, intent on this non-priestly task. He watched as the Bishop looked back at him, passed him his glass, and murmured the word, "Skoal."

And their eyes locked and Sean said, "Skoal, Patrick."

And then Sean knew what the Bishop was and what the Bishop wanted. And Sean accepted the consequences of this moment. And he realized that he didn't mind. He didn't mind one little bit.

7.

I form the light, and create darkness: I make peace, and create evil: I the LORD do all these things.

Isaiah 45:7

Thursday 13th September. Partner's Brunch. Father Sebastian had agreed to this second meeting with Mrs Patricia Hartnett with little hesitation. She was comfortable here. And he liked brunch at Partner's—combining breakfast and lunch had always appealed to his sense of economy. A few eggs over-easy, some pancakes, generously laden with fresh butter and genuine Vermont maple syrup, and some bacon. Exquisite. He'd once toyed with the idea of becoming vegetarian on ethical grounds, on a sanctity of all life basis, like Dr Albert Schweitzer. The bacon at Partner's had weighed heavy in the balance, could even be said to have been the straw that broke the camel's back. He felt like St Augustine when he said, "Make me good Lord, but not just yet."

But Trish Hartnett was today's issue. The parameters of the problem had been laid out last Sunday. And at least there were no more tears. Not this time. Father Sebastian had had his fill of tears. Everyone he met seemed to be crying these days. He tried not to begrudge them their grief. But it was a little tiring and even a priest needs respite from raw human misery.

Trish was smiling now as she sat opposite him, every inch the successful businesswoman; power dressing in black, her jacket barely contained her buxom form. She'd not been Springfield's Classical High homecoming queen for nothing. She knew where her assets lay and she traded on them, shamelessly, even with Father Sebastian.

Not that Father David Sebastian minded in the least. If asked, he would readily claim to be an adherent of the Susan

B. Anthony view of the sexes, whereby men and women were viewed as equal and sexuality confined to the arena of romantic love and expressed nowhere else. If asked, that is. In reality, like all the males of the species, his head was turned by a flirtatious woman. And Trish knew how to be flirtatious with the best of them. Seb was grateful to see she had pulled herself together, got back some semblance of direction. No histrionics today, God willing.

Tough though, this business. Trish was aware that Sean was playing away. Of that she was certain. Indeed Sean was almost flaunting the fact. So Trish had tried to be kind and understanding, and in the process allowed herself to appear stupid. Trish had not challenged him directly over the issue. And she was afraid to do so. But all this was breaking her apart. She couldn't even sleep anymore, or so she told Seb.

And Sebastian knew that Sean Hartnett was walking on the wild side. AC/DC. Whatever way you wanted to put it, this didn't bode well. But the confessional was the confessional. After last Sunday's brunch with Trish, he'd promised to pray on the matter. And pray he had, despite Officer Donna White's interruption.

What was all that about? He brushed the thought aside.

"What should I do Father Seb?" asked Trish Hartnett as she watched him consume his last morsel of pancake. She was so redolent with tension you could smell it.

He finished his mouthful, still uncertain how to answer. And he hated uncertainty. It was just too distracting. People needed answers. "We waste too much energy on uncertainty," he thought. And he believed it. He looked Trish over absentmindedly without allowing her hypnotic, green-gray, bedroom eyes to distract him. He liked the woman. Even had he not, he'd have wanted to help her. He sipped his coffee, giving himself time.

As Father Sebastian viewed things, there were three ways to deal with this, or indeed any other such circumstance. One was to advise her to please the other: To serve Sean regardless, and to hope for his reform. The second was to tell her to please herself, to act in her own interest. An annulment, though difficult to procure, might serve her best, given what Father Sebastian knew and she did not. The third option, the preferable option in this and every circumstance, was to do what was right. That course might differ from both of the above.

When Father Sebastian had been a year or two younger he'd had no problem knowing what was right. That still small voice had shone into his night prayer, telling him what should be done. But not now. Like St John of the Cross, he was enduring his own dark night of the soul. God no longer talked to him. Perhaps he never would again. Not with that burning clarity that Seb so loved and remembered. And it saddened him. So, all he had was his own instinct to go on. And his instinct told him what?

"Trish." He hesitated. He had too much authority perhaps. If he told her what to do she'd do it. He tried the Socratic approach. "What do you think is right?"

Trish looked understandably exasperated. "That's what I hoped you'd tell me, Father."

"And I will. But first I want to hear you say it."

Trish tensed for a moment; then the words came in a flood. "Sean and I have always found it difficult to communicate. Sean really did want to spend the rest of his life with me. But there are things that he never tells me about. Like where he goes when he is late coming home.

"What happened? I wish he would have told me. But he just comes back without an explanation; then if he says he still wants to make love to me, I feel angry. Like he didn't have a good enough time with her?

"Sean and I just don't talk enough. Most of that was my fault. I'm just so insensitive. I'm amazed I can take care of a cat. What? You need food? Oh, I thought you'd feed yourself!

"I want to work on my marriage. I want to understand what Sean needs from me. I want to be that person I used to be. And I'm finding it easier now. It's just that no one is around to see it because I pushed them all away. I'm trying very hard to repair my relationship with Sean. He means the world to me. He doesn't believe that, but it's true. I'm just afraid. It is so hard for me to be like okay if he leaves and goes and screws this other woman. And all I really want is to just grab him and kiss him and love him.

"It's hard. I need to talk about this. I'm trying to understand all this. I don't think I ever will. He needs space and I know he's tired of talking. He's talked out.

"I don't think he understands I'm not trying to fight. I don't blame him. I'm trying to get into that brain of his. I'm not trying to smother him or convince him to change. I've just got so many questions he can't answer. But I have to ask anyway. Because I know he thinks about the things I say to him. So I'm giving him something to think about.

"I want to make him happy. I love him so much. I'll do anything it takes to help him be happy again."

Then Trish looked directly at Father Seb, those normally wide green-gray eyes now small and mean and nervous. "Should I leave him?"

"Is that what you think you should do?"

Trish was irritated. "I don't know what to do. That's why I'm here." The last phrase was almost shouted. One or two of the other diners looked round. "Perhaps I expected far too much from marriage. Perhaps wild absolute love is illusory. I just don't know what to believe anymore."

"Very well Trish. No. You should not leave him. I will talk to him. You should give him one last chance. Tell him you want to make your marriage work. Give him a little time. Don't expect him to change at once. We will meet here again a month from now. And you can phone me, meet me, anytime, day or night between now and then. Anytime. I mean that. Indeed I expect that. Even in the middle of the night, call me if you need to."

"And if he doesn't change?"

Seb spread his arms. The gesture was one of great warmth and simplicity, large and full like a blessing. But the words that came with it were as cold as ice. "If he doesn't change, you must seek to have your marriage annulled. It will mean a formal application to the Vatican, but it is not that uncommon and I will back you. To do otherwise is wrong. That is absolute. I cannot countenance your continued suffering in a sham relationship."

And Trish Hartnett didn't cry. Indeed it seemed to her as if a weight of congealed jealousy had been lifted off her shoulders. "And you will talk to him?"

Father Sebastian nodded.

And despite his half-formed attempt to protest, she got to her feet, came round the table, leaned right over and enveloped him in an extravagant hug.

8.

I will say unto God my rock, Why hast thou forgotten me?
Why go I mourning because of the oppression of the enemy?

Psalm 42:9

Friday 14th September: And now of all times. Blast Bishop
Patrick O'Malley. This was all he needed. Though the thought
gave him pause. A blessing or a curse? Many would regard this
as the supreme badge of merit to which a young priest could
aspire. But Father Sebastian was not an ambitious man. An
ambitious young priest might have reveled in the prospect of
being chosen confessor to his Bishop. Not Seb. Never Seb. He
cared nothing but nothing for preferment. Why then had he
entered the church?

Because God was a cogent reality; dominating his existence.
A statement in need of an answer. Like the prophet Samuel he
had been called and had responded. And now this new call,
confessor to his bishop. As if he was not laden with confessions
enough.

"Forgive me Father, for I have sinned."

David Sebastian was tempted to say, "Yes my child." But he
restrained himself. This was no curtained confessional. This
was the Bishop's study and Bishop Patrick O'Malley was on his
knees in front of a mere common-or-garden priest. Admittedly
a common-or-garden priest in his best red-buttoned cassock.
Father Sebastian knew how to rise to the occasion.

Seb noticed that the Bishop had pinned a Claddagh to his lapel. An Irish good luck charm in the shape of a silver badge
comprising the heart of Christ held by the hands of Mary and
surmounted by the crown of God, representing, some say, love,
friendship, and loyalty. Characteristic of the man, thought Seb,
to wear such an affectation. And, almost lamely but with every

ounce of compassion he could muster, Father Sebastian said, "Yes Bishop. How have you sinned?"

And the Bishop told him. Just like that. Boldly. Sweating. On his knees. The Bishop to whom Father Seb owed allegiance, spat out his sin in short staccato sentences. And Father Sebastian found himself crying inside. Had it come to this? What penance then was worthy of the abominable crime? Or was it such a crime? Was he being homophobic? Maybe. But he could not but admit to himself that his shock would have been just as great had the Bishop admitted to an affair with a married woman rather than a married man. Indeed, curiously, he realized with a start that he would have been rather more shocked if the Bishop had admitted to a heterosexual affair. Was this some sort of politically correct reverse prejudice on his part? Seb found himself thinking of dear Angie and thinking this he thought, "There but for the grace of God," and he sighed. What penance for himself then? For our Lord tells us to seriously contemplate adultery is to commit adultery. To intend to, to plan to, to propose to commit a crime is to commit that crime in spirit.

And the penance came unbidden to his lips, his language contrived, artificially formal, but it seemed appropriate somehow. "Bishop. Each morning for a year from this day forward, as you wake from bed, you will remove yourself to your chapel, prostrate yourself to the floor, and say, 'God I am your servant', three times. And having said that, you will surrender yourself to the Blessed Mother and to her mercy. Can you do that?"

And the Bishop, in answer, prostrated himself in front of Father Seb, and said, "I can do that Father."

And Seb lifted his bishop from the floor, kissed him on the forehead, and, intuitively sensing the need for extreme gravitas, he reverted to the old Latin form long abandoned by the church as he said, "My child, *ego te absolvo*." And then, having released the Bishop from his sins, Father Seb added the formulaic words used by so many of his colleagues these days, except this time, for Seb at least, they were far from formulaic: "Pray for me for I also am a sinner." And then, immediately, Father Sebastian left the room, lest the Bishop see the tears that had come unwanted to his eyes.

9.

Thou believest that there is one God; thou doest well: the devils also believe, and tremble.

James 2:19

Sunday 23rd September: "The mass is over. Go in peace."

The mass was poorly attended in Father Sebastian's view. Could you expect better on a Sunday evening? This particular Saint's Day was no day of obligation. Though it was special for Father Sebastian. It was the Saint's Day for Padre Pio. The little Italian miracle worker was only canonized in 2002. He was beloved of millions, so much so that there was an entire satellite channel devoted to the saint, and all it broadcast was continual live footage of Padre Pio's flower-draped sarcophagus. Just that, hour in hour out. Strange how devotion manifests itself thought Father Seb. But Padre Pio had been Christlike. He once said, "The life of a Christian is nothing but a perpetual struggle against self; there is no flowering of the soul to the beauty of its perfection except at the price of pain." Padre Pio had been so devout himself that like Saint Francis of Assisi before him, he had carried the visible stigmata all his days, in imitation of the wounds inflicted on the crucified Christ.

Was such a thing a specious fraud as some had said? Was it a fraud that each Easter, in the tomb of our Lord, prayer mystically lit the taper for the candles in the Church of the Holy Sepulcher in Jerusalem? Was it a fraud that Christ raised Lazarus three days dead? Was it a fraud when our Lord himself was raised from the tomb on the third day? One notable Anglican bishop, a onetime Bishop of Durham, had once said so but continued to profess a belief in the Trinity, a position Father Sebastian found so bizarre as to be incomprehensible, if not absurd.

No. These were not vulgar frauds, thought Father Sebastian

as he walked slowly back home that night. Father Seb believed in miracles—not in some dewy-eyed way—but the miraculous was, he believed, a dimension of life. When he rationalized this he sometimes thought that devotion increased belief, maybe even transcending nature. He was even ready to concede that miracles may sometimes be perception intoxicated by prayer, God's mind stimulating our underused imaginations. That might work for visions like the burning bush or the moving finger. But he drew the line at regarding core transformations like the resurrection as mere grand illusions. To do so meant limiting the power of a God who could do anything. It was a denial of omnipotence. And it made miracle less significant than magic. Seb drew a definite distinction between magic and miracle, although he believed in both. Though both were forms of intercession in nature, magic was the supernatural manifestation of man's will in nature, whereas miracle was the supernatural manifestation of God's will in nature.

It took Seb a while to cross Sumner. The street was busy with traffic, even now, late as it was. But as the cars rolled down their progress was halted by bright yellow painted traffic lights that dangled from beams and crosswires like feeders for giant birds.

As he crossed Sumner he looked around at the brick-built tenements, offices, and shops that hemmed the street and stood sentinel for the well-kept clapperboard of the homes behind in their many pastel shades of red and white, brown, blue, and olive in the section of the city called Forest Park Heights. Springfield's nickname as "The City of Homes" was evident in this neighborhood—one of several "historic zones" sprinkled around the city for their singularly attractive stock of Victorian, Queen Anne, and Tudor houses.

Bound by Longhill Street with its prestigious large homes and mansions overlooking the Connecticut River Valley to the West and by the bountiful acreage of Forest Park itself to the South, this was a peaceful and friendly neighborhood of great diversity. Renowned Methodist, Baptist, Episcopalian, Seventh-Day Adventist, Evangelical, and Congregational churches were all nearby. Even a synagogue and a small Islamic Center were within short walking distance from the doors of OLPH. Pedestrians existed but not in New York numbers. Springfield is a car-friendly city where public transport is the domain of the poor; yellow school buses aside that is, which seemingly are everywhere, except of course now, at night.

It had been a gray and dreary day, he reflected, more early fall than late summer. The wintry sky had been relieved by that distant hint of brightness at low level that renders hope. But that too was gone obscured by night and neon. Seb felt his mood move toward the melancholy.

Crossing Sumner, he started meandering through the tree-lined back streets toward the small, gray clapperboard house on Cherryvale which was his home. He found himself reflecting on the issues he had been turning over in his mind a moment before. How much of church rite and ritual was mere sham and historic compromise. There could be fraud of course. He had no doubt that the occasional weeping Madonna in some remote Irish village might be the product of an overenthusiastic parishioner with an eye on the pilgrim trade. But there were miracles. He himself had seen prayer manifest itself in the healing of a little child with a hole in the heart and collapsed arteries and no prospect of life. How the ladies of the church-sewing circle had prayed little Samantha into life had been nothing short of astonishing. But it had happened.

Father Sebastian did this sort of thing sometimes, contemplated beautiful or satisfying issues to drive out thoughts that both disturbed and distracted him, like a host of squabbling children in the dark corners of his mind. That was what he was doing now he realized, repressing a morass of disturbing issues lurking at the back of his mind. How to deal with Sean Hartnett was one such issue. Then there was the business of the Bishop's confession. It had in turn raised issues about his own attitude to Angie Merrill that bothered him. The ongoing abuse she suffered was troubling him in a way that went far beyond the professional. And Bob Young's assault: What response was required of him there? The graze on his cheek had healed but the recollection still made him smart.

He was lost in thought as he walked home from the church along the dark, tree-lined back street. He didn't hear the footsteps as they came closer. But he heard his own sharp intake of breath at the searing glacial coldness of the blow that hit the middle of his back below the shoulder blades to the right of the spine. There was surprisingly little pain as he tried to spin round. He didn't manage to make it. He caught a glimpse of gray sweatshirt, then he found that his legs would no longer support his weight. There was a sound like a rush of flames climbing his back and a pain similar to that of the uncomfortable sting from a mild electric shock. He could smell the recently cut grass in the lawn next to the sidewalk. There was a make-believe quality to the moment as the street lighting withered away to a distant spark. Only then did Seb realise how desperately he was hurt. For a moment he felt as if he were asphyxiating. Then the darkness rushed in on him.

10.

For God so loved the world, that he gave his only begotten Son, that whosoever believeth in him should not perish, but have everlasting life.

John 3:16

Wednesday, 26th September: Sean Hartnett and Bishop Patrick O'Malley sat together in Bishop O'Malley's book-lined study in his Official Residence downtown next to St Matthew's Cathedral. They were watched over by volume upon volume of the lives of the saints and other weighty tomes. It was a cool, early autumn night and a log fire crackled in the grate. They faced one another, each sitting in a high-backed leather armchair, either side of the fireplace, a warm Bukhara hearthrug separating the space between them.

The Bishop had lain aside his cross. Even the heavy ring, symbol of his office, was not on his hand but rested, glinting, on the mantle shelf. The Bishop's simple black cassock belied his status. His feet were bare. Sean wore a T-shirt. It emphasized his well-muscled forearms, the product of hours working out at LA Fitness, as much as of his labors as a master carpenter.

They both sipped cocktails; stilettos again.

"Weren't you cold coming over here dressed like that?"

"Nah." Sean shrugged, his voice comfortable, even drowsy. "I don't feel the cold."

They had been talking of Father Sebastian, who lay in Mercy Hospital, run by Springfield's Sisters of Providence, lucky to be alive, the victim of a stabbing by an unknown assailant.

"Will he be OK?" asked Sean, returning without enthusiasm to the subject on everyone's mind.

"I believe so." The Bishop nodded. He toyed with his drink. His face was flushed. "Who could have done such a thing?" he mused for the second time that night.

Sean stretched out in his chair and stared at the ceiling. Then he answered without much interest, "God knows. Some druggy maybe—after money—'cause Father Sebastian had no enemies."

O'Malley bit at the thumbnail of his left hand. "I'm not so sure. Monsignor Davidson says he thinks someone assaulted him a few days earlier. Seb's face was bruised. He said he'd fallen over." The Bishop set aside his drink.

"You reckon?" Sean yawned, then took another sip from his glass. He didn't wait for a reply, "The whole fucken' church is talking about it."

The Bishop sighed, got to his feet and poked at the fire. "All Springfield is talking about it. This place is evil when it comes to gossip. Set the germ of a salacious idea in a Springfield mind and it multiplies like bacteria in a Petri dish."

"Hey, I confessed to him you know."

The Bishop was startled. He looked up from the fire, his piercing blue eyes seeking Sean's. "'Bout us?"

Sean drew his knees up, clasped his hands around them, and sat hunched forward, staring at the fire. "Naaa," He said slowly, "No. Not about us. Before us. About other men."

The Bishop returned to his chair. "Do you go with other men?"

"No Patrick. Not now." Sean stretched out his legs and leaned back in his chair. "But I know what it is to be lost. I've been bad. Seb told me what I was doing was adultery. N'he didn't seem so concerned about whether I was gay or not." He looked back at the Bishop then. "Is it adultery Patrick?"

Bishop Patrick returned to his chair before answering. Then he replied, staring down into his drink. "Yes, Sean, it is."

"So sex is bad eh?"

The Bishop smiled. "That's not what I said. One of the prime functions of life is the nurturing of life. Mankind continues because of the urge to procreate. It is the same with God. Our Father God needs us as a mother needs her child. Life needs life. Our purpose is to grow to be a worthy counterpoint to the creator. We are the spiritual seed in the seedbed that is the infinite universe."

"Yeh, and sex is bad."

"No. Sex is good. Adultery is bad."

"Bad like us."

"Yes Sean, bad like us."

"Are there degrees in sin? Is what the man who stabbed Father Sebastian did worse than what we've done?"

The Bishop looked up, but not at Sean. He stared into the fire. "Yes Sean. There are degrees in sin. There are greater sins than ours. Jesus tells us that to lead a child away from God is a great sin. And there are lesser sins. But adultery and murder, actual or attempted, are both mortal sins."

"Your answer stinks." Then more kindly, "Ranking adultery alongside murder's a bit steep," Sean added. "Is there no forgiveness then?"

"Of course there is. Christ forgave the woman taken in adultery as unhesitatingly as he forgave the thief on the cross. He taught forgiveness. His death was the ultimate act of forgiveness. He died for our sins, as a ransom price paid. He went to his death willingly that you and I should not die."

"And you and I, what the fuck's the hope for us if we keep on as we are? Is there forgiveness then?"

Bishop Patrick O'Malley continued to stare at the fire. "Yes, Sean. For you there will always be forgiveness. But for me, a leader in the church? St Paul tells us that those who claim to be leaders are judged more harshly than other men. For me—I am no longer sure."

And now it was Sean's turn to get to his feet. He stepped across and reached out to comfort his friend, cradling the Bishop's head against his chest, stroking the Bishop's raven black hair in the full knowledge that this act of compassion would have consequences. And he didn't mind.

11.

Nevertheless, to avoid fornication, let every man have his own wife, and let every woman have her own husband.

1 Corinthians 7:2

Saturday 29th September: Baxter had been drinking Budweiser beside the pool in his backyard at 185 Longhill most of the afternoon. It had been one of those hot Indian summer days; one of those so hot days that the sun on the water danced its reflection on the upturned branches of the nearby pines. Baxter had bathed in the sun so long that he felt as if his skin was stretched. The Stars and Stripes on the obligatory poolside pole hung limp against the liquid pastel blue of a sky in which clouds were, to Baxter's drink gentled mind, like steam puff intruders in a virgin womb. He liked the thought. He thought the clouds like sperm on water and the thought pleased him. The earth stood green and thrusting, masculine in contrast; whilst the cicadas thrummed, always thrummed, their monotonous tympanic sound. The night was coming and it was cooler now. The bugs were out. Midges come along at dusk in Springfield, conducting their small acts of courage with the suicidal persistence of miniature ninjas. He smashed at them, irritated. It was Saturday.

Things were not good for Baxter. The family business, Merrill Manufacturing, was an ancient one. The company had made the machine tools for the manufacture of the original Springfield rifles. It went that far back. Baxter had had new ideas. Baxter had shed much of the original machine tool business, sold it off in the belief that it was a liability when the high-tech revolution had come in the early Silicon Valley days. Instead he had invested in electronics, making computer parts on contract for IBM. Not the chips. "If only I'd invested in silicon chips," thought Baxter. "I could have done well." No, he had started making motherboards. Had tooled up for it. Invested heavily. Borrowed heavily. And he'd done well. At first.

Now those days were gone. Now Baxter drank. Especially on weekends. On the weekends he drank for America. Beer during the day, scotch and soda at night. Angie dreaded the weekends. It wasn't so bad Sundays when Baxter went to play golf with his friends. But Saturdays were bad. Baxter had all day to drink. Today was Saturday. Today he had consumed so much alcohol that the drink had overwhelmed his good side, exposing the raw, selfish animal that was Baxter on a dark day.

Angie was in the kitchen when Baxter came in from the pool. She was fixing supper. She'd made spaghetti with tomatoes and pepper and shrimp, the way Baxter liked it.

"Fix me a drink Angie."

Angie wondered what she'd do if Baxter were addicted to food the way he was to alcohol. What was it the British called drunks? Soaks? That was what Baxter was. More than a drunk. A soak. What would she rather, that her husband was fat or that he was a drunk? "Give me obese any day," she thought. Then aloud she said, "Supper's ready Baxter. Have supper first. It'll spoil."

"I said fix me a drink."

Angie did as she was told, pouring the Johnny Walker Black Label over the ice, then bringing it over, adding the soda. Just the right amount. Baxter was particular about his drinks. "Just a splash of soda," he always said. "Don't drown it."

He watched her as she started to move away, retreating toward the kitchen. She wore a loose blouse and a short skirt. Her fine legs went way up. Baxter had always thought her beautiful. Looking at her he felt the desire for her coming over him like a relentless incoming tide.

"Angie."

She stopped.

"Come here Angie."

She moved back toward him.

"Come here Angie."

She came over to his chair. Nervous.

He reached out then, running his hand up her thigh, stroking her higher, up under her skirt. "You wearing anything Angie?"

She shook her head. Baxter never liked her to have on underwear. He'd been on a trip once, to South India, to Bangalore, India's own Silicon Valley. He'd always subscribed to the Mark Twain dictum, "Be good and you will be lonesome." In India, he'd discovered that there were girls who wore no underwear under their vibrantly colored traditional dress. "My Ayah told me I shouldn't," one particularly pert Indian woman had told him as he'd reached up under her sari. "Knickers are dirty." And she'd been such a good lay. It had excited Baxter. It excited him now as he reached for Angie.

"Baxter, no. Please. Supper will spoil."

"Fuck supper. Come here."

Angie felt herself trembling. She was doubly annoyed with herself because she realized that there were many women who would be grateful for the kind of attention represented by Baxter's brutal brand of sexuality. But she so ached for something gentler. Seduction might be too much to ask but there were limits. She must stand up to him, or so she believed.

"No Baxter. Really. I don't feel like it now. I've been working in the kitchen. Can't we get supper out of the way. Then get cleaned up. Then I'll make it good for you Baxter. After supper. Really I will Baxter. Please. Later."

And Angie knew what making it good for Baxter meant. Baxter was particular about sex. Baxter was particular about everything. Sex with Baxter was all about pleasing Baxter. Which she didn't mind. Not at all really. It was easier in a way. But he expected her to enjoy it. Which she usually did. And if she didn't she pretended to. Of late she'd learnt to pretend well.

"Now Angie," Baxter growled.

She wasn't sure why she said "No" again. Maybe she was attempting to salvage some vestige of self-respect. The blow, when it came, was bad. Usually she saw it coming, had time to tense her stomach muscles. Not this time. It doubled her over, brought her to her knees like a slave girl.

She tried to stay down, like boxers do when the referee starts counting. Would it be easier some part of her wondered, to be hit by a boxer wearing gloves? She'd heard somewhere that two people a year died in the boxing ring in America alone. Far more have been killed since gloves were introduced than ever in the bare knuckle days. It could hurt your bare hands more to go for the face. Baxter rarely hit her in the face. That was because he cared what the neighbors thought. But Baxter wasn't going away. He was standing over her now.

She whimpered as Baxter grabbed her by her exquisite golden hair. He leant over her and pulled her head up with one hand, slammed his fist back into her stomach with the other, and then dragged her across the room to the rug. There he threw her down, lifted her skirt, spread her legs, and raped her. Raped her as he had done before, so many times. Except that in Baxter's mind this wasn't rape. For him marriage was a contract to which the woman brought sexual favors and the man brought financial stability. He didn't recognize this as institutionalized prostitution. He genuinely believed Angie was his to do with as he liked and she should know that.

fterwards Angie resolved that this was the end. She told herself she would pack her things in the morning and leave him. Just as she had told herself before—many times.

Chapter Three: October

For whosoever exalteth himself shall be abased; and he that humbleth himself shall be exalted.

Luke 14:11

Monday, 1ˢᵗ October: Bishop Patrick O'Malley paled when Molly announced the name of the woman at the door.

"Tell her I'm out."

The truth was the Bishop didn't want to hear what the woman had to say. It was all too embarrassing.

But there was to be no mercy that day. Trish Hartnett had followed unbidden into the hall. She marched past Molly. "Like hell you're out."

"Please Mrs Hartnett. Just take a seat. Calm down. Molly, fetch some coffee."

"You just can that order, Molly. I'm not drinking the Bishop's cawffee—and I won't be staying longer than necessary."

Molly was confused and stood a moment, frozen to the spot.

"It's OK Molly. Leave us please."

The Bishop nodded reassuringly, and Molly closed the door so abruptly that she inadvertently slammed it. She was distressed. The Bishop had his little ways, could be a bit pompous. But he had been kind to her and she was fond of him. She didn't like this situation one little bit.

Nor, of course, did the Bishop.

"Will you sit down Mrs. Hartnett?"

Trish shook her head. "No. I will not sit. What I have to say I can say standing."

"You don't mind if I sit down?"

"Please yourself. That's what you do, don't you? Please yourself I mean. You don't care anything for others. You call yourself a Bishop? You disgust me."

The Bishop said nothing for a moment, just looked at her. Then he buried his face in his hands like a six-year old and muttered, "I'm so sorry."

"Sorry? Tell God you're fucking sorry. Not me. You are sorry? I know everything. I had it out with Sean this morning. My Sean. He's been doing that, with you ... You are revolting, the pair of you."

Trish had expected today to be bittersweet. It wasn't. It was as foul as a day could be. Trish had had too many days like this since things had gone wrong with Sean. It was a long time since there had been days filled with laughter without fighting. Every day should be like that. She found herself thinking of Sean, of his soft flesh, his perfect mouth, and his dark eyes staring into hers.

After the stuff with the Bishop and knowing that he was sleeping with Sean, she really had not been sure what would happen when she got here.

The Bishop looked at her and for a moment, she thought he might cry. Gathering her dignity she mustered every ounce of calm she could manage. She said, "What did you think you were doing?"

"I am so sorry."

"You need to think about how it is wrong, lusting after another man. Those feelings should go away." She wanted to jump on top of him and beat the shit out of him until he exploded. She wanted to ask him, "Why do you want that. Why do you want to sleep with a man when you're a priest?" She just wanted to hit him so hard that he'd know how frustrated and upset by it she was. Beat his chest and ask why he did this?

But she knew the answer to that question.

She thought something clicked with the Bishop because then he said, "The way I behaved was wrong" But she knew he thought that it wasn't wrong.

"You still did it." And loved it, she thought.

She just wanted stability. She wanted her husband, the love of her life, and a family. She told the Bishop, "I will do whatever it takes to keep Sean."

She wanted to repair her marriage. And she wanted it to be that way for the rest of her life. And something was different now. "I don't feel such intense pain and longing anymore. I feel nothing but anger."

"It's not really like you think," the Bishop started to say, but Trish cut him short, overwhelmed by a new Tsunami of rage.

"Not like I think! What is it like then? Tell me."

"There are some in the church who no longer regard homosexuality as a sin."

"There are, are there? How appalling. Don't count me in that 'some'."

"In a free society, men and women learn to respect the rights of others."

"Respect?" Trish Hartnett paused a moment but not for long.

"And what you did with my Sean. Are you seriously suggesting that was not a sin?"

The Bishop looked up at her then. "No," he said, and then turned away from the merciless glare of her green-gray eyes. "It was indeed a sin, you being married."

"Us being married! You mean if Sean was a choirboy you could fiddle with him with a clear conscience?" The Bishop tried to respond but she didn't let him, using words like clubs to beat him with. "The whole church is full of child molesters. You can't open a newspaper without coming across a story about some priest who's been screwing his Sunday school children. Celibacy doesn't work for any of you people anymore."

The Bishop winced. He could scarcely argue. "There is a growing realization that what you are talking about is an institutional problem and not merely an individual problem. A problem that has to be faced up to rather than faced down. The church has a massive job of reaching the young and recovering its moral authority." He paused before continuing, "But just because I am gay does not mean that the entire system is at fault."

"You think you can dress up being a faggot with pretty words like 'gay'? You make me sick. Are you going to deny you committed a sin?"

The Bishop shook his downcast head.

"And how, Bishop, do you intend to pay for that sin?"

The Bishop spoke softly but deliberately. "With my immortal soul." Because that was what he believed, that his was a sort of Calvinistic double predestination. The concept whereby not only had God determined you would not go to heaven but that God had positively decided you were heading for hell. "I am damned," he said.

Trish laughed despite herself. "Well that's a comfort. I was always a subscriber to the Marty Feldman doctrine myself: life is as short as a butterfly's fart, but death lasts forever. On which basis, long may you rot in hell."

The Bishop sighed, "I expect I shall."

"And do you think that's enough?" She marched across to his chair, standing over him. "You should quit."

If O'Malley thought for more than a moment this merely meant cutting it out with Sean, he was to be instantly disabused.

"Will you stop being a Bishop?"

"If I must." O'Malley looked back at her. "But this is my vocation. I hadn't intended to resign."

"No?" Trish Hartnett allowed her lips to curl into a malicious smile. "And nor do I intend that."

"Thank you."

Trish narrowed her green-gray eyes. "Don't thank me. I want you where I can control you."

"Mrs. Hartnett, please. I don't want to be your enemy."

"Don't 'Please-Mrs-Hartnett' me. I'll show you your enemy!" Trish raised her right arm and pointed it at the mesmerized face of the Bishop. "You are your own enemy," she screamed. "Your enemy is you!" Her voice softened then, coldness replacing passion. "You will pay me a hundred thousand dollars or I'll have you unfrocked quicker than you can say 'homosexuality'."

The Bishop was visibly stunned. "But Mrs. Hartnett. You are rich. You don't need money."

"No. That's right. It's not the money. I don't need money. But I want to make you pay for what you've done. And you will. Then I'll give the money away."

"But I am a priest. I have no possessions. I have no money."

For answer Trish looked around. "That's all bull. This place doesn't come cheap. You can't tell me the church isn't wealthy. If you haven't got the money, find it. I don't care how."

"But I can't."

"You can and you will – or the story will be on the front page of the Springfield 'Republican'."

"But you'd wreck all our lives. Your own included."

"And you think I give a damn ... And Bishop, one thing more."

"Yes," he answered.

"If you so much as look at my Sean again, you'll have more than your immortal soul to worry about. I'll come after you, so help me God, and castrate you myself if I have to. OK?"

"Yes ... of course ... OK." And with that, Mrs Trish Hartnett turned and stalked from the room, slamming the door as Molly had done, but with Trish it was deliberate.

2.

And there shall in no wise enter into it any thing that defileth, neither whatsoever worketh abomination, or maketh a lie: but they which are written in the Lamb's book of life.

Revelations 21:27

Wednesday, 10th October: Father Sebastian was breaking himself in slowly. They'd kept him in Springfield's Mercy Hospital, the fiefdom of the well-regarded Sisters of Providence, for two weeks. The force of the knife thrust had been taken by his ribs. He'd been lucky. If it had been someone who knew how to use a knife, they'd have thrust the blade upwards and the wound would have been fatal. As it was his lung was punctured but they'd stitched him up and pumped him full of painkillers and, in the normal course of events, he'd have been convalescing at home—but the diocese was being extra cautious and forced his doctors to insist on a longer hospital rest than was strictly appropriate.

And Father Sebastian had acquiesced without real protest. He had a lot to think about, and he was mentally more exhausted than he cared to admit. But now he'd been given a clean bill of health and he was out.

He had accepted the invitation to drinks at Michael Hanlin's large Gothic–Tudor style house with its commanding position overlooking the Connecticut River on Longhill Street because enough was enough. It was time to face the world. They sat together in the huge oak-paneled living room at number 195. Just himself, Hanlin, and Richard Bryer. Hanlin and Bryer wore short trousers and sleeves in unstudied informality, as if summer were still present.

Hanlin was once wiry and sinewy but now just starting out plump. But he still retained the vestige of his lanky frame and boyish face. He had dark brown hair, as yet ungrayed, and kind if cynical, heavy lidded, world-weary eyes, with a sanguine, thin-lipped mouth.

Dick Bryer was a tall man, a former C.I.A. agent and Hanlin's best friend. He had crew cut short white hair, a round sun-stretched face, a strong nose, and one of those smiles that hangs around, lazy Southern style, displaying a cracked front tooth that added to the friendliness.

Hanlin's wife, Jane, was down in Florida looking after her invalid older sister, so this was an all male affair. Father Sebastian had been about ready to wean himself off the painkillers anyway. He'd set them aside after taking one early in the day, reasoning that Hanlin's alcohol would make a good substitute.

Which was OK. But he'd been glad of that first whisky from Hanlin's practiced hand. Neat twelve-year old Glenmorangie single malt on the rocks, and liberally poured. True amber nectar. He'd sipped it through a straw, the way he'd sipped the ice cream sodas the nurses had made for him in the hospital when he'd not been eating and they wanted to build up his strength.

"Hell of a thing, what happened to you. And you've no idea who did it?" Bryer had asked the question, his keen, sharp eyes watching Seb, friendly with an edge, like a sheepdog watching a lamb.

"None," Seb lied. Another sin. But how could he not lie? Should he express his suspicion, confess that the man who assaulted him a few days earlier had been Springfield's respected Schools Superintendent, the recently bereaved Robert Young? The lie itself creased Seb's forehead. He had always thought himself gifted with some measure of discernment. But was this small lie a kindness, a God inspiration—or was it an evil, and of Satanic inspiration he wondered? And he had no idea which. He was all too well aware that the mystic approach to life was more acutely subject to demonic influences than almost any other. Where then was truth? So elusive. Like cupping your hands to grasp water only to see every last drop fall through your fingers.

"Too much evil in the world," said Bryer, his laconic manner covering the fact that he scented the lie, expected it even.

Seb and Hanlin were drinking the Glenmorangie. Bryer had made a big dent in his BBC Steel Rail—the stronger spirits denied him because of rampant gout. "A bird can't fly on one wing," Hanlin said. He topped him up.

"Yes, evil," Father Seb was saying. "Reminds me of the compline prayer, 'Beware for Satan has come down like a roaring lion, seeking whom he may devour'."

"Poor Satan. He always gets a bad press," responded Bryer.

"Not if you're a Yazidi," said Hanlin.

"Meaning?" asked Bryer, who was well used to humoring his friend's desire to act the raconteur.

"Well, it's something I learned when I was in Iraq."

Bryer nodded. Seb looked up.

"They have this sect. The Yazidis. There are upwards of a half-million of them. Their holy day is Wednesday. They won't eat lettuce. They take as many wives as they like and their priests are celibate. The more zealous amongst them have been known to castrate themselves."

Father Seb grimaced, but then said, "Not such a bad idea."

Hanlin raised an eyebrow in astonishment. "Don't tell me you are tempted by women?"

"Is a priest not a man? If you prick him does he not bleed?"

"In your case. 'Yes', I guess. Well, who'd have thought it?"

"Get back to your story and leave the poor priest alone," grumbled Bryer in his singularly curmudgeonly way.

"OK. As I was saying, these people worship Satan."

"You're not serious?"

"Well not exactly worship him. They pray to the sun by day and the moon by night. But they respect Satan as the Peacock Angel, the first amongst the angels."

"That's bizarre," said Seb. And sensing there was more he added, "Go on."

"Their theology is interesting. They reckon that Satan fell from grace for his pride, just like the Muslims do."

Seb nodded. This he'd heard before.

"But they reckon that he repented. That he was redeemed by God and returned to heaven. And now the whole world is going through that same process of redemption. Or would do, if we could but repent of our sins."

"So not so bizarre after all I guess," said Bryer, demolishing yet more of his beer as an afterthought. "Eh Father? What do you think?"

"I think I could do with a refill."

Hanlin patted Bart, the Rottweiler Shepherd cross from which he was inseparable, then got to his feet to oblige.

"And in answer to your question. Anyone who's seeking redemption is not that far from God's mercy."

"What about that, 'No one comes to the Father but through Me' line attributed to Jesus in John's gospel?" asked Hanlin. "I thought you priests believed only us Christians were saved."

"Not exactly. Not in my case anyway. The way I see it, since you ask, is that we all face Christ when we meet God on Judgment Day. There is no salvation but through our Lord. That salvation is open to all. Muslim, Jew, Buddhist, whatever."

"A little heretical surely, Father Seb?" asked Hanlin.

"You would rather I subscribed to the doctrine 'extra ecclesia non salus'.

"No. I just thought we were straying from the official church line here."

"Not really. Pope John 23rd gave us the great spirit of ecumenism and started to look at the many facets of the diamond. Now the real problem is the subtle rise of secular dogmatism. They resort to slogans and thought dies. They have no appetite for complexity. There's hope for an ecumenical community of communities because that's the only way to bet. As regards salvation, Jesus gave us the parable of feast. When the invited guests were too busy to turn up on time, he turned them away and sent out for the beggars and the poor. We are the invited guests— but we are warned not to take our salvation for granted."

"And your assailant. He gets salvation?"

Seb smiled like he meant it. "I sure hope so."

"Well personally I hope he rots in hell, whoever he was," said Bryer.

"Which brings me to the point. We had an ulterior motive for bringing you over here."

Seb laughed. "Shame on you boys. I thought you wanted my company."

"We do," said Hanlin. "But are you intending to walk home through those back streets?"

"I don't really see why not."

"You don't? Well I'll tell you why not. Because Richard and I are going to take turns in my Hummer. We'll pick you up after church, or whenever you finish, and run you home."

Seb chuckled at the prospect of being collected in Hanlin's silver-gray Hummer H3—a scaled-down version of the monster the boys used in Iraq. "In that tank? You can't be serious. No, I'll walk."

"Then we'll be walking with you or arrange to have one or two trained operatives do so. At least for the next couple of weeks. Regard it as our bid for redemption. There'll be no argument. And they'll be armed."

"I'm not so sure that's such a good idea. You or your boys being armed, I mean. The idea of you killing someone to protect me."

"Seems pretty reasonable to me," said Hanlin.

"So would you take someone's life to provide transplant organs for people dying for the lack of them?"

"You don't catch me out like that. The street car enigma I have heard of. They use it to train troops. There's no parallel because in reality the guy who's out to get you is a murderer. He's doomed. The parallel we are talking about is a situation where a street car is hammering down on a set of points beyond which five people are tied to the rails. Switch the points and there's five saved but there's another guy tied to the other line. He dies."

"And so you switch them, I get the message. But I'm not five people, I'm just one. And God places an equal value on each one of us. Which means nobody takes a life to save mine."

"If you insist. No guns. But still we are going to watch out for you."

Seb laughed again, about to protest but Richard Bryer stopped him, raising his glass and using it to point by way of emphasis. "We're serious," he said.

And Seb, despite himself, was touched by their concern. "Thank you both. OK But no Hummer, and no guns, and for two weeks only. Else I'll feel like the President."

"Yeh. Well for us you're just as important," said Bryer. Which was true, he reflected. He meant it. He really liked this guy. "God knows who had it in for you; but no one's going to touch you on our watch."

3.

You shall love the Lord your God with all your heart, with all your soul, and with all your strength.

Deuteronomy 6:5

Thursday, 11th October: The Connecticut curved away from the South End Bridge, its great broad sweep meandering gently so you could see the best part of a mile at a stretch but no further, just far enough to see the top of the majestic roller coasters of Six Flags New England adjacent to the western shore of the river.

The water is gentle like a woman hereabouts. It doesn't race. Indeed where it meets the shore Agawam side it laps soft on sloping sands in places. Here and there close in the surface is rippled, betraying shallows in an otherwise serious body of water.

The shrubs, small trees, brush, Virginia creeper, and the like, on the Agawam side, run as far as the eye can see 'till the blue of the low hills in the distance. Whereas on the Springfield side the trees are more substantial, older perhaps, but there are less of them, the town running right out as it does to the ribbon of bluffs above the river that are unique to this northern shore where the ghosts of long dead Agawam Indians still rage against tomorrow.

They met on the river front bike path, that almost but not quite meets South End Bridge, failing to deliver the climax it deserves whereby it could link pedestrian Springfield with pedestrian Agawam. That hiatus kept the path quiet of people but not of noise this South end side as traffic roared to and from the bridge. Seb and Angie Merrill walked through the scrub maple that stretched down to the riverside. As before, Angie's dog, Titus, walked between them. Seb's stride was long and elastic. She had to walk nimbly to keep up with him.

"I had to give my minders the slip. They'll not be best

pleased when they report back to Bryer and Hanlin."

"Those two that follow you everywhere?"

Seb laughed and Angie laughed with him. "Yes. Just about everywhere. But for two weeks only. We have agreed. Well, I agreed so as to keep them quiet."

Angie looked at him, concern wrinkling her brow. "I wish they'd stay with you longer. I don't like the thought that you, of all people, might have an enemy."

"I'm sure it was just some opportunist, after money I didn't have." Seb smiled, then cut her short as she was about to reply. He stopped walking and turned to her. "We're here to talk about you."

She reached for his hand, holding it tenderly with her long fingers as a sister might, in genuine concern, perhaps unconscious of the effect her touch might have, or perhaps not. Staring at him she said, "I'm worried about you, Seb."

And he stood there a moment, feeling her small hand holding his. Outwardly he was tall, assured, clear eyed, erect; but inwardly he was bewildered. He relaxed his grip. "Now I understand why Orthodox Jews don't shake hands with women," he said with a regretful smile.

"Why is that?" asked Angie, smiling back.

"Because to touch a woman puts you in the way of temptation." He removed his hand from hers and placed it self-consciously in his overcoat pocket.

"Why Father Seb, I never knew you cared," she laughed.

And Seb laughed back, hoping she had not realized how much she affected him. "But seriously Angie, what about you and Baxter?"

His words cut the smile from her face. "Not good, Seb. When I married him, he was my superman. He seemed so assured. I didn't realize that he was a boy walking around in a man's body. His world revolves around sex and alcohol. We have so little in common. He doesn't discuss things with me anymore, he just descends into some morass of his own making and I no longer know how to reach him."

"Has he hurt you again?"

"He kicked the dog yesterday."

"I'm sorry to hear that. But that's not what I asked. Has he hurt you again?"

For answer she nodded. "Yes," she added a moment later. "He hurt me again."

"Badly?"

"Bad enough. Want to see?" And she started to lift her blouse with teasingly careful slowness but it was his turn to reach out a hand, to touch her, to stop her.

"No Angie. I don't want to see. I can imagine." Then he added, "This can't go on. For his sake as well as yours, you have to leave him."

"I don't know Seb. I'm not sure I can. I think about it often enough. I tell myself I intend to. But I never do." Then abruptly she changed the subject. "Why did Mary Young kill herself?"

Seb was startled. "You're not thinking like that? You must not. Absolutely not."

Angie laughed, "Of course not. Oh I don't mean I haven't thought of it. Who doesn't in the bad times? Is it a sin? To commit suicide I mean."

And Seb, despite himself, took hold of her, spinning her round to face him with such abrupt force that her long blonde hair flashed golden as it whipped out round her, like a sunburst. "It is a mortal sin Angie." His lips were drawn together. And anger born of concern mounted in him. "A mortal sin. It is the ultimate crime against the God who created you. It is a rejection of God's greatest gift, greater even than salvation, the gift of the life he gave you. You must never, never, even contemplate such a thing."

"I won't Seb." And Angie laughed breaking the tension. "I promise." And she felt childish, younger than her forty years, more like a schoolgirl talking to an adult.

Seb let her go then. The anger leaving him as abruptly as it had come, his face composed. "Good," he said.

Angie looked at him again, studied him as they resumed walking together. He was a kind man she reflected. Then her thoughts returned to Mary Young. "Is Mary damned then, for what she did I mean?"

"No Angie. No one is damned. Christ's mercy is as endless as the universe is vast. And Lord knows why she did it, but she must have had a reason." Then he reached out, grasping her arm again. "You will leave Baxter? Right now I mean. I am serious Angie."

But Angie didn't answer. She wouldn't lie to this dear man. She couldn't leave Baxter. Not just yet. Not with his whole world collapsing around him.

But Seb persisted. "Angie, I mean it. You must leave him."

"I can't. It would be wrong. I have to trust him, at least for the moment. I remember a sermon you once preached. You said that 'the person who trusts can never be mistaken, only betrayed'."

Seb shook his head. "Leave him Angie," he said. "I mean it. Leave him now."

4.

Whereas you were as the stars of heaven for multitude, you shall be left few in number; because you did not obey the voice of the Lord your God.

Deuteronomy 28:62

Friday, 19th October: Angie Merrill was a Rubenesque woman of forty. Her hair was a golden cascade above a beautiful childlike face. She had had a good day. She hadn't been working. Baxter didn't like the idea of the wife of the proprietor of Merrill Manufacturing having to earn a dollar. But she was on the board for the Springfield Festival and she'd been doing what she thought was a good job. One of her enterprises was to organize the annual visit of a small troupe from the New York Metropolitan Opera, who performed in Springfield's Symphony Hall each year. Today she'd finalized the details for the next visitation with her friend Jennie Moore, who was the accomplished, local symphony pianist who worked with the team from the Met on their visits to Springfield. She liked spending time with Jennie. They were close friends.

That was plus number one. Then there was Baxter. For whatever reason Baxter was in a good mood. He'd been kind to her, even courteous. He had been like that when she'd married him. When they'd made love last night it had been the old Baxter, soothing her, caressing her, and she had given herself to him without reservation, and she'd not had to pretend. That was plus number two.

Then she'd picked up a Quaker bumper sticker in a street market. It had pleased her and she'd slapped it on her car. It read, "God bless the whole world. No exceptions." That counted as plus number three.

And then she'd felt so great physically. The pummeling she had been getting from Baxter had abated lately and she had sort of healed. The bruises were still there but she didn't ache as bad. That together with the fact that it had been a glorious autumn day with enough blue in the sky to fill the ocean. And a day that had concluded thus far with a Springfield sunset that fell West across the Connecticut River in the skies above Agawam and stretched toward the distant hills at the horizon. A kind of fiery peach exploding into gray and pastel blue, streaking away into the infinite void of the darkening sky. Which all together made for plus number four and was best of all.

They'd had an early supper, some late season native corn followed by steak and salad. Then Titus started to bark. He did that, even before the door bell rang. She liked to think that the dog had sixth sense, the canine equivalent of female intuition; but Baxter said it was more likely the result of the sharper hearing of the canine species combined with the faint crunch of footsteps on gravel.

She got up. "Baxter, you expecting someone?"

"Yup."

"You didn't say."

"Nope."

She indulged him with a wry smile and went to the door.

It was Bishop O'Malley, boldly dressed in a purple shirt with a cross at his neck big enough to wave at a vampire. His hair was slicked down helping preserve the illusion of youth which he cultivated. His expression was serious.

"Please forgive me Angie but I need a private word with Baxter. Would you mind?"

"Of course not Bishop, come right in. I'll leave you boys alone in the den."

Which she did.

The den was Baxter's territory. He'd chosen the furniture. He'd fixed the walls. It was not to Angie's taste but he had a bar in there, a plasma screen television that was almost wall to wall, one of those Scandinavian stereo systems that was a techie's dream, and stacks of copies of Playboy and National Geographic going back to the days Baxter had been in short pants. And on each of the walls, which were windowless, Baxter had huge Andy Warhol prints. The genuine article including a pastel Marilyn Monroe. Angie didn't like them one bit but she didn't tell Baxter that. And last but by no means least there was a large mahogany desk trimmed with gold-edged leather that was clear and uncluttered save for an onyx pen set with a silver naked lady reaching for the sky flanked by two black pens set in holders at rakish angles.

Once Angie'd closed the door on the two of them, Baxter clasped the Bishop's hand in both of his in what Baxter regarded as a man to man handshake. Baxter broke off and went to the bar, asking his guest what he wanted to drink—"Scotch or Bourbon?" he offered.

"A bourbon, please, straight but on the rocks," responded the Bishop.

Baxter poured one large Jack Daniels into a whiskey tumbler, fixed himself the requisite Johnny Walker with a dollop of soda, and after handing the Jack to his guest, they both sank back into a pair of armchairs big enough to accommodate a sumo wrestler. Baxter opened the conversation.

"So what do you want Bishop?" Inquisitiveness twinkled in Baxter's friendly eyes.

The Bishop smiled. "Call me Patrick. It would make me more comfortable."

"OK, Patrick, what did you want?" smiled Baxter.

"God help me; I feel awkward just spitting it out."

"God help you? God help us all Bishop. Are you sure there is a God to help you?"

"Oh yes Baxter, there is a God. But he won't help me in this."

Baxter was in no mood to get to the point quickly. He was enjoying himself too much. "Why? Why is there a God I mean? If he exists seems to me he doesn't help much with anything. If God exists, who created God?"

The Bishop looked startled, then he relaxed and sighed, sinking back into his chair. "I'd noticed you'd not been much in evidence Baxter. You don't attend mass often, at least I presume that's the case. Are you in trouble?"

Baxter nodded, then took another slug at his ample drink. "But never mind me Bishop. You're dodging my question. Who created God?"

The Bishop sighed for the second time. "Now I wouldn't want to do that Baxter. Dodge your question I mean. God created God."

"Really?" said Baxter, genuinely surprised.

"And please call me Patrick."

Baxter nodded his assent. "Go on."

"Well God is eternal. Without beginning. Which is hard to grasp. It is hard for our minds to go backwards forever. Going forwards forever is easier. The scriptures tell us that the church is the bride of Christ and the product of this union will ultimately be a new heaven and a new earth. Beautiful as an idea don't you think?"

"I suppose," said Baxter, unconvinced.

"So who's to say that process does not continue, that there isn't a glorious greater purpose in all that is? For heaven read God, for earth read all creation. Everything goes on. But reborn better in the sense that it is more awesome than even this near infinite universe. Can you accept that?"

Baxter nodded. "I guess."

"So it is. And you can run the process backward in time. Or you could but for the fact that time itself is born new with each new creation."

"You've lost me now Patrick."

The Bishop smiled at the acknowledgment of his Christian name. "Our problem is that we find it hard to recognize that God the Father transcends time and space. He is the Alpha and the Omega. The beginning and the end. But that is not a temporal beginning. Nor does creation, the sum total of creation, the 'world without end' of our prayers, truly have an ending. Perhaps it doesn't even have a beginning."

Baxter was clearly puzzled and said as much. "As I read it you are suggesting all there is is a purposeless, endless cycle of life and death with no beginning."

"Well no beginning on the grand scale. This universe had a beginning but who's to say there aren't others. Some scientists postulate the possibility of a multiverse; many universes either side by side or concurrent.

But I digress. In terms of the world we know and love, look at it this way. The Holy Spirit is God working in the world. A vibrant life force but still God, still a persona. The creeds do us a disservice when they say that the spirit proceeds from the Father and the Son. That is true and less than the whole truth. The Spirit is the Hagios Pneumos of the New Testament scriptures. They used to call Him the 'Holy Ghost' but the name is unfashionable. That is what the Spirit is. The very ghost of the living God. The Spirit is here with us in this world, wrenched from the body of God as a child is wrenched from its mother. The supreme God transcends time and space which is why prophecy happens, why God can know the future."

"Enough Patrick!" And Baxter was laughing out loud now. "You have truly lost me and I'm not sure I even want to understand. You read science fiction?"

The Bishop smiled in turn and shook his head. "No, I don't."

"Well I do and my favorite author is Ursula Le Guin and you know what she says?"

The Bishop obliged by shaking his head as expected.

"She says the only thing that makes life possible is permanent, intolerable uncertainty, not knowing what comes next." He smiled. "But not you. You have the answers. And you believe in God."

"I do," answered the Bishop. "But I'm not going to knock uncertainty. I don't know what's coming any more than you do."

"Well that's good enough for me. I'll fix you and me another drink."

Which he did. And passing the glass back to the Bishop he said, "Now Patrick, what was your problem?"

But the Bishop shook his head. "No Baxter. You go first. Something is troubling you. You said so. What is it?"

So Baxter told him. He had always been one to wear his heart on his sleeve. But he didn't look at the Bishop's face. Instead he stared at a corner of one of the Warhol prints as he spoke. "Merrill Manufacturing is going bust. I'm finished, Bishop. Not even sure I'll keep the house. Angie doesn't know. Oh, she knows things are bad. I overextended you see." Now, almost reluctantly, he moved his whole head to match the Bishop's stare, eye to eye. "Anyway it doesn't matter what I did. Point is the business is finished. Just signed the papers with the lawyers and the banks two days back. A weight off my mind. They've given it a week's grace before we tell the staff. A week to run up more debt. Ostensibly it's a week to find a buyer. It won't happen. Anyway, either way, I'm finished."

The Bishop's heart went out to Baxter. He looked gravely at the broken man. He admired his stoicism. "Is there anything I can do?"

Baxter shook his head, his brow wrinkling momentarily, then he smiled. He looked at the Bishop with friendly eyes. "It's really not so bad. The end of a nightmare." And Baxter laughed. "Drink up Patrick. Now it's your turn. What's your problem?"

And the Bishop suppressed the hint of a frown, then smiled in turn. "Ah you can't help me. You can't help me at all Baxter. I came here to borrow money you see."

And for the second time that evening, Baxter found himself laughing. And the Bishop, to do him justice, laughed with him.

5.

Only be strong and very courageous, being careful to do according to all the law which Moses my servant commanded you; turn not from it to the right hand or to the left, that you may have good success wherever you go.

Joshua 1:7

Tuesday, 23rd October: "Those two guys with you all the time?" Officer Donna White indicated the street outside with her uplifted hand. She was visiting Father Sebastian in the parish office at OLPH on the corner of Sumner and Mount Pleasant—and this was official. With a soft, fair face and almond eyes she already looked young; her tailored jacket was deliberately cut just a little too big at the waist to cover her gun and the oversized jacket made her look younger; the effect was charming. It was ten in the morning.

Sebastian chuckled. He moved aside an overcoat draped across a chair back, offering Donna the seat. "Only till tomorrow. The two weeks are up then. And no—not all the time thank the Lord." Sebastian looked at her shrewdly. "But that's not why you're here is it?"

"No Father Seb. Your personal security is impressive. But that's not why I'm here." She shook her head and looked at the handsome priest. His dark, brooding eyes were almost mesmerizing. Such a waste, she thought. "Nope, it's that knife attack I've come to talk about."

Seb growled his response. "We've been through all that."

"Yup. But I thought I'd explore this again."

"In what way?"

"The 'who could have wanted you dead?' way."

"Somebody who had a habit to feed. Someone who needed money."

"And you attack a priest if you want money?" Donna's exasperation was genuine. "S'pose it weren't that. S'pose it was the person who wound us up over you being seen with Mary Young before she died."

Which is precisely what Seb had been supposing. But he wasn't going to share his suspicions with the police. To do so would compromise his position as a priest. They'd have to reach their own conclusions. "So?"

"What d'yu say we hypothesize Father. It could have been Bob Young. If he thought you'd been talking with Mary when she was contemplating suicide and not keeping him in the loop?"

Seb shrugged. All too near the mark, he thought. Though he so hoped it wasn't Bob.

"Or could have been the husband or lover of the woman you were with if that woman was not Mary."

Seb narrowed his eyes. He wasn't sure he liked the implication, but he couldn't fault the logic. Baxter Merrill. Seb shrugged the thought aside. And yet ... "I was not with Mary. I told you that."

"Yup. But you failed to say who you were with."

Seb shook his head from side to side. "And I'm still not saying."

"Obstructing the police is a crime."

"But you're not going to read me my rights and haul me downtown?"

"No," Donna forced a smile to cover her irritation. "Not this time." She shrugged. "If you're not going to help yourself, we can't help you. Tell me one thing though, Father Seb."

"What's that?"

"Any idea who beat you up a few days after Mary Young's death?"

Seb had been expecting this. He shook his head. "Nobody. I just fell and bruised my face."

For a moment Donna stared at the window beyond Father Seb's shoulder. She listened to the sound of a passing car. She breathed out slowly. "Priests allowed to lie, Father Seb?"

Sebastian's expression remained sympathetic. He leaned forward a little and said, "Nope. But then I'm not lying am I?"

"You're not?"

Seb laughed. "No. I am giving you a formulaic response when we both know the truth. I do that to make it easier for you. If I said that John Doe or whomever beat me up I'd be betraying that person."

Donna looked at the priest and realized for the first time that he exasperated her. "For a priest, you seem pretty screwed up Father Seb. There is no excuse for dishonesty."

Seb shook his head. "You are correct of course."

"And you're not going to tell me who hit you?"

"No."

"You know what Father Seb?"

"What?"

"I think it's past time you grew up and joined the rest of us in the real world." She narrowed her almond eyes as she said a perfunctory, "Good morning."

And she paid no attention to Father Sebastian's friendly, "Goodbye Donna." She turned and made her way to the door.

6.

He will wipe away every tear from their eyes, and death shall be no more, neither shall there be mourning nor crying nor pain any more, for the former things have passed away.

Revelation 21:4

Wednesday 24th October: Sean Hartnett had had a tough day at work. Tough enough to have almost dulled the sheen of his dark brown eyes and wiped the boyish smile off his face. That smile was one of his most endearing attributes. He was drinking bourbon on ice.

Bishop O'Malley was boyish too in his way, with that shock of black hair, a lock of which always seemed to manage to fall forward over his forehead. His delicate long-fingered hands were caressing a matching glass of bourbon. No stingers this time.

They sat, as so often in the past, in the Bishop's study in the Bishop's residence next to the cathedral up on that hill in downtown Springfield. The Bishop had phoned Sean at work to ask him to stop by on his way home. He came straight to the point. "She's blackmailing me you know. About us."

Sean was startled. "How's she doing that?"

The Bishop raised a forefinger. "She came to see me. Demanded money."

"She wants to punish us maybe."

"So she said." Bishop O'Malley smiled ruefully at his friend, "She's succeeding."

Sean wanted to say it would all be OK to tell Patrick not to worry. But he had never seen Trish like she'd been lately. She was cold. Unforgiving. Relentless in her anger.

"That's the hell of it. We have to be careful, Patrick."

The Bishop looked up, his eyes sharp. "We have to not see each other any more. I as good as promised her that."

ean stared into his glass. "Maybe it's for the best," he heard himself say.

"Are you worried?"

Sean nodded.

The Bishop smiled. He twisted around in his chair and reached out a hand to comfort his friend. "You know the story of the boy with the bicycle?"

Sean shook his head. His eyes grew distant and focused on the lapel of the Bishop's jacket.

The Bishop felt a tension he wanted to hide from his friend. Almost unconsciously, he screwed up his eyes and wrinkled his forehead before allowing his features to relax. Then he started his story, leaning back in his chair and staring at the ceiling as he spoke. "This boy was given a bicycle for his birthday but his family was poor and had to scrimp and save to afford the gift. What they'd not been able to afford was the little extras. There was no bicycle bell. No puncture repair kit.

"Anyway the boy was thrilled and rode his bike about all day. At the end of the day he got a puncture. Depressed and worried, he parked his bicycle in the yard behind the house and couldn't get to sleep that night for fretting about how he'd find the pennies for a puncture repair kit.

"The next morning he got up, went to the backyard, and looked at the bike. It still had a puncture."

The Bishop's piercing blue eyes searched for Sean's and when his friend at last met his gaze he added, "So the boy didn't worry anymore."

"Don't get it," said Sean. He had contorted his right hand to bite at the inside edge of his thumbnail.

The Bishop shrugged, "Worrying hadn't done any good."

Sean looked at the thumb he'd been gnawing and laughed. The Bishop had a story for any eventuality. He tossed them around like an old vaudeville juggler tossing oranges. But that still didn't deal with the problem. "What should we do?"

The Bishop shrugged again, and chewed at his lower lip like a schoolboy.

It was Sean's turn for a moment of inspiration. "We'll speak to Father Seb. She trusts him."

And Bishop O'Malley managed a smile. Clutching at straws was always useful, he thought. If only because it delayed facing the inevitable.

7.

And Delilah said to Samson, "Please tell me wherein your great strength lies, and how you might be bound, that one could subdue you."

Judges 16:6

Thursday, 25th October: Angie and Seb were back on the river side bike path. The two of them, plus Titus. In the distance you could still hear the traffic droning on. But the background sound was unimportant, and the silence between them was meaningful. It was colder now. Not cold. Just not hot.

The weather was changing. The air was crisp with an expectation of the onslaught that winter would bring. The trees had turned to their rich hues of crimson, reds, and yellows which marked the coming of a New England fall. Many had begun to shed their leaves, but the relative warmth of the past few weeks had heralded a blissful Indian Summer. Yet, nothing could forestall the impending autumnal cascade

Angie shivered a little and rubbed away the goose bumps on her arms. Though she was wearing a long skirt, all the colors of fall, and sturdy shoes, she had on only a light sweater. That and a light silk blouse served to separate her from immodesty. Along with an inadequate bra.

Seb watched her and noticed her shiver. He offered his warm coat which she ostensibly attempted to refuse whilst at the same time allowing him to place the jacket round her shoulders.

"I don't need it."

"You do."

She smiled at him, a contented smile that showed the edges of her teeth. One of those smiles to die for.

"Things are better with Baxter then?"

"Much. Far better, David. Better than I hoped for."

The familiarity startled him. "Only my mother calls me David."

"You mind?"

Seb shook his head as he stooped to pick up a stick. He toyed with it a moment before casting it aside. "No I don't mind." Seb watched her then as they walked side by side. "So you are happy?"

Angie was startled. "Happy?" The question surprised her. She shook her head. "You fall, you pick yourself up."

She brushed her blonde hair aside and broke step, pausing, looking up at Seb and searching for his eyes. "Everything is a compromise. Even marriage. There are no big loves, big hates. No, I am not happy. But I am no longer unhappy. I no longer want to kill Baxter." She smiled, then added softly "... or myself."

Seb grasped her by the arm, spinning her towards him, his brow furrowed in concern. "You never think that."

Angie looked up at him with a lingering regard that dwelt tenderly on him. Her wonderful, changeful eyes blinked. They were of the tenderest gray immediately about the dark pupils, merging into the deeper translucence of slate like the night sky in the predawn twilight.

She had been over this ground with him before. In her mind she thought, "Aw David, I'm a big girl now." But she said nothing.

He shook her then.

"Suicide is a terrible wrong that hurts those that love you. An infectious sin of the most evil kind. Suicide is murder and murder has been wrong since the day Cain slew Able."

For long seconds they stood there. He held her upper arms in a grip that would do credit to a wrestler. And she watched him, until at last she couldn't help herself. "David you are hurting me," she said in her gentlest voice, softly, like a mother to a child … without reproach.

And embarrassed, he let her go. They fell into step again; David, Angie, and Titus; three abreast. They walked on awhile. He felt awkward and self-conscious. He looked around at the still verdant autumn undergrowth—anywhere but at Angie. The woodland was thick with brambles on the upslope of the bike path.

"Did you come down here from your house the usual way?" he asked.

She looked obliquely at Seb and grinned impudently. "Want to see?" She took his hand and led him, childlike, along the path. "It's close by here."

The track, when they came to it, was barely visible from the bike path and twisted through the undergrowth. She let go his hand and started to climb, Titus at her heels. She spoke as she climbed, at one point almost crawling through a long culvert under both the railroad and the highway. "Before they built these noisy obscenities, this was the way to get from the river to the old summer tea house on the hillside above. From that point, there's a quite decent path to the house."

As they rounded the bend in the steep path, there it was ahead of them. The summer tea house was a little pagoda-style building with its two glass doors swung wide open to reveal a rustic bench. There was a wooden cross to one side on the otherwise bare walls of this small wooden structure, a mute reminder of his calling.

She turned as he caught up with her and doing so she stumbled a little and he frowned and reached a hand to help her. As he did so, she looked at him, her eyes locked on his.

She tried to regain her composure. She knew that she adored this man, priest or no priest. Whether she moved first was hard to tell in remembrance. She was standing apart one moment and the next he was crushing her with his arms, embracing her, kissing her as if the pent up passion of half-a-lifetime could be expiated in that one moment.

Her head fell back as his mouth slid to her throat. And she responded with her body, her breasts, thighs, pressed against him, letting him enfold her, opening herself to him without the semblance of conscious thought, responding at some animal level, all pretence brushed aside in the raw energy of the moment.

Had David Sebastian been rationalizing this, as he would later, he'd have been reminded of the way the psalmist speaks, of deep calling to deep. Now he just shuddered as he reacted to the sex of her; crushing her still further to himself, he folded her beneath him, his lips on hers, pushing her backwards between the open doors of the tea house, where she crumpled willingly onto the rough weathered wood of the floor.

His weight was on her now and, without thought, his hands were everywhere, at her breasts, at her thighs, reaching, not actually undressing her but instead pushing at her clothing, almost tearing it away, until the flesh of her was exposed. The air was almost redolent with the musk of him; he behaved like some rutting stag moving to mount his hind. And from somewhere deep within him, the man that had become this animal cried out to her even as he kissed her full lips and then down as his mouth found her now naked breasts.

And as she felt his hands moving to push aside the fabric of her long skirt, she lifted herself, helping him as he wrestled with the last vestiges of her clothing, aching for his hands on her naked flesh. Again she arched her body beneath him, moving by instinct now rather than design, her breasts tingling, her nipples tight.

"This is wrong,'" he was saying as he kissed her, as his hands explored her, as she gasped at the weight of him and the intensity of his frenzied actions.

"Angie, this is so wrong," he said, even as she writhed against him, all conscious thought gone, hearing but not hearing as she spread herself for him, infected by his desire, his lust so vitally acute that she trembled, the instrument that was her body singing in ecstatic, erotic response to his movements.

For Seb, there was something schizophrenic about this moment. Like once long ago with a high school girl heavy petting in a car, there was a part of him, unwanted but not unnoticed, that said this was beyond the pale, this line that he, now a supposedly celibate priest, was about to cross. And she was totally his now, to take. And the closer he got to indeed taking the squirming soft exposed prize that was Angie, to consuming every vulnerable lithesome morsel of her, the more that maddening inner alter ego grated and protested like a hockey mom at the PTA.

And he stopped. Puzzled like a dog doused in water, he tore himself from her, aware that in another moment he would be making love to her, and wanting that so much that it made his stomach hollow with the ache of the thing. And still he stopped, pulling himself away, stumbling backwards from the near-naked woman, her bruised body exposed raw beneath him, bearing the marks of her victimhood.

He was sorry then and tried to tell her so. "Angie ..." he said looking down at her, his dark eyes wide, panting as she was.

And she just looked back at him, her mouth open as she gasped for air, her body writhing a little still even now without him. She heard him then. Heard him as he said, "I am so sorry," in a crisp voice for what seemed the hundredth time.

Then she watched as his eyes hardened into stony brown disks, and he turned and walked away back down the path by which they had come. Her chest was still moving rapidly with her breathing. She was still not quite certain what had happened or why, still half expected him to turn back to her as she lay on the floor. Which he didn't. He just walked from her, seemingly forever, and her desolation, her profound humiliation, as she lay there, was absolute.

8.

How are the mighty fallen.

2 Samuel 1:25

Thursday, 25ᵗʰ October: Whilst Angie Merrill had been wrestling, albeit willingly, with Father Sebastian on the floor of the summer house at 185 Longhill, neighbor Sean Hartnett, master carpenter, friend of the Bishop, husband of Trish, was also wrestling; but he was in the arms of Alicia White, widowed mother of Officer Donna White. Alicia had him on his back, his right foot over his folded left knee, and she was leaning into him, stretching his taut muscleswith all the weight her slender body could muster.

Alicia was a personal trainer at LA Fitness, a new state–of-the art physical workout center crafted from what had been the old Basketball Hall of Fame down on the Springfield riverfront. Sean was one of her clients.

And Alicia was one of this world's better types, at least in the eyes of Sean. Sure she was a little odd. But then what American woman wasn't? Alicia had her eccentricities, like eating the whites of eggs on whole wheat toast for breakfast (the yolks being, according to Alicia, too high in cholesterol). And who was to gainsay her? She was a strong-minded woman. But she'd kept a good figure, despite being the wrong side of fifty. She wasn't conventionally cross-the-street beautiful but she had enough bubble to her personality to cover any shortcomings. And as a trainer she was one of the best. It was a job that she regarded as a vocation, a career in which whatever you did, helped, made a difference. She felt she was one of life's participants—not a mere spectator.

And Sean confided in her. On some things. His deepest secret, of the quiet hours spent with Bishop Patrick, was something he would prefer was his and God's alone.

Sean was confiding in her now.

"Things are bad between me and Trish," he said.

Alicia raised an enquiring eyebrow. "I'm so sorry to hear that Sean."

"It's not her fault."

"Oh," said Alicia. "I thought you two were the perfect couple."

"We were I guess. Or we could have been. My fault though. I hurt her."

Alicia leaned into Sean a little more heavily. Sean flinched. The intensity of her gaze bothered him. He felt as if she knew exactly what he was thinking.

She leaned into him again.

"Ouch Alicia. Cut that out."

"So just how did you hurt that lovely woman you married, Sean Hartnett?" She slapped his knee, indicating he should fold his other leg up and over so she could stretch that in turn.

"It wasn't like that Alicia. I didn't hit her or nothing," he said, shifting his position.

Alicia raised an eyebrow again. "You were playing away from home?"

Sean nodded. Alicia leaned her weight into him once again, a little harder than necessary. Sean didn't flinch this time.

"And she such a beautiful woman. And so in love with you if I'm not mistaken. You're a foolish man Sean Hartnett," she said, leaning back from him and standing akimbo, her hands on her hips like a circus ringmaster.

And Sean looked back at her. "You're right there Alicia. More stupid than you know. Fuck it. I think everything around me is so much shit. And she stays with me, like a flower on a dung heap. And I don't change, I won't ever; fucking stupid. That's me OK." And he wished that he could make things like they had been when he and Trish had first married. But he knew you couldn't. There was no going back, no such thing as water under the bridge, because in this worldview, he was the river, not the bridge.

9.

*These are they who have come out of the great tribulation;
they have washed their robes and made them white in the
blood of the lamb.*

Revelation 7:14

Friday 26 October: It was almost midnight. Bob Young was
out late, walking, along the winding roads of the Forest Park
neighborhood. Down Magnolia Terrace, past the mayor's house
on Pineywoods, and up Florentine Gardens toward Cherryvale
and back to Longhill. It was very late, even for a Friday night.
One in the morning and hereabouts most of the good Burgers
of Springfield were tucked away in their beds. The occasional
house had its porch lights on. Not many though.

Cherryvale was tree-lined like many other side streets in provincial America. Well-trimmed lawns with gardens covered
in mulch preparatory to winter's snow wrapping themselves
around the well-painted Victorian clapperboard houses. Even
in the moonlight, the gingerbread details of some of the finer
structures were clear. Every now and again there was a flagpole
with the ghost of an American flag

Bob didn't sleep so well these days and more often than not
walked by Father Sebastian's house late at night. It was an ob-
session with him. He recognized that in himself. But he had
every right. What had that priest been up to with his Mary?
What had she said to him? What had they been doing alone
the night she died? It gnawed at him.

Bob Young had found things difficult since the death of his
wife. His children, Jenny and Robert Junior, had always been
closer to their mother. They were grown up anyway. Truth was
he was lonely. He had got close to Angie Merrill, talked to her a
lot when they were alone on Churchwatch. Her marriage was in
trouble. She'd confided that much in him. She was a handsome

woman. But even she spent too much time with Father Seb.

The very thought of Father Seb made Bob angry. Donna White, Alicia's girl, the policewoman who'd made detective, had been round nosing into his business. Even implied that he'd been the one to attack Seb. Wanted to know where he'd been. How the fuck did he know? He'd beat the guy up. Sure. And he bloody deserved it. But knife him? The thought gave him a rare twinge of pleasure. Yes, if only he had.

He found himself thinking about death. He'd been doing that a great deal lately. The Dalai Lama said that you should contemplate your own death at least once each day. That death was a part of life. Bob did more than that. Death frightened him. The contemplation of death made it less terrible, like the child opening the dark cupboard to stare inside for monsters. Except you couldn't, could you? Stare across the void to the other side of death that is.

He'd studied Cicero at university. He remembered the four threats that old age brought on: retirement, weakness, less sensory pleasure, and approaching death. The way Cicero had it they all had an upside: authority, wisdom, and less distraction for the first three. And the upside to approaching death was it was a no-lose situation—either there'd be no afterlife and so no regrets, or there'd be an afterlife and a whole new adventure.

And where was Mary now? Had she ceased to exist? Or was she, a suicide almost certainly, in the very pit of hell with Satan? Was there a hell or was that all allegory? And if not what was there? No physical resurrection that was for sure whatever the antediluvian creeds of the church said. But a spiritual continuation of the inextinguishable spark of life? A tomorrow in which we all share a new existence as different from our current life as is the butterfly from the caterpillar? Perhaps.

Or perhaps not. Bob felt somehow distant from reality as he thought on this, feeling some pale shadow of an out-of body-experience, as if none of this mattered, life, death, his own existence, given the immensity of all that was

Bob stepped from the sidewalk to cross the little street. He was walking toward the intersection with Longhill, walking home. Then he heard the roar of the engine. Heard it for maybe three seconds. Long enough to turn and look into the brilliant glare of the headlights bearing down on him.

He could have saved himself had he been just the slightest bit quicker. But he froze a split-second too long. The great black bulk of the Hummer hit him square in the chest. He folded under the vehicle, too startled to do more than gasp as the huge weight born by the nearside wheel of the H3 crushed his ribcage. He was still conscious as he watched the vehicle recede into the dark. He gasped through the pain of his crushed ribs, fighting for air that just wouldn't come. His eyes were already misting as he saw the tail lights glow red. Then the light changed to white as the reversing light came on. By the time the tank-like vehicle had backed over his broken body, he was mercifully unconscious.

10.

Stay with me, fear not; for he that seeks my life seeks your life; with me you shall be in safekeeping.

1 Samuel 22:23

Saturday 27 October: Angie was the one to find him. Angie and Titus. She'd been hanging on for Baxter to come home, expecting him to give Titus his late walk. And he didn't come. Had he come she had no idea what she'd have said to him. Nothing she supposed. She was bewildered by the events of the day, her emotions raw. She knew that her marriage was over. That was true whether or not she ever saw Seb again. She wasn't even sure she wanted to see Seb again. What they had almost done made her feel dirty, in some way corrupt, as if she were responsible for destroying Seb. Perhaps she was, she reasoned. Though the rejection still grated. She shrugged away the thought. They were both adults.

And Baxter? She'd speak to Baxter in the morning. Resolve things somehow. Leave him she supposed. There was no other choice. She remembered that Seb had once said that these hard decisions and painful questions were only so impossible because you viewed them from the wrong perspective, from inside the relationship looking out. They should be viewed from outside the relationship looking in. Seb. Was that business just two days ago? How humiliating. She couldn't go to church again. Not now.

But it was way past late and there was no Baxter. Midnight came and went. So she found herself walking Titus across Longhill and meandering into the side streets of Forest Park, in the direction of Seb's place in the early hours of Saturday morning.

The streets were deserted. She had turned into Spruceland with its old Victorian houses set back from the road and walked on round to Cherryvale heading back for Longhill.

Then she found him.

She heard a feint moan, like the sound of a small dog whimpering, at the very edge of her hearing, before she actually saw him. And when she saw him she thought for a moment that she was looking at a bundle of rags in the street. Titus barked.

"Shsh Titus." She moved closer and gasped. This bloodied mess was a man. And not just any man, this was a friend.

She knelt, folding herself to the ground, cradling Bob's head. The injuries were horrific. She had the sense to dial 911 on her cell phone. Bob was falling in and out of consciousness.

He felt her move, felt the nearness of her, comforting in the darkness. "Angie," he said. "Is that you?"

"Yes, I'm here Bob. Help is on its way. I've called the ambulance and Father Seb's house is close. I can get him."

Bob's response was little more than a bare gasp. "No," he whispered. "Not Sebastian." And there was something desperate about the haunted eyes of the dying man.

Angie nodded. "It's OK Bob," she said, stroking the head she cradled in her lap. "We'll wait for the ambulance. Just the two of us. I'll stay with you."

And she did. It took time. In Springfield, cell phone 911 calls are routed through Eastern Mass before being forwarded back to Springfield Police Headquarters. The consequent delay cost Schools Superintendent Robert Young his life. By the time the ambulance arrived, Bob had not long heaved his last shuddering breath. And though Angie knew he was dead, she stayed with him, talking to him, caressing him, as if it still mattered.

11.

Above all hold unfailing your love for one another, since love covers a multitude of sins.

1 Peter 4:2

Saturday 27 October: The police and ambulance arrived together. The carcass of what had once been Bob Young was marked out, examined, and the street cordoned off; curtains twitched and neighbors gathered, and Angie was questioned. This was more excitement than this quiet, upscale, Springfield neighborhood was used to.

Somewhere a dog howled. Angie looked round for Titus. She had forgotten him but he was there, being petted by a concerned neighbor, someone she knew by sight from church. She nodded her thanks and made brief eye contact before turning back to respond to a man she'd heard introduced as the Captain of Detectives. Detectives Muse and White were also there. They were partners. Angie recognized Donna White. The way it worked in Springfield was the uniforms called in the Captain of Detectives and he attended with whomever he chose to call. For a big case he'd call in all eleven, the full squad. Even for a small case if they were available. Not for what the boys called the "gimmie" murders, the ones where a wife shot her husband and was found with a gun in her hand or whatever. Those were assigned right away to the team for that district. Springfield was divided into eighteen districts. Each detective had more than one. Muse and White were partnered up for districts nine, ten, and twelve. For a big case like this they'd hit it with everything the first 48 hours; after that the case starts to get cold. The Captain of Detectives would figure the scene and send for the sergeant of detectives for the night shift squad. The Captain of Detectives was talking to Angie now. She heard but not heard the officer's questions.

When at last she found herself able to think with clarity, her thoughts turned to Seb. Where was Seb? Could he sleep through all this?

And then she thought of Bob. Where was he now? Did the soul remain a distinct conscious entity as you entered the stream of eternity and merged with the infinite? She hoped so.

She realized she must be in shock. She heard someone say that the Medical Examiner was on his way and when he arrived he'd take precedence. The Medical Examiner checked out any unattended death, any suicide, and this certainly qualified. Someone told her they'd finished with her for now.

"Can we walk you home lady?" someone was saying.

She declined, shaking her head. "It's just a couple of blocks. Over on Longhill. I have Titus. Please, I need the space."

The officer agreed, "OK. We'll take your statement in the morning," he said

She left that place then, feeling eyes on her back, wondering what they were thinking.

But 185 Longhill, when she got there, was silent as the grave. Baxter was still not at home. She felt as if she were breaking apart, her emotions shredded, lonely, sorrowing, hungry, thirsty, yearning. She drank a glass of water, gave Titus some biscuits, locked the house telling the dog to hold the fort, and walked back out into the dark of the night.

When Seb answered the door it was 4 a.m. She was leaning on the buzzer, the weight of her body on the door jamb. She allowed herself to fall forward into him. Not caring whether she appeared melodramatic, too totally defeated and discouraged to even allow herself to care whether he rejected her. But he didn't. Nor did he ask a question. He ran her a shower and she discarded her bloodied and dirty clothes wordlessly as he averted his eyes like a schoolboy, gathering the soiled garments and handing her a robe. Later he took her to his bed and made to leave her there but she clutched his sleeve with such desperation, almost whimpering. She begged not to be left alone, and he weakened – and climbed into the narrow single bed alongside her. She was asleep in his arms in moments.

Later still, in the first gray light of dawn, she woke with a start, her slate-blue eyes wide like a frightened doe. He was still awake and soothed her then, and she reached for him trembling lest he again reject her. And he responded to her without hesitation, without word, covering her mouth with his and stifling her gasp as he entered her. And they at last made love in the half-light, before both fell back to sleep.

12.

This is the sign that the Lord has spoken: 'Behold, the altar
shall be torn down, and the ashes that are upon it shall be
poured out'.

1 Kings 13:3

Saturday 27 October: Trish Hartnett rarely attended OLPH
on Sumner these days for the traditional Sunday mass. Instead
she attended a Saturday afternoon mass for Springfield's
growing Spanish-speaking community at St Mathew's on the
Quadrangle, the massive nineteenth century pile next to the
Bishop's residence that the inhabitants of Springfield called the
Cathedral.

Warm and bordering on the ornate, the cathedral has a dis-
tinctly retro feel to its painted interior. A grand, pastel blue,
gold-roofed alcove in the Eastern tradition dominates the place.
There sits the Bishop, robed this time of year in purple, red, and
gold, watching as his priest and deputy, Monsignor Gilberto
Rodriguez, delivers the sermon for the separate Spanish mass.

Off to the right, all the fires of Pentecost explode in a mosaic
behind a baptistery built like a castle in the background to a
pre-Renaissance world.

Off to the left, in front of a safe place for the adoration of the
host, wait the assorted drums, guitars, and songsters of the vibrant music group which typically accompanies this service.

And boy they can sing! The noise fills the place, resounding
from wall to wall of this cavernous palace to God, which is by
now hot enough, whether from the Holy Spirit or some less
sacred cause, to strip the coat off your back.

And above it all, the Lord Jesus, a starburst to rival the sun in
blazing gold at his back, shadowed by an Alpha Omega Cross

feint enough to give the image of the resurrected Christ complete dominion, transcends the very heart of the cathedral, suspended in space and offering that peace we all yearn for but rarely find, in the welcome embrace of his once-crucified open arms.

But Trish Hartnett wasn't looking up. She was looking down at the floor, which was less spectacular, covered wall to wall with tacky gray linoleum. And here she prayed with the best of them but pointedly refrained from taking communion. And this day as always in recent weeks, she sat in the front row where the Bishop could be sure to see her. And when she wasn't praying she lifted her green-gray eyes to stare at the Bishop.

Bishop Patrick O'Malley had come to dread the 4 p.m. Saturday mass, when sure as eggs are eggs, the sensual woman who once ruled the roost at Springfield's Classical High would shroud her rich auburn hair in a resplendent Italian silk headscarf and watch him, nobody but him, from start to finish.

Unlike his more affable Puerto Rican deputy, Monsignor Rodriguez, our Bishop Patrick, wasn't given to the practice of pressing the flesh with the faithful after the service. Afterwards he liked to escape like some deus ex machina in reverse, disappearing into the cloisters and thence to his dilapidated adjoining home, much in need of a lick of paint, which was not likely to happen anytime soon given the sorry state of the diocesan funds since the compensation payouts started for child molestation by the clergy.

So the Bishop tried to dodge off in hope of escape.

But not this time. This time she was ready. She had figured out his routine.

As he stepped from the side door of the vestry, Bishop Patrick found Trish barring his path. It was raining and she was standing there, getting soaked.

"I want to talk with you."

"Later would be best."

Not later. Now."

The Bishop shrugged. He was not the kind of man to put off going to the dentist. Nor would he put this off. It was his character to deal with his problems head on. He led her back into the vestry. He had more than a shrewd suspicion that this meeting would leave him feeling violated, and he'd rather it not take place in his home.

Trish Hartnett was in no mood to pull any punches. "It's disgusting," she was saying. "Sean doesn't want to sleep with me. I guess I'm just not satisfying enough," she said. "Like I'm supposed to just be okay with the love of my life banging you, you disgusting little man. If your God exists, he must be as evil as sin."

The Bishop flinched. "God is perfect and cannot be evil. Nor can he create evil. But we have been given free will and can stray. We are free to follow God's plan or not. Free to make mistakes and learn by those mistakes."

"You think your words impress me?" Trish answered, "You pretentious fucking faggot."

The Bishop didn't respond. The example of Christ before Pilate flashed into his mind. Though he was no Christ, he quietly reflected.

"I have to live with what you've done," she said. "And I continue to pretend that I'm okay with it because I have to." Her words poured on, battering him like a torrent. "If I have any hope of ever really being his wife again, like before, I have to lay off punishing him. But fuck it! I have fucking feelings too. I'm tired of hearing, 'Sure I felt that way for a while but I dealt with it'. Yeah. I know what he did with you, and if he hated it so much, why do it in the first place?

"I think about things. It'll soon be Thanksgiving. I think about how happy I was last year when I was shopping for Thanksgiving dinner. And how I already know how I want to prepare things this year. But I get ignored even if I ask him what he wants for supper tonight, because he doesn't want to answer yes or no because he wants to see what else is happening first. Just in case there might be something better. I don't know. There isn't anything better, for me. I guess there is for him.

"Sometimes I feel so lonely and I hurt so badly. So much that I can't keep it in. I would think I didn't have tears enough anymore. Just when I don't think I do. It's like this bile in the back of my throat. I feel it rise and I swallow and try to keep it down and it's too strong for me. It breaks through.

"Then he thinks I want to fight. I don't want to fight. I just want to be his top priority again. I want to be the only one in his life again. Fuck you! So tell him it's no big deal. I don't even want to think about it. About you, Bishop, touching him and kissing his lips and laughing at his jokes, and he being in your bed. It makes me sick. And it hurts.

"And each time, I vow not to talk to him, because I just hurt. But I can never do it, because all I want is him, his love, his attention.

"I want that dream. I want Sean to take me in his arms and tell me he loves me and he'll never ever leave me

"But it won't happen."

The Bishop shook his head, unable to find words to respond as at last she sat down. The vestry held the basics for making coffee, and he went through the motions, knowing the gesture would be futile. "Can I pour you some," he said.

"No." Her monosyllabic refusal was the prelude to the inevitable question. "You have the money?"

Patrick O'Malley realized this was a game he could never win. His reply was both sullen and defiant, and equally monosyllabic. "No," he said.

"Why?" she asked, her curiosity seemingly genuine.

"I can't raise that kind of sum. I have tried. It is not possible."

"You leave me no alternative."

"You are not seriously suggesting you will expose me, with all the consequent gossip?"

"Yes. Unless that is, you retire from your position. Leave Springfield. Return to where you came from. Do whatever ex-Bishops do. Go to Rome on retreat or something."

And, as if a great rod were lifted from his back, he heard himself say, "No."

"You realize I don't have to go public on this. I can just write to the Cardinal in Boston and there'll be a private investigation – and you will be finished."

Bishop O'Malley smiled like a child at Christmas, the relief palpable as he found the strength within himself not to mind. "I realize that. The answer is still no."

And pretty Trish Hartnett's homecoming queen face crinkled, her eyes narrow with the spite she felt at the foul thing this man had done to her Sean. Her words, when they came, were measured, the emphasis strong on the first word of the sentence. "You will be sorry," she said. And she turned and left the room.

13.

The joy of our heart is ceased; our dance is turned into mourning.

Lamentations 5:15

Sunday 28 October: Trish Hartnett was fixing the flowers Sean had brought her. She was singing a Carole King song. "You make me feel," she sang. To Sean's ear her voice sounded like that of an angel. "You make me feel," the words went, "You make me feel like a natural woman." She had a good voice. If she'd been listening, Carole King would not have been offended.

Sean's mind drifted and soured. He interrupted and his careless words broke the precious spell like a ball through a window.

"It's not fucken' right, Trish."

Sean Hartnett was nervous. He had always thought this woman too rich for his blood, even when he'd first fallen for her. But now he knew what a colossal disadvantage her knowledge of his behavior had placed him in. He bit his lower lip and steeled his courage. "You can't go after him like this."

Trish narrowed her pretty green-gray eyes into cat-like slits, squinting at her husband. She was not going to make this easy for him. She felt abused as well as betrayed. It was a feeling that failed to dissipate. "Why can't I, Sean baby?" she purred maliciously. She picked up a glass of coke, and used a straw to stir the ice cubes absentmindedly as she looked at him.

"It's not fair Trish." He squared his shoulders to ease the tension in his muscles. "He's not a bad fellow."

"Fair?" She glared at him and he flinched like he'd been hit. "It's not a question of being fair. It's a question of justice. He's wrecked our lives. Well now he can pay. Justice as in retribution, Sean baby. An eye for an eye. You understand that don't you?"

She drew in a great gulp of air, gathering strength for the inevitable tirade that had become the only healing she could find.

"I hate you for choosing him over me. I hate you for thinking that's okay, for not telling me the truth, for making me feel worthless.

"How the hell am I supposed to forgive you for treating me worse than I ever treated you? I never made love to someone else.

"Do you have any idea how many tears I cry every day because you finally forced me to surrender my heart, and then you just left me feeling soiled and useless.

"I can't figure it out. If I'm so bloody great, why in the fucking hell do you fuck him? Why do you kiss him and spend time with him?

"I hope he's worth doing this to me, worth the possibility that you might just lose me forever. I guarantee you're going to regret this. You're going to feel so awful for doing these things to me. Like the way I feel now—only worse.

"I've never wished anyone would die in my life. But I wish he'd die.

"You know what? You just don't give a tinker's cuss how I feel right now. You don't care what you said to me, you don't care that you're sticking your dick in him after you stuck it in me. And I'm not fucking okay with that. I want to rip your fucking heart out so you can't hurt me.

"I'm not sure if we'll ever get back to the way we were because I can't stop being so fucking livid. Like I'm not supposed to be upset that you're with him instead of me?

"Shit! Why? You love me. Not him.

"I love you so much that I'll do anything to make you happy, anything, even if I die inside and have to cry myself to sleep forever.

"I hope he's worth it. You don't give a fuck. Congra-tulations. Have him."

ut Sean was shaking his head. "No Trish, it's not like that." And he looked at her. And looking at her he wanted to go to her, to stroke her auburn hair, to comfort her like he'd once have done. But he didn't. Instead he just said, "What we did was wrong. We've already paid, been paying. I pay each fucken' day when I look at you. Takin' it out on him ain't gonna make it any better."

And Trish realized then that he was right. But regardless she ached for vengeance. She needed her pound of flesh. If the Bishop wasn't going to give her satisfaction, she'd find some other way. The image of her Sean with that man in her mind's eye repulsed her.

"You're right Sean baby," she purred. "Nothing sets the clock back."

But she could set the record straight. He had played away from home. Well what was good for the gander ... Sure.

14.

Humble yourselves in the sight of the Lord, and he shall lift you up.

James 4:10

Monday 29th October: "It's three in the morning."

"You said I could phone anytime—day or night."

Seb recognized the voice. Pretty Trish Hartnett. Poor woman.

"You spoke to Sean?" Her tone was ice brittle.

"He spoke to me."

Her tone softened a little. "Same thing."

"Not quite. He came to me of his own accord. I didn't ask him to."

"And he told you everything? About him and that man? That bishop?" She spat out the last word with venom. Seb could visualize her contorted face.

But she was still talking. "Look. I want to see you and talk to you. The thing is I'm really frightened. I'm never going to stop loving Sean but I can't take it anymore. He's going to come to realize there isn't anyone else for him. When that happens, I will still love him deeply. At the moment Sean doesn't care about my feelings, and I hurt enough without Sean being awful because he's mad at himself for what he did."

Seb tried to speak but Trish wouldn't let him. "You're not calling me back because you're tired or because something more important has your attention. Sean is the love of my life, Father Seb, he's everything I have, my Sean."

"We should meet. Brunch tomorrow? Partners?"

126

"Now." The voice was edged with panic. "I want to see you now."

And Father Sebastian looked back to the bed. The bed where Angie had spent time with him in their shared brokenness. And he didn't want to see Trish Hartnett in this apartment. Not now.

"Can I come to you?"

Trish laughed, her laughter as frank and unexpected as snow in summer.

"Are you afraid I might come over and compromise you with the neighbors? My-oh-my. I'm flattered, Seb."

He laughed with her. And even as he laughed he was put in mind of a discussion he had had years ago at seminary. Every complex situation, every problem, had a gift in its hands, something that could be salvaged from the mess. Even the complex did not necessarily mean complicated. When a thing was complicated it was both complex and not easily untangled. And this sure was complicated. In all crises a measure of spiritual discernment was necessary; only then could you perceive whether a situation was divinely or diabolically inspired. And you didn't need to be a prophet to be sure that this was not God's hand at play.

Not that that should make a difference. It was Sean's duty to help. But he should be cautious. And he had his rules about meeting women alone. But was he beyond that now? He was already compromised way past anything in Trish Hartnett's imagining. What did it matter? His eyes ached and his head was heavy with tiredness, but even so he felt the tension ease as he made his decision.

"Yes," he said, "Of course. Come over."

15.

Yet thou in thy manifold mercies forsookest them not in the wilderness: the pillar of the cloud departed not from them by day, to lead them in the way; neither the pillar of fire by night, to shew them light, and the way wherein they should go.

Nehemiah 9:19

Monday 29th October: It was morning now. Seb was sitting making notes on a legal pad, trying to get his head round the Trish Hartnett affair. He thought if he set it all on paper he might know better what was needed from him. His handwriting was small, cramped and clenched up, full of underlining. It looked like he felt, he reflected. The door bell rang. He answered it.

"You look tired, Seb"

"Poor Trish Hartnett phoned in the middle of the night. She insisted on coming round."

Angie lowered her head mischievously to look up at him from under her lashes. "No rest for the wicked," she said, then regretted the words as soon as she saw the hurt look on his face. She reached a hand and cupped it tenderly to his cheek, feeling him as a blind person might, just touching him with her fingertips. "Dear David. I am sorry. This must be so hard for you."

He took her small hand from his face, holding it between his like a parent with a child, and led her inside, away from the doorstep.

She reached up then, to kiss him as he closed the door. But he stepped back from her, touching her moist, expectant, coral pink lips with his fingers. "No Angie. I can't think. I must think."

It was her turn to hesitate. She stepped back toward the door, nervous lest he see her eyes mist over.

"Of course, Seb. I understand. It was wrong of me to come here," she said. "I need to be going anyway. I promised to call in on the Hanlins after breakfast. The Millers are home from their posting, and they'll be there. I was at school with their daughter."

She was reaching to open the door to leave him, and she looked back at him. Their faces had that strange immobility that people's faces have when they are waiting for something to happen. And the suddenness of his reaction startled them both. With a sound that melded somewhere between a groan and a sigh, he enveloped her in a crushing embrace, more consuming her than kissing her. Pinning her back against the door, he reached at her clothes.

Later, afterwards, she lay beside him naked and unashamed, her clothes scattered where he had stripped them from her. And he was sleeping, face down, childlike, and vulnerable in his exhaustion. She struggled up on one elbow and half closed her slate-blue eyes against the sun streaming in from the window above the bed as she scanned his body. She decided as she watched him there that she'd have to take the lead on this. The choices were hers. She could leave him now, never see him again. And he could salvage his life, perhaps continue with the church. But it was her decision, not his. She knew that, and the knowledge gave her a strange sense of well-being and power. For the first time in a long while she felt in control of her destiny. And it felt good. Very good indeed.

16.

Show us thy mercy, O LORD, and grant us thy salvation.

Psalms 85:7

Monday 29th October: Vickie Walters had been upset. At first she thought she had done something wrong, offended him in some indeterminate way. He had totally changed his behavior. After chasing her from pillar to post, he'd won her heart. Then silence. She wondered whether he might be in some sort of trouble. But no, she must be the problem. It was something she had done.

And now she realized he was trying to teach her a lesson. He'd done it in such a mean way, just cutting off contact like that. And it hurts even now it was over. He was the most important thing in her life. Now she'd lost him. Still it hurts.

But for a little while at least, she had him back. He was here, with her. She could feel her heart melt just looking at him, this older man. He'd skipped work. It was late afternoon and he was on his third martini and already slurring his words.

"I'm going to give you some advice, Vickie." He smiled, "This one last time."

"Last time?" She heard the words and let them sink in. She felt short of breath, like a schoolgirl with a crush. She knew it was an ending. Sealing the loss. She'd been in denial, as she had always been.

He nodded. "First thing: friends, shrinks, boyfriends, that's all bullshit," he said. "You are the only thing that matters and you have to learn how to be alone."

He was waving at the barman using his glass like a boy scout with a semaphore flag. She watched him order another and shook her head in the negative in response to his raised eyebrow. She didn't need another drink. She tried to laugh at herself. Earlier she had said she wanted to be alone. Now she was.

"You can be alone and be happy with that," he was saying. He was smiling with his eyes, still waving his glass at the bartender whilst talking to her, impatient for the new drink he had ordered. His eyes were sober, clear; whilst his mouth, his demeanor, was that of a drunk.

"In order to be with other people, you have to learn to be with yourself." He reached out, resting his hand on hers. "When you can be yourself, that's the time you're gonna be ready to be around other people." He sort of leered at her then. "That's the time when people will go after you."

He let go her hand as the bartender passed him a new martini. The way he saw it, he was keeping it simple. He wanted his words to be meaningful to her. In his way he had loved her. But even he recognized that at fifty-four, he was a sight too old for a girl like this. His mother had taught him the Victorian code which meant that a man should never go out with a woman younger than half his age plus seven. Not that he was going to tell Vicky Walters that. He was more than twice her age.

Still, it had been fun. The love she'd felt for him was freshening. It blew through him like the wind. Lifted him. But now it was time for it to end. Sometimes things have to end because there's no room for them to go forward. Making time, treading water, was just not an option with this girl. He wasn't that cruel.

He picked up the chilled glass and sipped his drink. "It's very obvious what's going to happen. You are twenty-two. You are intelligent. You have more culture than people twice your age, but you are still twenty-two."

He watched her eyes fill with tears. He found that strangely arousing. He reached for her hand again. He watched her. She wasn't saying anything. He wondered whether he was being coherent. "You will disagree, because you see things different," he said.

She shook her head again. "No," she said, "I don't disagree," her words barely above a whisper.

"You are twenty-two," he said again. "You can't deny or change that. You are gonna behave like a twenty-two-year-old person, until you're not any more. You can try behaving like you're thirty, but it's not the same. It takes a lot of pain and those years to get there. You'll only understand when you see for yourself, when you live it." He set his glass down then. "And that's the last thing I'm gonna say about it."

Vicky Walters sighed and bit back the tears. So this was the end, she thought. Baxter Merrill was dumping her. Falling for this married man had cost her dear.

And Vicky garnered the last fragments of her self-respect, and finally summoned the strength of character to get up and walk away from the table without looking back. As she left the bar, the man she had loved stared blankly in her direction for a moment, before turning his attention to his drink.

CHAPTER FOUR: NOVEMBER

How forcible are right words! but what doth your arguing reprove?

Job 6:25

Thursday 1st November: They sat in the Hanlin's great oak paneled living room. Another three weeks and it would be Thanksgiving. The wind whistled through the eaves. It was evening. Father Seb, Angie Merrill, Dick Bryer, and Mike Hanlin were all drinking brutally chilled apple martinis, as had become their custom, except for Bryer who contented himself with his BBC Steel Rail ale. Hanlin's wife, Jane, had a garden club board meeting and had left them to their drinks. Marilyn Bryer had gone with her.

The white plastered ceiling roofed the broad windowed room, the whole of it framed in miniature rafters twisted into geometric shapes a century back by Italian craftsmen. The ceiling provided a chocolate box contrast to the somber dark patina of the stained mahogany paneling that covered all that was not window or fireplace.

And the great hearth with its polished wood- framed marble surround held a huge grate from which tongues of flame licked upwards from a fire in which yard long logs crackled in unending song. It was one of those fires you yearned to light even in summer just for the comfort of the thing, not so much for warmth as for reassurance in a bleak world.

And then the ornaments in ordered clutter, brass and brass and more brass, at the fireside and shelved on the walls. Burnished brass Arab coffee pots like soldiers marched in serried ranks around the room, the collection of an eccentric orientalist.

Hanlin and Bryer had called them together. They had an agenda. Hanlin was talking. His shock of black hair made him look younger than his years. He lowered himself into his chair. His dog, Bart, padded across and Hanlin leaned over to pat the animal as he spoke. "The situation needs resolving. We can't have the streets of Springfield becoming like downtown Washington."

Angie Merrill winced. She watched the reflection of firelight in the liquid in her glass.

"Sorry Angie. It must have been awful finding Bob like that."

Bryer interrupted. "Can we rewind on this, Father Seb? When you were attacked in the street, knifed that time, that wasn't the first time you'd been attacked was it?"

"All right," Seb sighed. "I suppose it makes little difference now. He's dead after all. Yes, Bob Young stopped me one time. He was angry. Someone had told him I'd been talking to his wife the afternoon she died. I denied it."

"And he believed you?"

"He hit me."

Angie was astonished. The others seemed amused, but the three words chilled her blood to ice. "You never told me that."

"No, I didn't." If anyone noticed the sheepish way he looked at her, they said nothing.

Bryer interrupted. "So it could have been Bob Young that subsequently knifed you?"

"It crossed my mind. I don't think so though. The person who attacked me wore a hooded sweatshirt. If it had been Bob, he'd not have concealed himself."

Hanlin broke in. "Bob thought you'd been having an affair with his wife?"

"I don't think so. Perhaps that I'd driven her to suicide. Or that I was withholding something. He really believed I'd been with her that day."

"Why?"

"Because, like I said, someone told him I'd been on the bike path with his wife."

"And you weren't?"

"That was me Seb was with," Angie said. "Baxter and I are having difficulties. I talked to Seb about it that afternoon."

"I see," said Hanlin. "So someone with a wish to make trouble tells Bob that Seb is with Bob's wife. Forgive me for this Angie but just to clear the air, could that have been Baxter?"

Angie laughed to mask the fact that what she really wanted to do was escape. But there was nowhere to flee. She stood abruptly. Her lithe figure was silhouetted against the firelight as she shifted onto the balls of her feet and smoothed and straightened her skirt. "Oh, I don't doubt that Baxter could be possessive enough. But no. He was preoccupied at that time, with the trouble at Merrill Manufacturing."

"So who killed Bob?"

"And why did Bob's wife kill herself? And why did it take the DA two month's to come to that conclusion, anyway?"

Hanlin grimaced. "We're getting nowhere." He signaled to Anna, setting her to work on another round of Apple Martinis and ale, then turned back to look at Father Seb. There was too much beating about the bush going on. Hanlin made a conscious decision to be more laconic from here on in.

"Seb. Could it've been a woman that knifed you?"

135

2.

They gave me also gall for my meat; and in my thirst they gave me vinegar to drink.

Psalm 69:21

Thursday 1st November: Angie Merrill saw the Lincoln Town Car when she arrived home at 185 Longhill. Baxter's car. He'd not been home for days. No word from him. Not that he'd gone missing. He'd been seen about town in his old haunts—in the bars and even going into the "Carnivale," Springfield's famous strip club. He just hadn't phoned her.

Angie let herself in with her front door key. Her heart was pounding so hard she could feel the thump. Not with guilt or fear but rather from the shear adrenalin rush of this moment of crisis. Which was what it was in Angie's eyes. She had no idea how Baxter would react when she told him. Violence was a given. Would he rape her? Possibly. She would accept any degradation, but she believed nothing would break her resolve.

She found him in the den. He didn't look up when she came into the room. She hated this room with its bright walls and garish prints. She wondered whether he really enjoyed the Warhol pictures. She'd have thought a Remington more his taste. But then Andy Warhol had the chic cachet, the prestige. Was it all sham, the life of this man she had once loved? He looked strangely morose. He grunted in acknowledgment of her presence without raising his languid brown eyes from the empty glass he was nursing. "That you, Angie?"

"Yes, Baxter, it's me."

"Fetch me a whisky, babe."

"You know something, Baxter?"

"What?" His voice turned sullen.

"You don't want a wife, you want a servant." She took the glass from his hand and stepped catlike across to the bar. She ignored the ice tongs and picked up the cubes one by one with the slender fingers she had once used to caress him. In her mind this was the last time she'd do this for him. She was making it personal, like performing a ritual. She carefully counted the ice cubes as she dropped them into a fresh glass, a heavy cut crystal tumbler. Four fingers of Chivas Regal. She handed the glass to Baxter, then sat opposite him, watching him. As he raised his glass to his lips she said it. "I'm leaving you Baxter."

"Uh huh," he said without looking up.

Curiously, she felt the anger rise like bile inside her. "That's all you can say after all this time?"

"What do you want me to say?" he asked.

Now at last Baxter looked directly at her and she noticed how red his eyes were. Had he been crying? No, not possible. It must be the booze. Whatever. It aroused no sympathy in her.

She studied the man who had been her life and whom, now, at last, she was leaving without compunction. "Nothing," she said. It was what he meant to her now after all. "Nothing," she said again.

And she turned and left the room—forever.

3.

And then shall that Wicked be revealed, whom the Lord shall consume with the spirit of his mouth, and shall destroy with the brightness of his coming.

2 Thessalonians 2:8

Friday 2nd November: Trish Hartnett answered the door. She recognized Donna. Trish thought in some ways Donna looked so very much like her mother.

"Mrs Hartnett. We are sorry to bother you. This is Detective Robert Muse."

The man was in plain clothes. Sports jacket and tie. Muse liked to wear a sports jacket to cover his gun, a semi-automatic, in the old days it used to be a revolver. He extended his hand cautiously, as if afraid the gesture might be rejected. "Forgive this intrusion, Ma'am. We need a few words if that's O.K."

Trish was both surprised and curious. Even a little worried. "Come in."

She was about to ask whether the Bishop had sent them, but some sixth sense stopped her. She wasn't quite that stupid. Though one thing was for sure, she thought, if Bishop O'Malley had called these two in he'd be smiling on the other side of his face soon enough.

"What can I do for you, Donna? Detective Muse?"

Muse might have tried to answer, but Trish Hartnett cut him short. "Cawffee?"

Donna was about to say no but Muse stopped her. His disarming pale slate-blue eyes were flecked with brown. He smiled and said, "Coffee would be fine. Cream and one sugar for Officer White. Black for me."

Muse had a full head of silver-gray hair, a broad full face, and powerful arms and shoulders, like a man that worked out. Despite his short stature he was the kind of man that women find attractive. Trish was no exception. She smiled back.

While Trish left the room to get the coffee, the officers took in the mantelshelf with Sean Hartnett's sports trophies, silver cups and college pennants. Pretentious thought Muse. "You think she did it?"

Donna shook her head, "No fucking way." Her small rosebud mouth clenched thin lipped in defiance, as if daring him to gainsay her.

He shrugged like a man indifferent.

The coffee didn't take long. "I always try and have a pot ready ..." Trish said, "... For Sean."

"That would be your husband, Maam?" said Muse, knowing the answer.

"Exactly right, detective, my husband. He's a self-employed carpenter. He often comes home unexpectedly, between jobs. I have work of my own, of course, but when I'm here, I keep hot cawffee always ready," she lied, but it seemed the expected thing to say.

Muse switched persona, Jekyl turning Hyde, becoming abruptly businesslike.

"Mrs Hartnett, I'll get straight to the point."

Trish sat down on a chintz covered sofa. "Please do," she said.

"We have received an anonymous letter, implicating you in the murder of Bob Young and the attempted murder of Father Sebastian."

Trish almost laughed out loud. She cupped her hands around

the hot coffee mug, seemingly too astonished to reply coherently. That bloody Bishop would pay for this she was thinking. But in her own time. "What did you say?" she asked, buying herself seconds.

"An anonymous letter," said Muse. He sized up Trish Hartnett. She was sure a beauty, and she knew how to package it. It looked as if she'd squeezed a sensual size eight figure into a size six dress. Short but feisty is how he'd describe her. Her full head of auburn hair was to die for, as were her seductively green-gray eyes. Sex on legs.

"Mrs Hartnett," he found himself saying. "Where were you between the hours of midnight and 3 a.m. on the night Bob Young died?"

Trish was irritated. "In bed asleep. Where else would I be?"

"And your husband can vouch for that?"

"No, actually."

Donna White broke in, "Why is that Mrs Hartnett?"

Trish appeared unembarrassed. "Well, Donna, Sean, and I have had some problems with our marriage lately."

She continued without embarrassment, as if she was talking to a close friend. "I told Sean last night that I cannot talk to him anymore, until he gets his life together, and realizes that he and I belong together."

In fact after her conversation with Sean, she drank the best part of two bottles of pinot grigio and passed out upstairs on the floor. She was thinking that she couldn't deal with him being with that Bishop. That she couldn't think about it or hear about it anymore.

She looked at Donna. "He knows where he should be," she said.

At least, his heart does she thought. She needed his love and his support. God it's not even about any of that, she thought. It's about him. Not what he does for me. "I have faith. It takes time," she said.

"I'm so sorry," said Donna.

I'll bet you are, Trish thought. But she decided to be civil. "Anyhow he was out late that night. I don't know what time he came in. I was asleep when he came to bed."

The detective switched gear. "Can we have a look at your Hummer, Mrs Hartnett?"

Trish didn't understand him, or at least pretended not to. "What's this? Some kind of show me yours and I'll show you mine conversation?"

Muse was not amused and indicated as much with his taught expression. "Look Mrs Hartnett, our solve rate used to be 94% and now it's 60%. We're short staffed and overworked but we're on a mission to turn things around on the Springfield Force. Which means we take murder personally. So please, don't mess with us.

our Hummer, Mrs Hartnett. The car. Where is it?"

If she hadn't understood him to begin with, Trish understood him now but seemed little the wiser. "The only Hummer in this town is the one owned by Michael Hanlin. He keeps it in his driveway down on Longhill."

Muse wasn't into playing games. "We know about Mr Hanlin's Hummer. It's yours we're interested in."

Trish was too much the schoolgirl at heart not to be amused at the potential for double entendre. She pursed her lips into a baby-doll pout and tilted her head to one side, "Why Detective Muse, I have no Hummer. Not the kind you're looking for anyhow."

Donna spoke, her words terse, like an adult with a child, "Mrs Hartnett, this is serious."

Then Detective Muse cut in, his words cold like ice, "A woman answering your description took an H3 Hummer out on a one month hire from a rental car agency at Bradley International Airport in Windsor Locks two weeks back."

This is too much, Trish was thinking, but she kept her cool. "It wasn't me detective, I swear." Trish smiled her best smile. "Are you so sure she really answered my description?"

"We don't have to be sure Mrs Hartnett. She produced your driving license and used your credit card." And like a good mouser with cornered prey, he waited, savoring the kill, before he added, "Where, exactly, is the vehicle, Mrs Hartnett?"

4.

Therefore, behold, I will this once cause them to know, I will cause them to know mine hand and my might; and they shall know that my name is The LORD.

Jeremiah 16:21

Saturday 3rd November: "Don't you give me any bull; you know what I'm talking about."

"No, Mrs Hartnett. Truly I don't." Bishop Patrick O'Malley tried to fend her off with words, a little frightened of this volatile woman who had stormed her way into his home. Pretty she might be in the normal run of things but enraged and red faced she looked like a gnome on acid.

"Please Mrs Hartnett, believe me."

"I should believe you! You—your whole life is a lie."

Bishop O'Malley bowed his head. Her words cut through him, hurting at a profound level, pricking at the inside of his chest like a foretaste of mortality. "But I swear on all that is holy, I did not send that letter. I'd swear on my immortal soul if I still had one."

Trish Hartnett sighed. She felt the fight go out of her. She collapsed into the armchair in the Bishop's study— the same one where Sean had sat so many times before.

The Bishop found himself thinking how much was chance. How simple it would have been if he'd never met Sean. He thought of the Blaise Pascal maxim, "Had Cleopatra's nose been differently shaped, the history of the world would have been altered." So much was chance from the stray bullet on the battlefield to the stray encounter on the street. And in another sense nothing was chance. Chance only shaped the environment. Man made the choices. Chance sets the stage and we are the players and life is and can only be what we make of it.

He realized then that she was talking again.

"I love him so much," she said, staring at Bishop O'Malley without looking at him. "It's so hard not to be like we used to be. I don't know how long I have to wait, but I know now that Sean and I will end up back like we were before.

"I just have to learn to be patient. Patience is important in a marriage, especially with Sean, because he's more sensitive than most men. I need to learn more patience for those times when things are going badly. The more patient I am, the easier it will be for me to talk to him.

"Father Seb told me that I should work on getting my head together now, so that if I do end up back with Sean, I'm a better person for his sake and if I don't, I'm a better person for my own sake. Seb makes sense. He's a good man. After my talk with Seb, I just feel better.

"Although better doesn't mean that much. I've never loved anyone enough to wait like this when I went through breakups before I met Sean. I just found a new man. But now, no one else will do."

And saying that, she wondered if it was true. But it was true now, which was what mattered. "I will be here when my Sean realizes that he needs me in his life. For the moment, I'm okay with waiting."

There were tears in her eyes. The Bishop reached out a slender long-fingered hand to comfort her. She stiffened, and he moved away, as if slapped.

"I am sorry," he said.

The palms of her hands felt slick with perspiration. She gripped the arms of her chair tightly to stop her hands from shaking.

The old anger welled up in her. An ocean of it, demanding expiation, "I bet you are. Thrilled I should think."

"No, Mrs Hartnett. I am sorry. You don't deserve this." He hesitated, "The police only questioned you in your home? They didn't take you in for questioning?"

She shook her head, irritated.

"Then they cannot be sure of their ground. I am certain that's the case. This will all get cleared up. It is some terrible misunderstanding."

Trish Hartnett looked up at him, her green-gray eyes catlike, narrow. "You better hope so, Bishop. 'Cause if I go down, you can be damned sure I'll bring you down with me."

She paused. She realized that sounded weak and she wanted this man who had caused her such an ocean of pain to feel something of the pressure she was under. She got to her feet so she could look down at him. Then she delivered what she intended as the body blow.

"If I am ever arrested and tried for Bob Young's murder, I will see to it that my defense lawyer brings out every detail of your relationship with my husband. You will be finished here."

And as she stood over him, the Bishop thought, but didn't say, "It was your precious Sean as much as it was me. And he enjoyed every second." But even as he allowed himself the luxury of the thought, some part of him realized it was, in actuality, all over, his time as a Bishop, and worst still if that were possible, his relationship with Sean, all finished, done with, along with his immortal soul. And the thought broke him.

She watched him visibly wilt as she gazed at him, savoring the moment. Then she turned and left him at last.

5.

Sharp arrows of the mighty, with coals of juniper.

Psalm 120:4

Monday 5th November: The Merrill home was built on a bluff where the Indians once camped, the narrow yellow clapperboard picked out by small cream-framed windows. There had been some early, heavy snow this year, normally rare before Thanksgiving, and small drifts highlighted the deep corners of the eaves and the roof over the wraparound porch. Great trees, two times and more the height of the house, reached for the sky and in the process half-hid the ancient mansion, A few were Scots Pine. Fully a third were scrawny but tall, wind ravaged fir, shallow-rooted and known locally as widow-makers. The balance asserted by deciduous trees, a myriad of species including oaks, maples, chestnut, apple, and ash as befits ancient woodland, most already stripped naked by this fall's onslaught, their branches seemingly frail against the cold, all quite bare but for what remained of a few red oak, multicolored, in their best autumn dress.

Baxter Merrill opened the door at 185 Longhill. It was three in the afternoon, but he wasn't at work. There was no work for him to go to anymore. "Angie isn't in," he said, the words automatic like a check-in clerk, a reflex to the face that smiled into view.

"You look a mess, Baxter."

He knew he looked a mess. He didn't need anyone to tell him. "Angie's not here," he repeated, ignoring her comment.

Trish placed her arms akimbo, like a hooker talking to a cop. "You gonna let me in or am I just gonna stand here?"

She let her arms drop to her side. Baxter looked at her then, looked at her like a man looks at a horse, his languid brown eyes

146

appraising her, skimming slowly along the curve of her neck, the sweep of her arms. His glance dropped down to her thighs, strapped into a skirt that was little more than a handspan from waist to hem, framing the impression of her sex, and enhancing the illusion that she had legs that went right back up to her shoulders, despite her modest height. All the above together with breasts to make you think you'd died and gone to heaven. Not quite Dolly Parton breasts. These breasts were full but well proportioned; breasts that invited you in like looking at the open door of an Aladdin's cave, hinting at the treasure beyond, alluded to by the outline of her nipples against the cotton of the flimsy T-shirt that was all she wore despite the cold.

Baxter's gaze, reluctantly, left her body and returned to her face. She was smiling, her green-gray eyes held the confidence of a woman who knows her strengths and was playing to them; her auburn hair cascading about her like the frame of a picture almost too exquisite to define. Her head was tilted slightly to one side as she examined him in turn.

His response was softer now but his words were the same. "Angie's not here," he said.

Trish Hartnett smiled. "Baxter, it's you I've come to visit, not Angie."

And to do him credit, Baxter laughed. He opened the door a little wider, bowing and sweeping his arms with a Musketeer-like flourish that belonged South of the Mason-Dixon Line. "Do come in then, Mrs Hartnett."

"Trish will do fine Baxter. Call me Trish."

"Angie's left me Trish, you know that?"

Trish nodded.

"Of course you know that. This is Springfield. Everyone knows everything in Springfield."

"Not everything Baxter." She looked him over just as he had her. "You gonna just leave me standing here in the hall?"

"No, of course not. You wanna come into the den? It's more my space than the rest of the house."

"Sure Baxter, that'd do fine."

He talked as he led the way. "You heard about Merrill Manufacturing?"

"Yes. I'm sorry. Not your week is it? First, your company and, then, your wife."

Baxter laughed. "Troubles come in threes I reckon. They'll probably take the house next. Still you reach a point when things can only get better."

They were in the den now. Trish looked around at the garish prints, the black leather chairs. Her decorator's eye was not impressed. But she shrugged and let herself down onto the sofa, taking her shoes off and curling her feet beneath her.

Baxter raised an eyebrow. He felt like a schoolmaster faced with a precocious pupil. "And why did you want to see me Trish?" he asked.

Trish looked back at him. "Did you say something about a drink?"

"No I don't think I did. But since you come to mention it, what would you like?"

It was then that Trish decided to act on the impulse that had led her over here in the first place, though one part of her felt she shouldn't make this too easy. Anyway, she needed the time, if only to ready herself for what she had in mind. "An Old Fashioned please. On the rocks if you wouldn't mind."

Baxter grunted. "I'll have to go out into the kitchen to prepare it."

Trish smiled her best little girl smile. "Why, that's kind of you Baxter."

Baxter grunted again and grabbed the bottle of Makers Mark. He wandered off.

As she watched him, her mind turned to Sean. She'd had another text from Sean to say he'd be working late this evening. She wondered if he'd come home drunk. "When he drinks, he gets horny," she was thinking. She wanted Sean to be hers. To be hot and here. Not with that Bishop. And she remembered how he used to say he missed her every second he wasn't with her.

How she wished it were still true. But now although she still truly loved him, she was unable to have him in her arms. Fuck him. She would teach Sean a lesson on taking things for granted. It was time to prove to herself that she could do without him.

But this was Baxter's home. And Baxter was away in the kitchen fixing the drinks. It took Baxter time to fetch the orange peel, the bitters, and the sugar cubes and to get the crushed ice from the kitchen fridge. But he didn't mind. Better this than dwell on his troubles. He was only moping about anyhow.

He kicked the door with his foot on his way back to the den, his hands holding the two brimming tumblers. Not his favorite drink, but he was never one to be picky. "So exactly what did you want with me Trish?" he asked.

And Trish answered him.

"Revenge Baxter. Just revenge."

She was still on the sofa but she'd stretched her short frame out like a vaudeville tableau, one hand behind her head, one draped toward the floor, palm outward; one leg folded at the knee, the other slack, her small ankle slack, trailing the floor. And from ankle to outstretched hand every square inch of Trish

Hartnett's body was as naked as the day she'd been born and as exquisitely formed as God could have ever shaped woman in the myriad years since time began. Or so thought Baxter.

Baxter was wise enough to know when he'd died and gone to heaven. This was one gift horse he'd not question. And he felt the old familiar dull insistent ache as he placed the glasses on the table at her side.

As he moved to her the desire pulsed through him and he stripped aside his shirt and kicked away his pants before covering her, flesh on flesh, quickly, urgently, lest she'd change her mind. And he scarcely heard her as she whispered the words once more like a caress, "Revenge Baxter. Just revenge." She gasped then, surprised and unready as he took her. And for just a moment her eyes misted with tears. But Baxter didn't notice. Then the passion finally managed to consume her sadness and take hold of her and she raked his back with her nails, urging him on as she arched her body and shuddered in response, and nothing mattered anymore.

6.

Many shall be purified, and made white, and tried; but the wicked shall do wickedly: and none of the wicked shall understand; but the wise shall understand.

Daniel 12:10

Monday 5ᵗʰ November: "You called me here to take your confession, Bishop O'Malley?"

They had exchanged the usual pleasantries and Bishop Patrick O'Malley had failed, so far, to get to the point, hence Seb's question.

The formal way in which the two men addressed each other was a contrived thing, a deliberate artificiality initiated by Seb when the Bishop had taken him as his confessor. He did it to distance himself and the Bishop had played along.

"No, Father Sebastian. There is another matter I wish to discuss with you."

Seb looked at his bishop a moment before replying. He was unused to the reversal of their roles. He the cat. The Bishop the mouse. He could almost swear the man was embarrassed. "What is it Bishop?" he asked.

Bishop Pat O'Malley decided to do away with the normal formality. "Seb. May I call you Seb?"

"Of course Bishop."

The Bishop indicated that the taller man should sit in an armchair. "Seb, take a drink would you? For my sake. It would make me more comfortable."

Normally Seb avoided daytime drinking but he was no stickler.

He agreed to a glass of red wine. The Bishop poured himself a port cask Glenmorangie, neat.

"In a sense, given my problems, of which you are all too aware, I feel less than qualified to raise this matter with you."

Now it was Seb's turn to feel embarrassed. He cupped the glass of wine with both hands. "Please go on," he said not meaning it.

The point is that I am still your Bishop. And ..." O'Malley hesitated. He placed down his whisky and ran his fingers up through his lank black hair. "There is a matter that came to my attention." The changeover was seamless. The Bishop cloaked himself in authority as simultaneously, Seb was stripped of his pretentions and left vulnerable.

Seb decided to make it easier. "You want to talk with me about Baxter Merrill's wife, Angie?"

The Bishop looked at the younger man, his blue eyes narrowed, the authority of his office dictating his behavior. "Exactly, Seb. An old lady of the parish mentioned that she had seen you together and ..." Again the Bishop hesitated, "Need I go further?"

Seb stiffened, then slowly he allowed himself to relax, facing the inevitable. "No Bishop. I do have a problem. I would have brought the matter to your attention soon enough had you not called for this meeting." Was that a lie he wondered? Would he have really? He shrugged the thought aside and continued. "I have grown fond of Angie," he said.

"I think, Seb, under the circumstances you may call me Patrick."

Seb hesitated for no more than a heartbeat. He looked directly at the Bishop, his brown eyes unblinking. "Thank you, Patrick."

Pat O'Malley sighed. "I presume this has gone further than a mere expression of kindness. Were that not the case, you'd have been telling me to mind my own business by now."

Seb nodded, again embarrassed by the direction this conversation was heading. He had rehearsed the discussion in his mind but now he found himself tongue tied—like he'd been caught with his hands in the cookie jar. Which, of course, he had.

But the Bishop smiled gently. "Have you had any past difficulties of this kind?"

"Not of a serious nature."

"Forgive me if I avoid prevarication. You have never wanted to screw a woman before?"

Sebastian, despite himself, felt shocked at the Bishop's lack of circumspection. "I would not be human if I did not feel sexually frustrated occasionally."

"We all have our difficulties. How would you normally sublimate them, through confession, prayer, food, alcohol, talking it through with a friend? Or would you revert to masturbation, like many of our colleagues?"

Seb was confused. "I don't believe you can be truly celibate if you masturbate. Masturbation is a form of sexual practice, albeit crippled and unsatisfactory. As for my sexual frustrations, I try not to sublimate them Bishop."

O'Malley smiled. "Your strictures on masturbation are a little harsh. If we all adhered to them there'd be no priesthood. But to the issue at hand." The Bishop chuckled. "No pun intended. When you say you try not to sublimate your sexual difficulties, you surrender to them?"

Seb's response was rapid and on the edge of panic. "No, I have tried many approaches. But usually I deal with this sort of thing through prayer."

The Bishop mused. "Hmm. I find alcohol better myself. You have had sexual experiences before."

Seb was not phased by this, he knew the Bishop liked shocking people out of their complacency. "Only as a young man, before I was called to be a priest."

The Bishop smiled. "Everything is relative. You are young now. But preordination sexuality is dangerous. Some would argue that it's kinder never to have shown the rabbit to the greyhound, if you get my drift. Have you been discontented with celibacy?"

"No. At least not before."

"And you are now?"

"I am no longer sure. They say Saint Peter was married. Paul counseled celibacy. There have always been two approaches. I am not sure we are right to take an extreme view and rule out a married priesthood."

"But you accept the *diktats* of Rome on these matters?"

Seb answered grimly. "Yes."

"And you have failed to live by them?"

"Yes."

"And so too I."

They stared at each other until Seb broke the silence. "I was aware of the inevitable sexual tensions, but they have never been a problem until Angie."

The Bishop changed tack, "Is Angie unstable?"

"She is going through a bad time. She has been abused. She has left her husband."

"And you were counseling her?"

"Yes."

"And there was a measure of transference, of dependence, on Angie's part, would you say?"

Seb wasn't angry. He had no right to be. He responded automatically. "You imply that I took advantage of her."

"Did you?"

Now at last Seb felt angry but controlled his emotion staring fixedly at the floor. The question was just. "Perhaps."

"So, did you exploit her vulnerability, or perhaps was she less innocent than she seemed, perhaps she exploited yours?"

Seb felt the tears well up and cloud his eyes. He stood and walked to the window, unable to face the Bishop. "It wasn't like that," he said lamely.

But the Bishop didn't relent. "And this encounter, was it trivial for you?"

"No," Seb spun round. "It may have been many things, my motives may have been seriously flawed, my behavior atrocious, ridiculous even, but one thing it was not—it was not trivial."

"Was your reaction in this encounter involuntary? Was this something you could have controlled?"

Seb reflected a moment. "It would be easy to say no but the reality is different. We can always control our actions. Perhaps I didn't wish to."

"So you were in a state of sexual vulnerability and this woman came and took advantage of you?"

"No."

"No. I didn't think so either. So you are completely responsible. You exploited a vulnerable woman?"

"No, I honestly believe that's absurd. Though it may seem that way."

"It more than seems that way, unless, that is, you are in love with her."

Seb failed to respond.

"So you are in love with her?"

Seb remained silent but nodded his head. He lacked confidence. The Bishop waited and eventually Seb replied.

"I am not quite sure of my motives; not quite sure where desire ends and love begins. I guess it's like the chicken with the egg. I'm not sure which came first. But now there is love on my part. Whether that means being in love like in the chick flicks is another matter. I ache for her when she's not around. In what degree that's loneliness, love or mere sexual frustration, I find it hard to distinguish. All three I suppose."

The Bishop nodded. "I don't want to overstate the importance of motive. We are Christians after all. I am inclined to think that the most Christian of lives was that lived by Mahatma Gandhi. He was an avid reader of the New Testament, and he fought for his beliefs successfully using passive methods of resistance against tyranny. And he believed that ends could never justify means. He wrote that means must determine ends and, indeed, that it is questionable in human affairs whether there is an end. The best we can do is to make sure of the method and examine the motive.

"The Japanese have a proverb: The difference between the worst and the best of us is no greater than the wing of a butterfly—and in that tiny separation lays everything and nothing.

"So," the Bishop sipped his drink, his long-fingered hands caressing the glass. "Would you like to tell me about it? From the beginning if you could."

Father Sebastian looked at O'Malley. Not the confidant he would choose for himself, this wounded man, his Bishop. But perhaps in some way he was empowering the Bishop by opening up before him, restoring this broken prelate, healing him. It was a gift Sebastian could offer. And in all conscience he owed this man honesty. He was still his Bishop after all.

And Seb, falteringly, like a schoolboy reporting to his master, told the Bishop everything.

7.

And Jesus said unto him, No man, having put his hand to the plough, and looking back, is fit for the kingdom of God.

Luke 9:62

Monday 5th November: He wondered if God got lonely. Yes he supposed. We were after all created in his image. Perhaps that was what it was all about. Creation. A response to the loneliness of God. That was the hardest thing, he reflected, about celibacy. It wasn't the absence of sex. It was the loneliness that made it difficult. Not to be able to share your life with just one other person. The absence of that intimacy. And he recognized the downside, that it was a perversion of loneliness that drove much of that sin that was adultery—that drove him in his betrayal of his commitment to the church by undertaking this affair. But he needed her, like God needed the lost sheep, with a desperate yearning that transcended sexuality. She looked at him then, her eyes opening in languid thoughtfulness. "You told him everything?"

Sebastian nodded.

"Everything?"

David Sebastian watched her. He liked looking at her. The long curve of her neck could best Berlin's bust of Nefertiti. The way her hair cascaded about her was magic. And now she was naked he liked watching her all the more. The soft down of the faint hair on her forearms. The concave hollow of her belly. And then there were her breasts, beyond delightful. He ached to bury his face between them. And yet she wasn't perfect. She was that little bit plump, her backside exquisitely Rubenesque, her waistline betraying the feint striations of stretch marks, from a time when she'd once been too overweight, this particular flaw making her all the more attractive in his eyes. Not that he was having a Shallow Hal experience. He was quite conscious of there being more of her than many men would find attractive. But if all men liked the same thing, there'd be a sight more fighting and there was enough of that already.

And again he felt uncontrollably aroused. He had had her just now, and he should be replete he told himself. That he wasn't was the product of years of abstinence or so he believed. The ache was mounting in his groin, and he knew it would soon be unbearable.

And she knew it. She blushed then. "Stop looking at my breasts," she said, embarrassed.

"I can't," he said.

She lifted her body from the bed where she'd been lying, with her head on her hand. She sat up so she could look down at him. "So what did the Bishop say?"

Seb found it hard to concentrate on conversation. With Herculean effort he tore his gaze from the fulsome body of the woman looming above him and looked into her slate-blue eyes. It didn't really make it any easier. "I expected him to tell me to leave you," Seb smiled. "But he didn't."

"He said what then?"

Seb reached up a hand and caressed her shoulder, stroking her down her spine so that she trembled just a little as he talked. "Well I told him everything. I had to. Then we prayed together. Then he said that the decision was not about you, so much as about the church. That I should decide whether to stay with OLPH and he said he'd give me time for that." Now it was becoming difficult for her. She moaned slightly but she wouldn't let go of the topic. She shook her shoulders as if to shake away his hand. "But he means you to continue officiating?"

Seb shook his head. His hand had moved down to her waist,

resting there a moment. "Of course not, He will ask Monsignor Davidson to reduce my duties. People will assume it's for R and R reasons, given all that's happened. He says to let them think that."

Angie smiled. "So you get more time for me." She laughed and reached over and pinched the inside of his thigh. Then shrieked as Seb pulled her down, her laughter stifled into a moan by the weight of him as he gathered her up, swung her over onto her back and pushed her legs apart with his and pressed himself between her thighs. And she responded with an inward gasp, and for a last rational moment she realized how much she loved him. Then his mouth covered hers, and she felt both suffocated and consumed as the passion in her took over and she surrendered to the raw heat of the moment, reaching for his buttocks like an animal, pulling him in deeper still and urging him on with her slender hands.

8.

Behold, the LORD thy God hath set the land before thee: go up and possess it, as the LORD God of thy fathers hath said unto thee; fear not, neither be discouraged.

Deuteronomy 1:21

Wednesday, 7th November: Seb was breaking all the rules now. Going to Trish Hartnett's baby pink house all by himself.

He was past needing the old rules. He was treading water spiritually, marking time, assimilating new realities. He had discussed things with the monsignor and the older priest had talked with the Bishop. As a consequence he was no longer required to celebrate communion. But the Bishop had decreed that in other respects his parish duties were to continue unabated. And even had the Bishop decided otherwise, Trish Hartnett was a friend as well as a parishioner. He could not refuse her cry for help. Her phone call had been desperate.

He'd rung the bell but the door was open, on the latch, so he'd just walked in when no one came. He called her name.

She called back then. "In here Seb."

He found Trish. She didn't look good. She was curled in the corner of a cream colored leather couch in the sun room.

The sun room looked over the garden and was lined with windows as it should be, floor to ceiling but for a yard and a half of brickwork rising from the dull red of the tiles that marched across the floor; tiles hid in part by thick cream carpet spread like a lawn out on which sat cane tables, chairs, and sofas with olive-colored cushions on which to rest your bones. Then there were the houseplants. A big ficus tree dominated one corner; a succulent creeper, bright red flowered, drowned out the other. Between these in clumps and clusters on pot stands and tables ranged little baby cyclamen and purple violets to great flowering cacti and assorted, exotic house plants in cascades and splashes of green, rust red, white, and pink.

Trish was cocooned in a zip-up bathrobe, a toweling affair. Her feet were up on the sofa and she had little pink rabbit slippers on, like a child might wear. Her shock of auburn hair was lank and wet from the shower, without so much as a towel to bind it. Her eyes were red from crying. She was smoking a cigarette. She didn't get up.

Seb noticed the cigarette. He'd never seen Trish smoke but he didn't comment. Instead he said, "Shall I fetch you a coffee?"

Trish looked up and smiled despite herself. "You won't know what to do," she said. But he said he would and she let him, so he rummaged around in the kitchen and made the coffee and brought her some. He told her he'd added some good old maize whiskey, Jim Beam. He thought the bourbon would help. She didn't say anything, just took the coffee. They sat there a while in silence. Seb knew when to be quiet. He sipped his coffee and waited. She lit another cigarette and smoked it through before she spoke. Then she said, "Seb?"

"Yes."

"Am I damned?"

"No one's damned Trish. God doesn't work that way."

"I don't want to go another day feeling like I do so I'm telling you exactly what's on my mind."

Seb nodded. "Go ahead."

"What about Judas? He was damned."

"Perhaps. On the other hand there's a non-canonical Gospel of Judas in which he's painted as Jesus' favored disciple who was only doing as he was told by an omniscient Christ."

Trish screwed up her nose, her skepticism apparent. "So that's predestination. The church believes in predestination?"

"Whether Judas had a choice or not is a question that has exercised worthier minds than mine. He will meet his maker on judgment day along with the rest of us. Until when, according to the doctrine of the church, he sleeps, waiting the last trump. I don't know. But I do know that it's a grave sin to call anyone a lost soul."

He paused, looking closely at Trish. She seemed calmer. He continued. "As regards predestination, the church believes that predestination is the certainty of salvation for some: that in a sense there are some that God has chosen."

"Well that's depressing. There are no choices at all then?"

"Oh no. That is far from the truth. Nobody is forced to accept salvation. Not in the eyes of the Catholic Church. God may have chosen you and may have marked you for redemption as one of his elect but you can still ignore the gift of grace. Christ died for all mankind but not all avail themselves of the benefits of redemption. Similarly God predestined no one to sin, let alone hell. Just as no one is saved against their will so no one can be damned without being wicked.

"Having said which things are predetermined in some degree when it comes to the events that take place each day that passes. That is a sort of predetermination rather than predestination—in the sense that God knows the future. Not in the sense that you have no choice in the matter. You determine that future."

"Sounds convoluted to me." Trish lit another cigarette and kept it in her mouth whilst she spoke, making her pretty face somehow slovenly thought Seb. But he understood—or thought he did. She needed to degrade herself. It was like that with people sometimes.

"Not so convoluted really. We have a transcendent God. We are an immanent people."

"Sorry Seb. That's convoluted where I come from. There is destiny. Fate if you prefer. We don't necessarily determine our futures. You just have to look at horoscopes and stuff. Some people are without hope."

Seb shook his head. "Astrology is forbidden to us as Christians. Perhaps because it can so easily be used to generate fear. Some say it is as bad as witchcraft—and it's more prevalent."

"Explain," said Trish, curious despite herself.

"Witchcraft in its best form is just magic. The use of the other's belief and trust for healing. There's a fine line between that and Christ's use of the Spirit of God to heal. The primitive shamans were often the only healer available to the tribe. Are they then always evil? But astrology is more dangerous. Astrology is fundamentally flawed. It is based on the premise that there are forces that deny us free will, that determine our future in some degree. Astronomy is an act of denial of the supreme divine gift that is free will. Without true free will there is no purpose to life. All is futile. This one diamond we mustn't chip away at."

"That's all very fine. I don't know about free will." Trish screwed up her eyes. "All I know is I'm damned whatever you say—in this life and the next."

"I doubt that Trish, I really do."

Her sadness boiled into anger. "I was drunk as fuck last night." She looked up at Seb and wondered whether her language might offend him. But she was past caring what anyone thought of her. "I was freaking the fuck out and I'd been in some bar. I went walking down the street at nearly 2 a.m., somewhere in Agawam, drunk as a skunk in a beer barrel. So drunk, that I had no idea where I was or where my car was. I'll spare you the details but finally I got sober enough to find the car and get back to my bed. I didn't get to sleep until 5 a.m. I've had about three hours sleep. I'm bushed.

"So I flipped with Sean this morning. I was like, what the fuck, I worry my fucking ass off. I nearly exploded I was just so fucking mad. He just doesn't even come home most nights, and I don't know if I'm going to cope.

"Life has become such a rush, and I spend my time running around like a blue assed fly. And whatever I'm doing I can't help thinking about Sean.

"He sent me a text last night when I was at the bar to say he'd be late. That was when I seriously started drinking. I'm sure he could have come home early. I'm upset with myself that I didn't ask him to. He knows I miss him so much, when he goes off.

"I just need Sean. I want to be able to have days like today when I'm whacked out and not sure what's going on, but I can come back home and fall into his arms. Just let him make things better, make it all go away for a while. Take a hot shower and then just sit together on the couch. I need him.

"I need a break. Life is crazy and unpredictable. Friends are unreliable. Sean is gone. I want him to be here. I need him back here. I'm not some love-sick teenager, attention-grabbing. I'm just lonely and I've been trying to keep busy and do what I can. But nothing changes. I always end up sitting here with a drink, and thinking of the love of my life. Thinking of him and hoping he's thinking of me."

She paused then, shaking herself as if to come back from the place her mind was in.

"You think? The police believe I murdered Bob."

"Did you?"

"No."

"And I believe you."

Trish looked up at him then and twin tears tracked down her face. "But there's other stuff I've done."

And she told him then.

And he listened.

9.

For what is a man advantaged, if he gain the whole world,
and lose himself, or be cast away?

Luke 9:25

Thursday, 8th November: They'd been out to supper together which was a first. They'd gone to a discreet out-of-town Chinese restaurant in Longmeadow, an elite district Seb insisted on calling "Longghetto," because of the town's flat refusal to allow any low-income housing to receive zoning permission within its boundaries. It was a place where neither was likely to be recognized. Still, the frisson of risk added an edge to their meal.

Seb had been talking of the things that mattered to him—of his family, of his call to the priesthood, of his belief in God and the sanctity of life. Angie had just listened mostly. It was all about him, but she didn't mind. He had been there for her when she'd needed him. It was his turn now.

Later, they were in her car. He was driving. He had intended to drop her back to her new place in the nearby Georgetown district, but she put her hand on his arm, "No, yours," she said. He knew this meant she would stay the night and he was uncomfortable with the idea. This was going too fast for him and these bridges, once burnt, could not be crossed again. Not too fast for Angie though. She had thrown herself at their shared new world and the new dawn it represented for her. She wanted him to move in with her in her new home.

Angie's words broke in on him then, earnest and keen edged from the passenger seat of the car. He could feel her looking at him as she spoke, watching his face for reaction. "You know you were talking about the sanctity of life?" she asked. She wanted to understand him, this man that made her feel so good.

He nodded. "Yes."

"That's really important to you? All life?"

"Yes," he said again.

"But you're not vegetarian."

"No," he said. "But if I were no longer a priest, I might become a vegetarian."

"Why not now?"

He smiled. "Don't want to put anyone to any trouble," he said. The minute he said it he noticed how lame it sounded but it was the truth.

"So all life is sacred?"

"Yes."

"I had an abortion once."

He pulled the car over, in close to the sidewalk. The road pavement was glistening black in the streetlight. It had been sleeting. It was late. He turned to face her. "What did you say?"

"I had an abortion."

"Why?"

She was nervous now. She'd just wanted to be honest with this her new love. "I was young. In college, actually. There was a boy I liked. I was careless. I was afraid of what my parents would think."

"But how could you do that?" He was disturbed by this new revelation, and he genuinely wanted to know. He didn't care how immature he sounded.

She watched him, her head tilted a little to one side, like a cat, her slate-blue eyes wide, appraising. "You talking as my priest or as my lover?" she asked. She was a little frightened inside by how cold his voice sounded.

"I can never be your priest again." He frowned bitterly. "I'm not sure I can ever be anyone's priest."

She smiled and reached a hand over to smooth his brow. "I've been reading up on it," she said. "On celibacy I mean."

He didn't say anything. He had turned back to stare blankly ahead out of the windscreen, so she went on. "There weren't many celibate priests before Pope Gregory reformed things in the sixth century. Certainly not in the Western church. Monks were celibate, not priests."

He turned to face her again. "Maybe I should become a monk," he said. And then, "You never said anything about this at confession."

"About having an abortion you mean?"

He nodded.

"You were my priest, not my lover." She hesitated a moment. "Does it make a difference?"

"Yes. It makes a difference."

"Why?"

"Because you're talking of a new life. And I'm not Jesus. However much I'd like to be perfect."

She smoothed his brow again with the tips of her long, slender fingers. "I don't want you perfect," she said.

"Some things are better left unsaid."

She dropped her hand and tilted her head again so her hair fell to one side, glistening in the half-light like a shimmering golden curtain.

"Why?"

"Christ told the truth. But he didn't tell the whole truth. He knew when to remain silent."

"And this hurts you, so I shouldn't have said it?"

He didn't say anything. Not that he was lost for words but that it did hurt, the thought of a littler life snuffed out. This conversation had gone as far as he felt like going. And she knew what he thought. They already had something of that magic, that knowing the mind of the other that comes with a deep love.

And this knowledge hurt her in turn. More profoundly than he knew. She kissed him then. First on the cheeks, then on the lips. She was frightened she might lose him, unable to admit, even to herself, how much he meant to her, despite his narrow mindedness.

Later at his place as they took each other, there was an awkward edge to their lovemaking for the first time. Like they both knew there was a whole mountain yet to be climbed.

10.

Take heed now; for the LORD hath chosen thee to build an house for the sanctuary: be strong, and do it.

1 Chronicles 28:10

Friday 9th November: Vicky Walters had phoned from Pazzo's Bar, back of the Basketball Hall of Fame.

Springfield, the City of Firsts. They invented basketball in Springfield; alongside the ice skate; the first U.S. armory; the Springfield rifle; the first U.S.-manufactured automobile, the Duryea car; the Indian Motorcycle; and so many other points of trivia. Why Springfield even boasts the first zip code—01101—or so they say.

And this was a first for Father Seb. He had never been to this place before. But when Vicky phoned she sounded upset so he had come right over.

He found her nursing a dirty martini: good gin, a splash of olive juice, and one or two olives, stirred not shaken, and poured ice cold into a chilled martini glass. It was the favored drink of F.D.R.; at one time Roosevelt had mixed it for Stalin. But she was no Stalin. Vicky looked every inch the frail elementary school teacher, with a face young enough to be confused with those of her pupils. "Dollar to a dime they'll have asked her for photo ID in a place like this," Seb thought.

She sat alone at the 30-foot, mirror-backed, mahogany bar behind which marched wine bottles like soldiers framing row after row of spirits.

From somewhere piped music of a better stamp was piercing the gloom of the smokey lamps. The Beatles sang, "No Reply."

Lisa, the bejewelled, well-bosomed barmaid, was leaning across sharing a plate of mozzarella cheese sticks with Vicky in an attempt to offer consolation to the sad figure cut by the elementary school teacher.

Vicky's pretty young face turned toward Seb as he walked in. Her lower lip trembled and her features grew pinched. She bit back the tears. Lisa made herself scarce.

"I'm sorry Father Seb," Vicky was saying.

Seb flinched. He knew he was compromised by his own behavior. He half-wondered what he was doing here. He felt unworthy to offer help to this broken child. "You don't need to apologize for anything."

"I needed to talk to you."

"Of course."

"Will you take a drink, Father?"

He asked for a coffee which Lisa provided before retiring discreetly to the remotest corner of the substantial bar, busying herself with polishing the glasses in best bartender style.

"So?" Father Seb asked as soon as he'd sipped his coffee.

Vicky looked down at the table as she spoke. "I'm pregnant, Father."

"Ah," said Seb. And without pause he slid his coffee toward Vicky Walters and took her martini from her hand. "You'd best not drink then."

She looked up at him then. "I'm so sorry. I'm alone, you see," she said. "That's why I'm not keeping it, Father Seb, the child I mean."

"That's your prerogative. But in case you change your mind, alcohol is not good for the child you now carry."

Vicky said nothing. Just stared, vacantly, at the coffee that Seb had substituted for her drink.

"Do I know the Father?" Seb asked.

She nodded.

"Will you tell me his name?"

She shook her head slowly from right to left and back again.

"Is he married?"

She nodded, adding, "Is it wrong to have an abortion?"

Seb shrugged. Before his recent conversation with Angie his answer might have been different. "For some things a simple yes or no answer works. Is it wrong to commit adultery? Yes. It is wrong." He didn't pause, his words flowed ahead removing all hint of disapproval. "Is it wrong to have an abortion? I'm not sure it's a matter of right and wrong. Things are not that simple." He noticed Vicky's involuntary grimace at his equivocation. She wants me to say what she expects me to say, he thought. Then aloud he said, "Christ told Saint Peter that what he bound on earth would be bound in heaven. What he meant, in my view, is that we follow our instincts and that determines God's judgment of us. In a sense we judge ourselves. What seems right to you is right. What seems wrong to you is wrong." He paused and studied her. Her reddened eyes were fixed on his. He glanced down at the redundant martini he was now nursing and continued. "Have you told him? The father of the child I mean."

She shook her head.

"Perhaps you should."

"He has just dumped me."

"That's not the issue."

173

"In what way is it not the issue?" Vicky bridled. "Why the hell should it mean so much to you? I am alone, and I am pregnant and I am getting an abortion."

"If you are so sure about this why did you call me?"

"Abortion, is that wrong?"

Seb smiled. There was no way she was going to let him wriggle off this hook. "That depends."

"On what?"

"On whether there's any alternative."

Vicky laughed. "Fat lot of use you are." Then she sighed. "Is life sacred, Father?"

He thought a moment.

"Have you heard of the Goldilocks enigma?"

Again Vicky shook her head.

"That the universe is neither too hot nor too cold but is just right for life, like Baby Bear's porridge?"

"So?"

"So everything that is created is just one immense cradle for life. It is God's central concern, the gift of life. And yes, life is utterly sacred, however much we wish God Almighty to play to our rules."

"This is supposed to be helping me?"

Seb shrugged. "You called a priest, not a doctor. What did you expect me to say?"

11.

And when the Lord saw her, he had compassion on her, and said unto her, Weep not.

Luke 7:13

Saturday 10th November: "You want a drink?"

"Coffee maybe if you've got some. Father Seb said I shouldn't drink. Not with the child."

Trish Hartnett narrowed her green-gray eyes in hard-edged curiosity, like a cat, or a snake maybe, or a teenager. "You're keeping it then?" she asked.

Vicky was defensive. "I didn't decide yet. I don't think I want a child." Vicky's shoulders slumped as she allowed her frailty to show. "When I found out I was pregnant I was so confused. I couldn't sleep. I was sad all the time, not able to think how I could get myself out of the situation. And all the time I was thinking how I'd let my parents down. I was so miserable at the idea of being a single mother."

Vicky was playing with her hair twisting it in her fingers school-girl fashion. She had hair long enough to sit on and was wearing a little Afghan style jacket and a long skirt. Transport her back thirty or forty years and paint a flower on her cheek and she'd make a hippy, Trish thought, and the thought irritated her. This child-mother to be didn't know which way was up. She caught herself wondering whether her marriage to Sean would have been better had she let him make her pregnant. Had he wanted that she wondered. They'd not discussed it. Trish poured Vicky's coffee. "You'll have to cut your hair."

"What?"

"Your hair. You can't seriously be a mother with all that hair."

Vicky laughed.

"You've been speaking to Seb about this?"

Vicky nodded. "Wasn't much help. He went on about the three bears' porridge."

"Meaning life is precious and the universe is just right for it?"

"Yeh. And the wages of sin is life." Vicky opened her mouth in mock amazement, "You mean he says that stuff to all the girls?"

Trish laughed in turn. She poured her own coffee. "He wasn't much help about my Sean either."

"Your Sean?"

"He's having an affair."

"I'm sorry."

Trish shrugged "I fucking hate him. He's supposed to be the love of my life, for Christ's sake, the fucking love of my life.

"I keep telling myself to be strong, it'll be OK. But I'm not strong. And I'm not OK.

"It takes everything inside me not to break down in front of him when I see him. Perhaps I should. But I won't. It hurts so much. I could just send him a text right now and tell him I miss him and I love him so much and I need him.

"But it wouldn't make any difference. And that's what stops me." Trish smiled. "Still it's no good sobbing about it." She shook her head. "But this wasn't about me. It's about you. We're both in the same boat really. Everyone around us is in love and everyone's happy and we have to stand around and look happy for them. It makes me sick.

"We're alone and our dreams have become colossal tragedies."

She sighed. "All I want is my Sean back."

Vicky reached out a hand. "I'm sorry," she said again.

"Don't be. All men are bastards."

"Don't use that word."

Trish looked surprised.

"That's what my child will be if I have him. Or her."

"Don't."

"Don't what?"

"Don't have the child. An abortion is easy. You're only a few weeks gone. You have no commitment to the man who did this to you." Trish paused. "That's right isn't it? You're not committed to him?"

Vicky shrugged as if the question were unimportant. "No."

"Does he even know?"

Vicky shook her head.

"Don't tell him then. Just get rid of it. I'll go with you. I'll help you." Trish smiled at this child mother-to-be, her attitude softer now. Life was so unfair. She was just a kid. She didn't need to destroy her future over this. It was unconscionable. "Really Vicky dear. I mean it."

And Vicky Walters smiled. The kind of smile that came from deep inside and meant something. "Thank you," she said.

"For what?"

"You've ..." She hesitated, grasping for the words. "You've empowered me."

Be wise now therefore, O ye kings: be instructed, ye judges of the earth.

Psalm 2:10

Sunday 11th November: "So why for God's sake did Mary kill herself?"

Mike Hanlin and Dick Bryer sat together in Peter's Grill in the Marriott—as anonymous as you could be amongst the bustle. They were drinking coffee. It was late afternoon.

There was a third member of their little troop. She was Dr Paola Subani, the family physician that Hanlin and Bryer shared in common with the late Mrs Mary Young. They had invited her over to milk her for information; and she knew it.

At 56 Dr Paola wore her years badly. Her breasts sagged, her face was prematurely wrinkled, but she remained attractive largely because her habit was to flirt.

It was an unconscious reflex action—her flirting. Had she been told that was what she did she'd have been quite surprised. But she did, and men always like a flirt.

However this afternoon she was not true to type. She was being cautious. She just shrugged in response to Bryer's question.

Mike Hanlin decided to bring an end to the incipient hiatus. He resorted to the obvious distraction. "Look, let's can the coffee. Perhaps they can bring us something stronger." He raised his arm to flag down the nearest waiter.

Dr Paola lifted her head. She still had good hair, fine, black and curly. She liked to think of it as her crowning glory and she more tossed her head than shook it. "Coffee's fine for me, but you boys go ahead."

Which they did. Ordering bourbon on the rocks and a BBC Steel Rail beer. "You sure?" said Hanlin.

Dr Paola wanted to say "Yes" but intended to say "No." She surprised herself when she said, "Well OK then. A glass of white wine; anything but Chardonnay."

Mike Hanlin made small talk as they waited for the drinks which came swiftly, hotel style, with little glass bowls containing potato chips and olives respectively.

"Getting back to Mary," Dick Bryer said once they had all wished one another good health. "You understand Dr Paola? Why we ask you these questions I mean. It may be pertinent to the murder inquiry. Is there anything, anything at all, that you may have withheld from the police to spare the family's feelings—anything that you feel unable to share with the police at this stage as a consequence?"

Bryer saw her hesitation and pushed his advantage. "Anything, anything at all, Dr Paola. It would really help."

Dr Paola didn't answer at once. Instead she sipped her Sauvignon Blanc thoughtfully. Mentally she had an "Aw what the heck" moment. At last she commented, "Well, there was something."

The two men lent slightly forward. "Yes?" said Bryer.

Dr Paola paused a long while, sipping her wine while she considered. "This goes no further? I have your assurance on that."

The men nodded. "Of course," said Dick Bryer.

"Well I was concerned for the family. I didn't want to bring out Mary Young's private life when I spoke with the police. I saw no need. However since you've promised to retain confidentiality, I will tell you that Mary Young was taking Paxil for depression."

"You prescribed that?"

Dr Paolo pursed her lips and sucked in her cheeks in one those smirkish you-should-know-better-than-to-ask smiles, "No, she bought it on the Internet. I warned against it. I would have prescribed Prozac. Paxil may be a good workmanlike anti-depressant, but it is known to have side effects on occasion."

"Such as making you feel suicidal?" interrupted Bryer.

The doctor nodded, more somberly this time. "Not as a rule. Paxil is a useful drug. But sometimes it may not be, well, the drug of first choice."

"Wow," said Dick Bryer. He whistled. "That may explain a lot."

Hanlin interrupted. "Wait a minute Dick. This is important. He looked shrewdly into Dr Paola's eyes. "There's something else isn't there?"

Dr Paola snapped her head round, locking her eyes on his. "Yes there is. And as a matter of fact it turned out fine. There was nothing to worry about. But about two weeks before she died ..." Dr Paola returned to her wine before she continued. "Just a couple of weeks before she died—she asked for an HIV test."

13.

*But he that heareth, and doeth not, is like a man that without
a foundation built an house upon the earth; against which the
stream did beat vehemently, and immediately it fell; and the
ruin of that house was great.*

Luke 6:49

Monday 12ᵗʰ November: Anna Maria Gonzalez worked three
days a week for the Hanlins and two days a week for the
Merrills. She was an illegal, like one in five of the Mexican
population of Springfield. And being an illegal was a severe
disadvantage. Thirty percent of all federal prison inmates
are illegal aliens. Anna had been smuggled across the border
with her mother when she was just six years old. Now she was
twenty-six. She'd spent the past ten years working with various families as a housemaid and then expanded her utility by
attending bartending school and a culinary course so she could
help her employers at social functions, as well. She'd been with
the Merrills for eight of those ten years.

Anna worked for Angie about the house. Normally she
didn't see Baxter who would be at work down at Merrill
Manufacturing at the times at which she was conducting her
duties.

Anna was caught in a generation warp, neither quite American
like her peers nor quite Mexican like her mother. The insecu-
rity this fostered made her shy—a feature that enhanced her
currency amongst the Chicano boys after church. And she had
a sultry, full-lipped beauty that complimented the kind of full
but the right side of plump figure that most men admired and
most women were embarrassed by. She had been out with a
series of men but been steady with none for any length of time.
But one swarthy boy, who spelt his name Manuell but who used
the colloquially popular form of 'Manny', had been chasing her

more avidly than most for much of the past two years.

He had asked her to marry him twice.

She liked him. She had decided she would accept him if he asked her again. It wasn't so much that she loved Manny but he was nice. And at twenty-six she was still a virgin, which was unusual even in the Latino community. And she so wanted to have children and a place of her own. She loved children. The biological clock might not be such an issue for women with access to elite health care. But Anna belonged on the wrong side of the tracks. Plus most of her peers—even her fellow undocumented would-be immigrants—were married and on their second brood. Maiden Aunt status grated, though she hid it well.

And now, she was working at the Merrill house. She felt uncomfortable there with Mrs Merrill gone and Baxter about so much. He was there now. He'd been drinking. He was leaning against the frame of the kitchen door as he sipped at a cup of black coffee, watching her load the dishwasher.

Baxter was watching as she bent down to place soiled cutlery in the knife rack of the dishwasher. He was thinking that her well-rounded ass was delightful. And as he watched her he became aroused. This was of itself commonplace. Baxter was drunk. This too was commonplace. They were alone together. This had become commonplace. The juxtaposition of the three factors made the ensuing events almost inevitable. He put his coffee cup down, walked over, and placed a hand firmly on each side of Anna's buttocks. He didn't say a word. And neither did Anna. Not a word as he put one hand round her waist and the other up her skirt and shifted her, bending her over the kitchen table. She trembled. Her whole body trembled, which excited him immeasurably. He didn't see her face. He had not attempted to turn her round. Instead he leant across her, using his left hand to hitch up her skirt, whilst his right reached round her, across her shoulder, and down across her breasts. He prepared to push himself between her thighs.

Anna's emotions, meanwhile, had run the full gamut; starting with shock; then arousal, despite herself. And then fear as she realized that this chain of events would lead to her losing the virginity she had so carefully guarded—and to a middle-aged drunk.

So she screamed. And Baxter froze. But Maria was still screaming and Baxter found the noise intolerable. He knocked her to the floor.

"You Chicano bitch." He grunted as he fell upon her. She screamed again but it didn't seem to stop him. She tried to curl into a ball bringing her knees up but even that failed to stop Baxter.

She stopped screaming then. She felt the weight of him, relentless. His passion continued to arouse an echo in herself and she was repelled and disgusted by her own reaction. She had to stop this. She gasped words without thought. She didn't know what she was saying. She was almost incoherent. Then she pulled the remnants of her tattered self-respect together and mouthed the words, "I will tell them."

Which did not stop Baxter. "You asked for it," he said. His voice came to her through a haze as he tried to force her knees apart—and then succeeded.

"I will tell them about before," she said between sobs, writhing away from him as she spoke.

And Baxter paused. "Before what?"

"Before with the lady. Six months ago. When Mrs Merrill was away."

"What?" Baxter was genuinely puzzled.

"I came into the living room. I know. I heard what she said to you."

And at last Baxter climbed off her. Not because he was afraid of what she might say. He didn't really care. But rather because he had lost his appetite for her. Part of her wanted him. He knew that. And he wouldn't have stopped short of forcing himself on the woman if that was what it took. But not without more of a response. She was annoying him now.

"Do what you like bitch. But get out of here," spat Baxter. "And don't come back."

14.

Tuesday 13th November: "You can't be serious mother?"

"A car's a car as far as I am concerned."

Officer Donna White raised an eyebrow in exaggerated astonishment. "Parked right there, outside LA Fitness downtown , where you work most everyday of the week. How could you fail to notice that monster?"

Alicia White flushed up. "You were the ones who were supposed to be looking for the thing. How come none of your boys in blue saw it? Anyhow, how did you know it was a Hummer?"

"We didn't. A neighbor saw a vehicle he thought might be a Hummer drive out of Cherryvale late that night. And then there were the tire tracks in the blood."

The conversation conjured up graphic pictures in Alicia's imagination. She had that sort of mind, where if you said a thing she saw it. Troubled, she walked to the window and looked out onto the wind-lashed garden. Autumn was tightening her grasp. Donna was still talking.

"We could tell, if it was a Hummer, and which model, from the tire tracks."

Alicia turned to look at her daughter," So you are convinced it was Trish Hartnett?"

"Personally, yes. Though it is strange she persists in her claim to have had nothing to do with the vehicle."

Alicia frowned. "That's not strange if it's the truth."

"But it's not the truth. For one thing there was a postcard in the glove compartment; a postcard from Maine, from Bridgeport, where Trish Hartnett has a cabin."

Donna had always been a true American in the guileless, what-you-see-is-what-you-get tradition. The mother could read the daughter like a book. And Alicia could see her daughter keeping something back, her face tightening.

"And?"

"And there's stuff we're keeping to ourselves at the moment. You do that sometimes. Hold back stuff 'till the arrest."

"Like?"

"Like—and this is confidential, Mom—there was a door-key left in the vehicle. It fits Trish Hartnett's home. Plus a compact with her initials."

For a moment Alicia stood akimbo, wide eyed and open mouthed. "You're not serious?"

Donna nodded. "I am."

"Then she's guilty as sin."

"In my view, yes. But it's all circumstantial. We can't actually prove that particular vehicle killed Bob Young. It's been steam cleaned. And too much time has elapsed. There's no physical evidence."

"So she gets away with it?"

Donna's face turned grim. "No. We get an indictment from the Grand Jury down at the Hampden County Hall of Justice. Then we arrest her. When we're ready. Then we sweat it out of her."

Alicia White frowned. "You're sure are you—that no one's framing her?"

Donna's grim face broke into a smile. "Oh for God's sake Mother ... Really!"

15.

And the devil said unto him, All this power will I give thee, and the glory of them: for that is delivered unto me; and to whomsoever I will I give it.

Luke 4:6

Wednesday 14th November: "This was an appropriate place to meet," said Seb.

They were in the Bishop's study. The marble mantelshelf framed the hearth. To either side a couple of large wing-backed leather armchairs. The other walls book lined to middle height, above which were pictures, well framed and eclectic, of Springfield in the past—one of Kimball's Hotel, another of the old Union Station, and the third one of the iconic Italianate bell tower flanked by the impressive symphony and city hall on either side—the unofficial symbols of the City of Springfield. A television stood in one corner. Standard lamps occupied the others. A large sofa faced the fire. And everywhere papers covered almost all available flat surface.

The others present were Donna and Alicia White—and the Bishop.

"As good a place as any," Donna replied.

Seb nodded. "You brought your mother."

Donna smiled, "She brought me. This meeting was her idea."

Seb smiled in turn. "So what can we do for you, ladies?"

Alicia was the one to answer. "They think Trish Hartnett is guilty."

Seb nodded. "I understand that to be the situation." Seb's words hung in the air, sounding pompous, even to Seb.

188

"The more I think about this business, the more I think Trish is being framed. Is there anything you haven't told the police, for whatever reason?" Alicia hesitated, "Maybe just something small?"

Seb nodded again. "There was. There were things I withheld from Donna. But I've shared them with her now."

"How come?"

"The circumstances have changed. These were confidential matters. For various reasons, the situation has moved on."

"I can't believe Trish Hartnett's guilty. Is there anything you haven't said that might help?"

David Sebastian looked at her again, his dark brown eyes thoughtful. "Not directly. But ..."

Donna broke in. "If you know anything you must share it."

Seb turned to the Bishop. "This relates to a confession."

Bishop O'Malley visibly paled.

Then Seb added, "A confession by someone since deceased."

"Go on," said Donna.

The Bishop nodded his encouragement. "If the confessant is dead, normally the rules still apply. However, if a life is at stake, as in the case of a possible miscarriage of justice in a murder investigation, in my view in extremis, the normal rules need no longer apply. You have my dispensation to speak."

Seb smiled grimly. "All right then. But I need everyone's agreement. Anything I say now is between us. It goes no further without my permission?"

The others nodded. "Agreed," said Donna.

"Well you'll remember that this all began with Mary Young's suicide?" Seb didn't wait for their acknowledgment but continued. "Just two days before she died, she confessed to me that Bob, her late husband, was not the father of her eldest child. Jenny."

"What?" Donna and Alicia spoke in unison, both open mouthed in their total astonishment.

Seb ignored them. "She'd had an affair, years ago. It was short lived. Jenny was the consequence."

"You know with whom?" asked Donna.

Seb shook his head.

"You know but you're not saying?"

Again Seb shook his head. "The point is that she had got it into her head that the paternity of her child was going to come out."

"Was she being blackmailed?"

Seb shook his head. "Nothing of that kind. She'd had another affair, recently."

Alicia shrieked. The thought of perfect Mary Young having a dark side was incomprehensible. Seb frowned at her, and she raised her eyebrows and bit her lower lip, still astonished.

Donna spoke. "And you know with whom and you're not telling?"

And again Seb shook his head. "No, I don't know. She didn't say. But I do know that she thought she'd contracted some sort of disease, and that somehow or other Jenny's paternity would be exposed."

"And you told her that was nonsense I presume," said Bishop O'Malley.

"Exactly. I told her to go to the doctor and get herself checked out."

"Which she did?"

"She said she had already done so and it had been OK. I said if it was still bothering her to get checked again. She may have. But she died two days later."

"You think that all this preyed on her mind? Drove her to suicide? The guilt perhaps?"

Seb nodded. "It's a possibility." He paused, then added thoughtfully, "Though whether any of that will help establish Trish Hartnett's innocence is, I am sorry to say, debatable."

16.

I have stuck unto thy testimonies: O LORD, put me not to shame.

Psalm 119:31

Thursday 15th November: Manuel, Anna's young man, the boy who went by the colloquial appellation 'Manny'," was in the coffee shop. Anna was late. Very late as it happened. He was drinking his third "Garibaldi" coffee, espresso with a twist of lemon rind. Occasionally he glanced at the door in expectation. Then for a while he stopped himself, on the watched-pot-never-boils principle. Instead he thought of her. Her long dark hair so sleek and deep dark brown; her full face; the bright summer dresses she wore even as winter closed in; her laughter and her energy. He was more than in love with the girl. He was besotted.

She was twenty minutes late now. He tried her cell phone but it flipped to answer. He wasn't worried. Not worried she'd stand him up anyway. Anna was not that kind of girl. He planned to ask her to marry him again. He had tried twice before and she'd refused. This time, just maybe. However long it took. He would wear her down. He knew she loved him really. She just hadn't come to realize she did.

And still she didn't come. He was annoyed now. Annoyance meshing the genuine worry he had begun to feel. He tried to phone her again. Answer phone still. He wasn't gonna leave yet another message. He'd go round. She lived in the the the cheap high-rise rentals down by the cathedral. Not that they had start-ed cheap. But units had been reserved for affordable housing, and—over time— they had all become cheap with drugs and increasing petty crime taking its toll. Crime had exploded in Springfield back in 1986 when crack came in. The city had be-come much more violent overnight. Crack makes a would be car thief a shooter, always chasing that first hit. Crack is cocaine mixed with baking soda and crystallized. You smoke it. The difference between heroin and crack is with heroin you can get a quick score but with crack you need more and that can mean three or four thousand dollars in a weekend. Downtown the violence was worst. Manny didn't really like her living there, but her Mom was in the same apartment block, and she wouldn't move. When they got married he would move her out. That was for sure.

Still, Anna could take care of herself. She carried Mace and one of those "screech" alarms. Manny had made her do that. He paid the bill for the coffee and gave an overly generous tip. He did that. Tipped too much because he couldn't bear embarrassment. He knew the waiter knew he'd been stood up. Knew it because he always came here to meet Anna—for no other purpose. And it was a small place.

Manny drove across town to Anna's. He parked on the street risking a ticket.

Anna's apartment was 65A on the sixth floor. The door was slightly ajar, which was crazy, in this place at least.

Manny pushed at the door and the vista transformed. No more the chipped dirty plaster of the hallway corridor walls. Here in Anna's space, all was perfect. The pictures, the furniture, the freshly well-painted walls. He called her name then. Nothing.

He rapped on the already open door. "Anna? You here?"

Still nothing, so he moved inside, his disquiet growing with each step. The small living room was as he remembered it. Tidy, polished clean, ornaments, and child-like toys, a cabbage patch doll on the sofa, a teddy bear on the bookshelf, a brass pig as a doorstop with a money-box slit. He moved to the bedroom beyond. The door to that was also ajar. The curtains were partly closed, the room half in shadow.

And there she lay, fully clothed, asleep on the bed. "Anna, for heaven's sake." He stepped across the room to the bedside. He noticed a glass of water on the table. He reached to shake her. Then he froze and he sighed the one word, "No ..."

Then slowly Mikhail reached out to touch her. But he couldn't. His hand sank to his side and his knees folded as he started to sob. It was much too horrible. The gash in her throat too final. She was lost to him forever.

Anna lay on her back, her beautiful hair spread wide as if deliberately to frame her exquisite face. The blood was splashed onto the coverlet in a crimson smile, like the laugh of a clown. Maria was undeniably dead. Her throat cut low to the shoulder. Her own pretty mouth sagging open in shocked protest. Her eyes, mercifully, closed.

17.

From that time Jesus began to preach, and to say, Repent: for
the kingdom of heaven is at hand.

Matthew 4:17

Friday 16th November: "Sorry to trouble you, Mrs Hartnett,
but we need to talk."

Donna White was uncomfortable and Trish Hartnett could
see that. Trish had answered the door with a glass of iced sherry
in her hand. She raised it and tossed back a gulp in wry salute
to the young detective, and Detective Muse who stood to the
right behind her dressed in jacket and tie as always. For Muse
public perception mattered. He was an old-fashioned cop and
liked to be turned out neat. The Department gave detectives
a hundred dollar a year cleaning allowance. Muse spent way
more than that a month. "If you're at a scene who cares," he'd
told Donna when she'd asked, "But otherwise during the day
I always wear a tie."

"You'd better come in then, hadn't you," Trish was saying.

Muse couldn't help but smile. At 29 Trish Hartnett was not
the same Trish as the 17-year old Springfield Classical High
homecoming queen. Now she was all woman, every ripe curve
defined by a figure-hugging red dress with a satin sheen good
enough to gladden the eye of even the most jaded roué.

Muse caught himself being won over merely by the look of the
woman and the realization was the mental equivalent of being
doused in cold water. Refreshing. He narrowed his eyes. This
stunner could well be a merciless killer. The issue was not how
good this witch looked, but rather where the hell did she keep
the broomstick?

And Trish Hartnett noticed as she walked them to the living

room. For one brief moment, Detective Muse had 'Cloud Nine' written on his face and it gave her a little skip of the heart. And now it was gone. Like switching out a light. And it saddened her.

Which in turn angered her. She stopped herself clutching her glass in a white knuckled grip as she gestured to them to take a seat. She must calm herself, she thought. Too much passion in this heart of hers made her far more vulnerable than she dared admit. Her father used to tell her that a certain amount of order and discipline were necessary to allow the world to function. How she wished he was here now. But her father had died prematurely and her husband, Sean, was the last person she could turn to. No, she had to face this one alone. She had to learn to do what her father used to tell her. "Don't so much live for the moment," he'd say, "As cherish the moments you've lived."

She looked at them both. "So officers, what can I do for you this time?"

Donna White ran her hand back through her hair which was cut like a boy's, little wisps of hair feathering her forehead. She placed her notebook primly on her knees and smiled at Trish, trying her best to put this woman, her mother's friend, at ease. But the hammer-blow answer was delivered, almost with relish, by Detective Muse.

"We have received another anonymous letter, Mrs Hartnett." He paused, watching for her response, giving her an opportunity to interrupt. Which she didn't. So he continued, "And this one implicates you in the murder of Anna Gonzalez." Then, in apparent afterthought, he added, "Have you anything to say?"

18.

But whoso hearkeneth unto me shall dwell safely, and shall be quiet from fear of evil.

Proverbs 1:33

Saturday 17th November: "Vicky?"

Baxter had been doing nothing. He did nothing most of his days at the moment.

"You'd better come in."

Vicky Walters was wearing her brightest smile when he answered the door. But it dissolved when she saw the man she had loved.

"I was so sorry to hear about Anna."

Baxter shrugged. "Yeh. The police were with me earlier. They have no idea who did it."

He led Vicky into the house she had never entered when he'd been with Angie.

"I am so sorry, Baxter. About your marriage too. I heard you and Angie had separated." She hesitated but screwed up her courage. "That wasn't because of me Baxter, was it? I don't want to be a home wrecker, really I don't."

Baxter, to his credit, didn't laugh. "No Vicky. It wasn't you." They were standing in the sun room. Then perhaps a little cruelly he added, "No. It was over between us."

Baxter looked at this too-young-for-him girl. She had abandoned her usual hippy garb for a short yellow skirt and yellow top and jacket. It looked new. The thought crossed his mind that she might have bought this outfit for this meeting. If so, he was flattered. She was pretty, her long brown hair cascading like a silk fan from her shoulders.

She sat then, abruptly, on the sofa in the sun room. She took her jacket off and put it beside her, like a barrier, lest Baxter sit next to her. She couldn't think clearly. She knew what she had to say but couldn't bring herself to tell him. She couldn't bear to look at him. Her arm rested on the little table beside her, the sunlight from the window glistening on her bare shoulder. She was conscious of everything, of Baxter watching her, of the tears that were already brimming into her eyes, of how she must look.

And to Baxter she looked magnificent. Like many men, Baxter was aroused by a weeping woman, empowered. But whereas in others, the reflex action might be one of compassion, for Baxter other emotions were dominant. He was never one to think. He simply reached for her jacket. Moved it to one side, took her face in his hands, and kissed away the tears.

To start with.

At first Vicky wasn't aware of what he was doing as his hands moved lower and his mouth moved to her neck. Then she felt his hands caressing her and she stiffened, moving her head away.

"No Baxter, please," she said, as his hands continued to move over her with an insistence with which she was familiar. She knew that part of her wanted this, had wanted this from the morning. And even as she cried, she felt his hands lift her blouse, pulling at it, releasing her breasts. And Baxter knew, as he kissed her, that she was ready for him. He reached down then, and pulled the clothes from the woman, until he had her stripped naked, still weeping. He remained fully clothed, only pausing to loosen his belt; and, without any attempt to undress himself, he lifted her from the sofa, carried her to the rug, and took her.

And Vicky, the tears still coming in great gulps so that she could barely breath as his mouth covered hers, surrendered to him, yelping as she raked her hands down his back and back up under his shirt. He paused then, long enough to strip away his own shirt, then moved back on top of her and made love to her with all the fevered passion of his broken soul.

Afterwards, as he lay on top of her, his full weight so heavy, she told him. She said, "Baxter, I'm pregnant with your child."

"Uh huh," said Baxter as he lifted himself a little, taking his weight on his elbows, and looked down at her. "You want a drink?"

Surprised by his equanimity, she shook her head. "Bad for the baby."

And Baxter moved from her, making her sigh as she felt him leave her.

"Baxter."

"Yuh."

"You heard me?"

"Yuh."

"You don't mind?"

And Baxter looked at her then. Angie had never given him a child. Not that he'd wanted children. But something stirred within him, and he looked down at her then, naked, young, full of need. She was way too young for him but what the hell.

Nah Vicky. I don't mind." And he buckled his belt and went to fix his drink, whilst Vicky still lay there, just lay there, for the first time in a long while feeling truly good.

"Baxter."

Baxter paused.

"You don't need the drink." She arched her back and looked at him slyly. "Have me instead."

And Baxter laughed. "You gonna reform me?"

"Nah Baxter. Nobody could do that."

But she knew that soon he would take her again. And she ached for the completion that this second and less hasty act of sex would be, and as he came back to her side she felt her small hand moving, almost instinctively and without her volition, towards his thigh, knowing that next time it would be good. And she shuddered in anticipation.

And he doesn't mind, thought Vicky. And for her nothing mattered. Not now. Nothing at all. She knew in her heart, in her soul, that her man had come back. That he was hers. That she owned this old bear. And she wasn't ever going to let him go.

19.

He that hath an ear, let him hear what the Spirit saith unto
the churches; To him that overcometh will I give to eat of the
tree of life, which is in the midst of the paradise of God.

Revelations 2:7

Sunday 18th November: Trish Hartnett watched her husband
swim back and forth in the pool in their back garden—the covered pool had been winterized for the season.

eemed a rarity these days, they both being home together. She
looked at his well-muscled shoulders as he powered, arm over
arm, through the water. This had been her man. Her feelings for
him still ran hot and heavy. She was sitting, nursing a Margarita.
She watched as he completed one last lap, then used the momen-
tum to help haul himself from the pool in one slick movement.

Trish caught herself thinking, "He's a poser, this man of mine."
But she didn't mind. That was the least of it. She even liked him
for it. Men with low self-esteem were, in Trish Hartnett's worldview, energy sapping and tedious. But she wished Sean would
drag her out tonight. Wished he would give her a reason to put
on makeup. It wasn't that she specially wanted to go out. It was
that she wanted to have a reason to tell Sean she loved him.

"He's probably thinking about the Bishop right now," Trish
thought. A dyed-in-the-wool Republican, Trish had backed
hockey mom Palin. But from nowhere the thought crossed her
mind now she should join the Tea Party, the new all-American,
centre-right bloc that cared more about power than principle
and put abortion and gay marriage lower on the political agenda
than the right to a job.

Sean was surprised, almost, when Trish offered him a towel
with as much nervous reverence as a refugee with a white flag.
Then she spoilt the moment. "Do you believe in the sanctity of

marriage, Sean?" she was saying.

Sean looked up at her. A momentary wave of anger engulfed him. He snapped at her as he took the towel. "You gonna fucken' lecture me Trish?" he said. "You know, what I reckon's best?" He didn't wait for an answer. "If it floats, fucks or flies, rent it."

She was shocked, hurt even. "You'd do that," she said, "Sleep with a hooker. When you've got me?"

"People shouldn't be so down on hookers. They save a lot of marriages. They're a public service I reckon. I bet they make a fucken bus load of men here in Springfield alone a lot nicer to know."

"Think of the women," she said. "They didn't choose those lives. They were forced into them by drugs or poverty. Some of them are trafficked across borders for the sex industry."

"That's too bloody ridiculous. This is Springfield, not Miami."

"Still don't stop it being wrong. Porn and prostitution is what's destroying modern America."

"Porn now? What you gonna do. Have a book burning? You're sick Trish Hartnett."

"Am not either. They always push the boundaries. The television is worst. The stuff kids see on cable. The sex and the violence. It's poisonous."

He ignored her. He was rubbing himself down with the towel. But whilst his eyes were red with chlorine, hers were red with tears. And he saw that as in the same moment he noticed how the green silk sheath of the dress she was wearing seemed to mold itself to every curve in her body. He asked her then without consideration, but not awkwardly or unkindly, "Those fucken' killings Trish. They down to you?"

And she shook her head. "You could believe that?" she asked.

"Of me?"

And she watched him as he dried himself off. He was always alert, always watching out for her, when he was around. She'd trust him with her life—but never again would she trust him with her heart. In a moment of insight she found herself thinking, "I love this man, but I don't like him."

"So many deaths, Sean. Mary Young's suicide. Bob Young's murder. And now little Anna, the Hanlin's maid. They even tried to kill Father Seb. At first it all seemed make-believe. But then you realize the deaths are real. These are people you know."

Sean moved to her then, still wet from the pool. His hands caressed her. How she had wanted this moment. She felt him unzip her dress, felt it slide to the floor.

By the time they were both naked her whole body was shaking. She felt his flesh on her flesh, the cold dampness of him. She didn't know how they moved to the bedroom but he stripped aside the quilt and she lay back on the bare sheets. She didn't say a word, not daring lest it break the spell. Instead she moaned as she offered him all she had in this act of sexual healing, giving him her body, and with it the very heart of her. His mouth sought hers and covered it as he stretched across the bed and bore down on her with all of his weight. She stroked his head. Then she found herself moaning as the passion in her caught her unawares and she arched her spine and shuddered, raking her fingernails down his back. Later she watched him as he slept, grateful for this act of love.

20.

Discretion shall preserve thee, understanding shall keep thee.

Proverbs 2:11

Monday 19th November: LA Fitness. Sean Hartnett pushed the weights alternately, punching at the ceiling with slow deliberation. He wasn't counting. Alicia White did that for him. "OK Sean. That's enough."

He sat up slowly then replaced the weights.

"You have a great torso Sean. But your legs are weak. We should work on your legs."

"Yeh," Sean smiled. "Not sure I care about having fucken' great legs." He looked appraisingly at his trainer, "You on the other hand."

Alicia White knew she looked good for her age. And she liked the compliment, which she ignored. "Time to stretch. Right leg first."

Sean obeyed, leaning forward, one leg folded, one stretched right back, mimicking her. "Great hair Alicia. New color is it?"

Alicia smiled back. "Auburn highlights." She switched legs. "Yeh I like it." Then she paused. "You OK Sean?"

"I guess." To change the subject he said, "Whadda you hear about Angie and Baxter Merrill?"

Alicia nodded. "They broke up. Shame really. But you could see it coming." She looked at Sean. He was still stretching. She appraised his strong arms like a professional craftsman. "All my own work," she thought. "Rest a minute," she said.

Sean took the cue and lay flat on his back on the matting, his hands folded behind his head, as if he might be about to do sit-ups.

"Sad about Anna though. Getting herself murdered. Such a sweet girl, too. I can't see anyone wanting to kill her."

"You don't talk with your daughter then?"

Alicia's cheeks colored. "Well, yes, I guess. But not in the past few days. Not since Anna's death."

"Ah." Sean closed his eyes. "Then you wouldn't know?"

"Know what?"

"That someone's written an anonymous letter accusing my Trish of having something to do with it."

"That's ridiculous."

"Course it is. More likely to be Vicky Walters."

Alicia White's gray-blue eyes widened in astonishment. She sank to the floor conspiratorially, then propped her back against the workout bench. "What did you say?"

"More likely to be Vicky Walters." Sean's eyes were closed still. He had a world-weary mien to his face. "She moved in with Baxter before the dust was settled, almost as soon as Angie moved out."

Alicia was genuinely amazed. "But she's young enough to be his daughter."

Sean opened his eyes, his old boyish smile back for the first time this morning. "Since when did that stop anyone?"

Alicia didn't want to go there. "Who'd want to send those letters though—about your Trish?"

"Letters? Plural?"

Alicia blushed again. "Donna sometimes tells me things. I knew there'd been one letter—about the Bob Young killing. I didn't know there'd been another."

Sean looked at her. "I swear Alicia. If I knew who was sending those anonymous letters ..." He took his right hand from behind his head, holding it high, clenching it first into a claw, then a fist, so tight that the veins bulged. "Y'unnerstand?"

Alicia winced. "I still can't see it. Any of it. I mean Vicky Walters isn't capable of killing Anna. Nor is Trish. Neither of them could have done it."

"N'maybe it was Baxter who killed Anna."

"And why would he do that?"

Sean's eyes narrowed. "That one never could keep his pants buttoned. He hits on everything in a skirt. Bet he tried to give it to Anna, and she turned him down."

"That's no reason to kill her."

"Huh?" Sean smiled. "Maybe," he said. "Since you know so much about everything tell me this: Who would have pretended to be my wife, used her credit card and license to rent that Hummer?"

"Can't say it makes any sense. It'd have to be someone who knows her, wouldn't you think?"

"Maybe." Sean paused. "You know this all links back to Mary Young's suicide."

Alicia raised an eyebrow, "You sure?"

"Uh huh. Sure I'm sure." He looked at her then, square in the face. "And you know what?"

"What?"

"I know why she killed herself."

"How could you possibly know any such thing?"

"I know 'cause Trish told me something."

"What would Trish know about it?"

"She was friendly with Mary."

"Mary was my age."

"Uh huh. So? We are friends aren't we? Being a different age is no big deal. And Trish and Mary had that church thing in common."

"Oh."

"Yeh. My sentiments."

"So?"

"So her daughter, Jenny."

"Yup."

"Mary told Trish she wasn't Bob's child."

Alicia somehow managed to close her mouth which was wide open in astonishment. "That's ridiculous. Not Mary Young. Anyone else I'd believe it." Then Alicia laughed. "Not pure ice queen Mary?"

Sean nodded. "She was afraid Bob would find out."

"If he hadn't found out all these years, how'd she think he'd find out now?"

"She didn't say."

"It's not that uncommon. They say one in ten children has a daddy different to the one they think they've got."

"That's ridiculous."

"Well I heard it on the radio."

"And that makes it true? That many on the wrong side of the blanket?"

"Well in Bob's case, could have been quite innocent. Maybe Bob had a low sperm count."

"Lay off screwing for a few days and you ratchet up your sperm count they say."

"Really?" Alicia raised an eyebrow. "Well I'm sure they'd have tried that. Anyway, if she'd been desperate for a child she may have tried something else."

"Fucked someone else you mean."

"You've got a foul mouth Sean Hartnett. No I mean a sperm donor. Artificial insemination. It happens more often than you men think. There are websites for it."

"That's disgusting." He noticed the look of disbelief on Alicia's face and added, "Jacking off when you could make love, I mean."

"Did it occur to you that some women might not want to make love to someone other than their partner? And what about gay couples? Or single parents that don't want husbands? They exist you know. Not everyone regards men as God's gift to the universe."

"Still need us for the sperm though."

"Don't count on it. Time'll come when you'll be replaced as obsolete."

"Sure—and you'll all screw robots."

"Watch that mouth of yours Sean." She laughed. "Maybe so. One thing I do know. There's more satisfaction in a five-inch vibrator than there ever was in a man."

"Yukh. Now who's being crude? You can't be serious?"

"No—not really," she lied. "But I just wanted to see your reaction."

"Anyway, this time around, it was a man not a machine, and not Bob Young either."

"She said whose child it was?"

Sean looked up and smiled.

Alicia almost shrieked. "Whose? You're gonna tell Sean Hartnett!"

"You'll keep it quiet? You won't let on?"

"On my mother's grave."

"You won't even let on to your daughter?"

"Cross my heart and hope to die."

Sean leaned in close so his nose almost touched hers. His eyes narrowed, almost cold. And he told her. "Baxter Merrill," he said. "It was that sonofabitch Baxter."

21

Nevertheless I have somewhat against thee, because thou hast left thy first love.

Revelations 2:4

Tuesday 20th November: Donna White arrived in the early afternoon. She had told him she would come over as soon as she could. She needed to talk to him, she'd said.

She took his right hand in both of hers. "Gee, I'm glad to see you looking better after all your troubles."

"I'm all right," said David Sebastian. "But there's much that isn't. We need to sort this mess out ..."

"I told you that," Donna said. "It's why I'm here."

Seb frowned, "So?"

"So we now have two murders, one attempted murder, and one suicide. In addition to which we have three anonymous letters, all typed on a standard computer word processor, all almost certainly by the same hand. One implicating you in some ill-defined way over Mary Young's death, one accusing Trish Hartnett of murdering Bob Young, and now a third accusing Trish Hartnett of murdering poor Anna Gonzalez."

"I didn't know about the last letter," said Seb. "Does look like someone's not too keen on Mrs Hartnett."

"On top of which, Father Seb ..." Donna hesitated. "Oh— do I still call you Father Seb?"

Seb had the decency to blush. "You call me Seb. We don't need the formality."

"I used to look up to you, you know." She didn't give him time to respond. "On top of which you are having an affair with Mrs Merrill; Mrs Hartnett is having an affair with person or persons unknown; and Mr Merrill is having an affair with Vicky Walters. And God knows what else in this messed up town."

"Sounds like Peyton Place."

"Fortunately that particular antediluvian soap is before my time."

"Anyway," Seb shrugged, "I am sorry to hear about Vicky Walters. She's a little young for him."

"Well that's the understatement of the year."

" Where do you get this from? Your mother?"

"Uh-huh. Some of it, at least. Vicky Walters has moved in with Mr Merrill. Has Mrs Merrill moved in with you?"

"No."

"What infuriates me is that people know things and don't tell me."

"Of all the funny things to do."

Officer White looked up sharply, her deep brown, almond-shaped eyes narrowing suddenly. "Don't mess with me Father Seb." She looked away from him then, staring out of the window. "The information you gave us checks out. It seems that Mary Young's eldest—Jenny—was not Bob Young's child. Who's child was she Father Seb?"

"I have no idea." It was Seb's turn to look infuriated. "And that's the truth."

Donna believed him. She said so. "My mother has picked up some gossip to the effect that the father may be Baxter Merrill. Does that ring true?"

Seb shook his head in amazement rather than denial. "Possible, I guess. I really couldn't say."

Donna nodded. She turned to leave. Then paused, turning back to him. "You believe priests should be celibate?"

Seb returned her gaze. He felt like a defiant child. "It helps," he said.

"And what you did is a sin?"

"It is."

"And will you leave the church or leave Mrs Hartnett?"

Seb's gaze fell to the floor, like an errant child. He didn't answer.

"Tell you something, Father Seb."

He looked back at her then. "What?"

Donna White's brown eyes were hard, bitter-dark, "The church may forgive you," she said. "But I don't."

22.

Let not mercy and truth forsake thee: bind them about thy
neck; write them upon the table of thine heart:

Proverbs 3:3

Wednesday 21st November: The Bishop's study had become a refuge of sorts for Sean Hartnett. The carpet had a design of pale brown circles and stars inside a flower-patterned border worn faint with age. Sean stared down at it now, his bourbon glass held resting on his crossed knee. He was talking to the Bishop but he didn't look up at him.

"I don't get it. I mean I know I should bein' a Catholic and all. But what's the point of communion? Is it a sort of magic trick to make us better, the spiritual equivalent of a get well tonic? Or is it just some sort of symbol to say you belong to the Christian club, like rolling up a trouser leg for the Freemasons? And do you really think that it's literally God's blood? That's what's always struck me as strange?

The Bishop smiled at his friend. "This really matters?"

Sean nodded.

"Very well. Then yes, unlike the Protestants, who are generally unhappy with the idea of transubstantiation and generally believe that the bread and the wine represent the body and blood, we believe they actually become God. That means that they take on the substantial nature of God, just as wood may take on the substantial nature of a table. Perhaps that's not quite it. The Orthodox generally call Holy Communion a 'mystery' and don't try to explain it. There's a sense in which food, once it's consumed by a human being, becomes a part of that human being's substance. But that's smaller than the truth. When Christ said, 'This is my body', the bread retained the appearance of bread but in a very real sense took on the substance of his body.

In a similar way, when we recite the creed, we talk of our Lord being, 'of one substance' with the Father. That does not mean that Christ and the Father *look* the same in any physical sense. But none the less they are the same. Do you follow?"

Sean shrugged. "I guess."

"As for communion being a magic token to make you well in some spiritual sense or an outward symbol of the membership of some Christian club, well yes actually, I'll go with both of those. But it is rather more than that. Christ said, 'Do this in remembrance of me', so it is also an offering by you in loving memory of and commitment to Jesus. More still than that, it is the outward sign and symbol of the New Covenant by which we merely offer to love one another whereas Christ in his turn went to suffer death for the redemption of our sin." The Bishop smiled. "We square on that now?"

Sean nodded and smiled for a moment in return before bowing his head in thought, his brow creased in concentration.

"But there's more than that on your mind is there not?"

Sean nodded again.

"Go on, Sean." Patrick O'Malley was smiling at his special friend, his warm blue eyes crinkled at the edges. "Spit it out."

"Trish and I are making a go of it," he said. He looked up at him and his dark brown eyes locked instantly on the Bishop's. "I mean it Patrick. We are making a serious try at it this time."

Patrick O'Malley sighed. It was his turn to drop his gaze, to study the well-worn carpet. "I am glad, Sean," he said. He meant it. "She needs you. Now more than ever with so much suspicion falling on her."

"She didn't do it." Sean's words were a sharp, staccato burst. His eyes burned into the Bishop's forehead, as if daring him

214

to gainsay him.

"Kill Bob Young you mean?"

"Uh huh." Sean nodded. "She didn't do it," he repeated.

"I don't doubt that. But who did?"

Sean replied with a belligerent edge to his tone. "Well it wasn't my Trish is all I know."

Bishop Patrick nodded kindly. He didn't say anything.

Sean watched his now former lover and softened. "You gonna be OK?" he found himself asking.

The Bishop looked up and as he did so he used the slender fingers of his left hand in womany fashion to brush a lock of hair back in place. "Of course," he said.

Sean hesitated, "Without me, I mean."

The Bishop looked up again. "We can still be friends?" It was more a statement than a question.

Sean shook his head. "I don't think so," he said. "That wouldn't work."

"Ah," said the Bishop, as if acknowledging some profound truth, which in a way he was. "Perhaps it is for the best. You distract me. I need to go my own way, if I am to make a difference. Clarence Darrow once wrote, 'You can run with the pack, in the middle of the pack, but if you want to do something, get to the edges and peel away'. It is past time I was doing more constructive work."

"Will you be OK?" asked Sean for a second time.

The Bishop nodded. "Fine," he said. Then he leaned back in his chair and looked at the ceiling. He felt as if he could stare right through it at the night sky beyond, stare right into the very heart of the God who had both created him homosexual and in so doing had also predestined him to a series of events that had led to his ultimate damnation.

"Eloi, eloi, lama sabachthani?" The Bishop whispered Christ's crucifixion lament.

"What the fuck are you talkin about?" Sean said. Then more gently, "You forget Patrick, I know what that means. Bible knowledge is one of the benefits of a good catholic upbringing."

The Bishop smiled again. "I am not going to pretend that the loss of your friendship is a small thing." He paused, looking closely at his friend. "We each carry a cross in our different ways. Losing you is, in its way, an Armageddon experience. Christ dealt with the cross by embracing death, by emptying himself as he breathed his last with the words, 'It is finished'.

"So between us it is finished?"

The Bishop held up his hand to stave off the interruption from Sean to what was, after all, a rhetorical question. "No, I know I cannot compare this ordeal to the crucifixion in a literal sense. But we all learn from life and are made greater because of it. This has been painful but beautiful. Cleansing. And now it is finished. There is a beauty in that too. Now my life moves on as does yours. In that sense, my dear friend," and the Bishop paused for emphasis, "I will be OK without you."

23.

If we say that we have no sin, we deceive ourselves, and the truth is not in us.

1 John 1:8

Thursday 22nd November: Trish Hartnett's day job was well paid. She worked at interior design, by and large in the non-residential field, though she sometimes took on private commissions. Trish was at home. Trish was often at home these days. She worked in a partnership with two others and had handed across almost all her clients. It wasn't merely that she felt under pressure. It was because the word was out that she was a suspect in the Bob Young murder case, and she didn't like the interested looks. She didn't like being the object of curiosity.

More importantly, she was home because it was Thanksgiving. This was the earliest the feast could fall in the calendar month and it was a warm day with an Indian summer feel about it. She and Sean had been invited to upstate New York where her retired parents still maintained their large family home in Saratoga. She'd declined. Too many explanations. She just wanted to be with Sean. They could have gone to spend Thanksgiving with Sean's sister, but it'd have been awkward given the circumstances and they'd politely declined that invitation, as well.

So Trish had decided to cook a New England style turkey with a special oyster-laced stuffing, and she'd been preparing the bird. She'd have made pumpkin pie like her mother used to, but Sean didn't go for pumpkin pie much, and this Thanksgiving was going to be all about Sean. So she opted for Marilyn Bryer's recipe for pecan. She knew he was trying to make a new start and it mattered.

Sean was out jogging in nearby Forest Park. She missed Sean so much at that moment that she just couldn't take it. So she texted him and told him so. Then he texted back to her that he missed her as well. "So much," he added.

She was aching to be in his arms. She felt stressed and needed him to make her forget it all like only he could. "Just wrap me up and love me," she thought.

She was wearing bright red underwear, the frilly kind. She'd bought it because she thought that Sean would find it kind of hot. She so wanted Sean to hurry home. She was beyond lonely. She wanted to make herself matter to him. So she threw herself into the cooking as if, if she made the food perfect, everything would be perfect.

She was in the house when Detectives Muse and White came calling. She wanted to say, "Haven't you got anything better to do on Thanksgiving?" but she stopped herself. Truth was this Thanksgiving Day visit was Muse's idea not Donna's. Donna had protested. But Muse insisted. He didn't like the way the new kids let things slide just because it was a holiday. "We're professionals," he'd said to her. The eleven-man homicide squad worked Monday through Friday on three eight-hour shifts round the clock starting 4 p.m., midnight and an 8 a.m. day shift. Then they each worked every fifth weekend in two-man teams. Muse liked working weekends. Witnesses were more often home and you could get more done. Same for Thanksgiving and they'd drawn duty that day. Least they didn't have the night shift. They'd be home for dinner.

"You'd better come in," said Trish.

They did.

Trish decided to make the best of it. "You want cawffee?"

Donna declined. "We need to ask you a few questions Mrs Hartnett. Is that OK?"

"Do I have a choice?"

"No. I am sorry. We need to talk to you."

Trish shrugged. She noticed Muse hadn't said anything so she ignored him. "OK, Donna, go ahead."

Donna White only hesitated for a moment. "What reason would you have to dislike Father Sebastian?"

Trish was bewildered and said so. "I thought you were investigating the death of Bob Young?"

"We are. Just answer the question please." This from Detective Muse.

Trish acknowledged his presence with a nod, then turned back to Donna. "I have no reason to dislike Father Seb. Quite the contrary."

"You were very close to Mary Young, weren't you?"

"Mary and I were close friends, yes."

"Very close?"

"Yes."

"Do you blame Father Seb for her death?"

"Heavens no, Donna. Of course not."

"Someone does."

"Well I don't."

Donna didn't miss a beat as she switched her line of questioning. "Did you resent Father Sebastian's affair with Angie Merrill?"

"What?" Trish Hartnett gave every impression of being surprised.

"You can't pretend you didn't know of it, Mrs Hartnett." Donna didn't wait for an answer. "Have you been having an affair with Angie's husband, Baxter Merrill?"

Trish Hartnett's features paled as the blood drained from her face. She had been standing but now she sat. She said nothing.

Donna waited. Then, in the absence of an answer, she continued. "Did you attempt to kill Father Sebastian out of some misguided sense of loyalty to your lover, Baxter Merrill? Or was your attack premised on your loyalty to Mary Young? Did you think that Father Sebastian caused her death in some way?"

At last Trish Hartnett looked up. "Mary's death had nothing to do with Father Sebastian."

"What did it have to do with Mrs Hartnett?"

But Trish Hartnett shook her head. Tears were welling behind her green-gray eyes.

Detective Muse interrupted, "You'd better answer Mrs Hartnett. We already have good cause to suspect you of the murder of Mr Young. We now have reason to suspect that you may have been Father Sebastian's assailant."

Trish shook her head again, saying nothing. A single tear ran down her cheek.

Donna knew the way this thing might go, should Trish fail to cooperate fully. "Please Mrs Hartnett. You are in a great deal of trouble. You must tell us whatever you know."

Trish shook her head then bit her lower lip and raised her eyes to stare directly at Detective Muse. "I have nothing more to say."

Muse raised his right hand and combed it through his silver-gray hair, wrinkling his forehead at the same time, as if the action enabled him to think more clearly. "Very well, Mrs Hartnett. You leave us no alternative."

It was Donna who interrupted this time. "Please, Mrs Hartnett. This doesn't have to happen."

Muse waited, partly in deference to his colleague, but partly because he himself was uncomfortable with what they were about to do. But Trish remained impassive. There was an inevitability about this in any case. In Massachusetts arrest warrants are issued by Grand Juries that sit for three months at a stretch handling case after case like shelling peas. Unbeknownst to Trish she'd been arraigned by the District Court and indicted by the Grand Jury that morning. At last Muse spoke, his voice labored and weary.

"Very well Mrs Hartnett. You leave us little alternative but to arrest you on suspicion of the murder of Robert Young and the attempted murder of Father Sebastian. You have the right to remain silent."

He paused before continuing. Mostly to be sure she understood. He knew these words off by heart. "Anything you say or do can and will be used against you in a court of law. You have the right to an attorney. If you cannot afford an attorney, one will be appointed for you. Do you understand these rights as they have been read to you?"

Trish nodded. "Yes, I understand," she said.

Which was not enough for Detective Muse. As was his practice, he removed a piece of card from his pocket, an eight by eleven sheet on which the customary words were inscribed, and read them line by line asking Trish to initial each line on the card as he did so. When he got down to the station he would have her read the card again. That way there could be no comeback later. Though he always went by the book and told the defendant he or she had the right to consult with an attorney, he knew that they very seldom asked for an attorney straight out. "They'll just try to outslick you," he had told Donna when she first hooked up as his partner. And generally he was right. His basic rule of thumb was, "If I get name, address and date of birth and you don't lawyer up, I am gonna get something helpful." And he was already way past that with Trish.

And as they recited her Miranda rights, Trish Hartnett felt a greater sense of calm than she had felt in weeks. An intolerable burden had been lifted from her shoulders.

24.

There is that speaketh like the piercings of a sword: but the tongue of the wise is health.

Proverbs 12:18

Friday 30th November: "So she's coming here?"

"Well I could hardly refuse. Personally, I think it's rather flattering. Not to say exciting."

"Yeh." Dick Bryer shrugged. "If you say so. A quarter-million dollars bail. That's a lot of money."

Hanlin raised a sardonic eyebrow. "Not for her. Not much at all. She's pretty well healed. Before the bail review hearing it was going to be way higher I'm told. You realize she only actually has to find ten percent if she's willing to use a bail bondsman. It's cash or surety and if she uses a bail bondsman she loses the ten per cent altogether but that'd be nothing for her. She's lucky to get bail at all actually, on a capital charge. Very seldom a murderer gets bail. Only ever happened once before for Murder One in Massachusetts. That was the Big Y supermarket murder. Where the wife killed the boss."

Bryer nodded, "Yeh. And that woman was as guilty as sin."

"They have to relinquish their passports."

"Who?"

"People who get bail."

"I should bloody well think so for murder in the first degree."

And so she came. Trish arrived straight from the Police HQ on Pearl Street, downtown, a huge bunker-like building more appropriate to Mussolini's Rome than to Springfield, "the City of Homes." It was massive. In the eighties it had been HQ for 650 sworn officers with 32 on homicide. That number had been reduced to 350 today. Back then they called homicide the "Elbow Squad" because they were so keen to get their pictures in the papers with their collars they held them by the elbows for the press photographers. Some things at least had improved.

They sat Trish on a sofa and drew chairs up facing her, separated only by a low, glass-topped table on which sat cups of coffee poured by Jane Hanlin.

Dressed in a broad flower-patterned suit over which her auburn hair cascaded, she was, as always, a picture. Initially she said nothing, just nursed her coffee. The two men were patient. They made no small talk. Instead they waited.

"I have come to you for help."

Hanlin nodded his encouragement. "Go on," he said.

She did, answering their unspoken question. "I have always respected you both. I can't ask the police for help. They have me down as a serial killer."

Hanlin smiled. "Perhaps not a serial killer, Mrs Hartnett."

"As good as. I'm accused of the murder of Bob Young and the attempted murder of Father Seb. And they are questioning me about the death of both Mary Young and Anna Maria Gonzalez."

Bryer whistled. "You need something stronger than coffee."

"Cawffee is fine."

Hanlin got straight to the point. "So, what have they got on you Mrs Hartnett?"

"Trish, call me Trish." And she explained.

"Just that someone used your credit card to hire a Hummer?"

"That and the anonymous letters."

"The letters are irrelevant. Poison pen letters are not evidence. What about motive?"

Trish hesitated then said, "What the heck." She paused a moment then continued. "They have all sorts of strange theories. One is that I was having an affair with Baxter Merrill, and that I felt his wife had betrayed him because she was having an affair with Father Seb which I, in some way, wished to avenge."

Hanlin chuckled quietly. "Sounds a bit convoluted. Is this Springfield or "Desperate Housewives?"

"Oh it's Springfield all right."

Hanlin cut in. "And were you?"

Trish had the grace to smile. "Not at the time of the attack on Father Seb."

"But before that, you had such an affair?"

Trish shook her head, "No," she said.

Hanlin narrowed his dark eyes. "But since the time of the attack, you have had such an affair?"

Trish tossed her auburn hair. "And if I had? Why is it that men can play around but women can't?"

Breyr's experience at the CIA had taught him the value of pushing the envelope. He'd already decided to treat this like an interrogation. If he pulled his punches, it would not help her. "So Sean's been playing around?" he asked. Trish bit her lower lip. Her response was just a nod of the head.

"You know with whom?"

Again she nodded. "It's over now," she said.

"And the name of your husband's ex-paramour?"

"I'd rather not say. And, really, there is not much else that I can tell you."

Hanlin sighed. "Very well Trish. We'll do what we can. But you're not helping yourself if you withhold information from us."

Trish nodded. "Thank you," she said. "Really, thank you."

Hanlin smiled. "Well, I'm not sure how much we can help," he said. "But what can be done, we will do."

CHAPTER FIVE: DECEMBER

Greet ye one another with a kiss of charity. Peace be with you all that are in Christ Jesus. Amen.

1 Peter 5:14

Saturday 1st December: She had moved her stuff out of the house the week after she had left Baxter. She had taken a small but attractive town house in the Georgetown neighborhood off Dickinson Street bordering Longmeadow. She could afford it—just.

And this time, David Sebastian had come to visit. And she could tell right off that all was not well. Seb had that lowering look that men get when they feel pressured. A woman would get angry in similar circumstances perhaps. Not a man, at least not a man like Seb. You had to push a man's buttons to make him angry. Otherwise, in circumstances beyond control, the male reaction to pressure was often a sort of sullen immobility, like an ox put unwilling to harness.

Angie recognized his mood as uncharacteristic. This was not her David, not the man she had grown to know and love. She had been in this world long enough to know that there were two ways to lift the male of the species out of depression. One was to kick them out of it, to goad them to anger. The other was to love them out of it. She chose the latter course, her perspective being that sex was the ace card in the mature woman's armament.

Inevitably perhaps, it was a hasty business, more like lovemaking had been in that other world an eternity ago, with Baxter. Afterwards he fell asleep, and she bore his weight a while and then gently pushed him aside, soothing him awake.

For a while they lay together, he leant over and kissed her forehead, and her eyes, and cupped her face in his hands, leaning on his elbow to do so, kissing her once briefly on the lips. Then he climbed from the bed saying, "Angie, we must talk."

And there was something in the words that sent a chill to the nape of her neck, a frisson of fear running through her like a physical thing, and she knew what he was about to say before he said it.

"We have to end this."

"You are going back to the church?" she asked with a bravado she didn't feel. She wasn't going to let him see her cry; though the tears were there and would come, later.

"Not exactly. Not the Catholic church per se. But there's an ecumenical seminary up in Detroit. It has a good reputation. They'll give me refuge for now. I'll teach a little. I've had discussions with them."

"You'll move away?"

"I think so. It seems best."

"Now?"

"Soon. When this is sorted." He was dressing as he spoke.

And Angie Merrill watched him. Watched as her world came to an end.

"I'm sorry Angie," he was saying but his words made little impression. "I think it best. I hope you can forgive me."

She didn't look at him. She felt so desperately hurt. All she wanted was to be alone, to curl up and cry and lick her wounds. Was this her fault? Had she seduced him, damaged him in some way? Should it be her that asked his forgiveness for subverting his mission in life? For taking him from the priesthood?

She felt him stroking her hair and she closed her eyes as if by so doing she could make him disappear. She knew the tears were there, great oceans of them, building inside ready to overwhelm and engulf her.

He had asked her forgiveness. But sometimes forgiveness was not in the mix.

Did she want his forgiveness? No, his love was all she wanted, unconditional love. And that he wasn't prepared to offer, not in the way she needed him at least.

And should she then forgive him for this thing he was doing, this abandonment, this betrayal? Why? It served no purpose other than to satisfy him, the man who had used her. God, Baxter was a saint alongside this one, for all that he beat up on her. What this one had done was truly abusive at a far deeper level.

Forgive him then? This one she need never forgive, not 'till the day she died. Nor would she.

He tried to kiss her one last time but she turned her head away as her humiliation was replaced by anger.

"Go," she said. "Go now."

He smiled weakly. Then he left.

2.

In the mouth of the foolish [is] a rod of pride: but the lips of the wise shall preserve them.

Proverbs 14:3

Saturday 1st December: Lisa the bartender sat with Vicky in Pazzo's Bar. But this time Lisa was a customer, as well, and liked it. They sat in a banquette opposite the long wooden bar. Both girls looked well in their different ways. Lisa was wearing a white waistcoat and shirt with a wide black belt worn high over a tight black skirt that was little more than a pelmet. She had gold and black jump-up shoes, the things with wedges. Her hair was in a ponytail, and she was draped in cheap and cheerful jewelry. She turned heads.

And even Vicky was looking good. Not for the first time lately. She'd abandoned her neo-hippy dress code for a short cutaway dress in white tinged with purple and a black jacket. She'd pulled her long brown hair into a ponytail like Lisa, and she had neon plastic sunglasses pushed high on her head. The effect was to make her look her age, which for Vicky was unusual.

"I'm worried Vicky," Lisa was saying. "I've only been here two years. I got no legal status."

Lisa didn't look it but she was a Dominican, a Latina, Hispanic like fully a fifth of Springfield's population. Vicky smiled. She liked to be giving advice these days, helping people, on the other-people's-troubles-take-your-mind-off-your-own basis, which in a way was part of the reason she'd chosen to be a teacher.

"You really needn't worry. You've got a social security number; that's half the battle. You'll be able to get naturalized in a year or two if you keep your nose clean." Vicky's eyes crinkled mischievously, "Or marry an American if you want to sort it out sooner." Vicky looked down at her coffee and then looked up slyly at her friend. "That's what I intend to do."

Lisa was so preoccupied with her own troubles she didn't register. "You don't need to marry an American. You're American yourself."

Vicky smiled. "Oh yes I do. The baby remember."

And Lisa, to do her credit, shrieked. "You're going to marry him? The man that knocked you up? Gee girl, that's great!"

"Well I think so. Leastways we've moved in together. Well I've moved in with him, yesterday. God, Lisa, I'm so excited."

"And you're keeping the baby?"

Vicky nodded, "Mmm. Yup. I am."

Lisa was genuinely thrilled. "Geez V, that's great. So who's the guy?"

"Baxter Merrill."

"Oh my God, Vicky!"

"Well don't sound so thrilled. He's not that old."

"Vicky." Lisa reached for her friend's hand. "I don't give a damn how old he is."

"What then?"

"God, Vicky. He tried to hit on Anna before she was killed."

Vicky pulled her hand back and straightened in her chair, "So? He's a man. Men are like that. Anyway, I wasn't with him then."

"Sure, Vicky, but it's worse than that."

Vicky was getting irritated. The rasp in her voice showed as much. "How worse?"

"Manuel, Anna's man. You know Manuel—Manny?"

Vicky nodded.

"He thinks Baxter Merrill may have killed Anna Maria."

"That's ridiculous. Anyway they say the police are questioning Trish Hartnett over all those killings. Not that I think for one moment she's guilty. Still ..."

"Not for Anna. They haven't charged her with that. And Manny says Baxter Merrill had a motive."

"Which was?" Vicky was angry now, and beginning to show it.

Anna had told him she had something on Baxter not long before she was killed."

"What precisely?"

"I don't know."

"No, you don't, do you? Look here Lisa. Baxter Merrill is a good man. He's my man. He's the father of my child."

And Vicky got to her feet and marched out of the bar.

3.

*Forasmuch then as Christ hath suffered for us in the flesh,
arm yourselves likewise with the same mind: for he that hath
suffered in the flesh hath ceased from sin*

1 Peter 4:1

Monday 3rd December: Baxter's thoughts were all over the place.
He found himself musing about Trish Hartnett. He remembered the way she had been when he'd found her naked, waiting
for him like some latter-day Matahari in the den. Exquisite. He
shrugged the picture from his mind's eye. Could she possibly
be a killer? He conjured up a mental image of Trish Hartnett,
Delilah-like, à la femme fatale, slipping poison into the mint
julep. No it just didn't ring true.

The letter did though. He glanced back at it for the umpteenth
time. On a Sumner Elementary School letterhead, the type-
written note was from the Principal and asked him to drop
by the school today at 4 p.m. after the staff and students had
gone home.

It had to be about Vicky, of course. She probably wanted to tell
him to lay off a girl young enough to be his daughter. So what,
if you loved someone? And he did love her, in his way. Maybe
her being with child was a factor. Vulnerability usually stirred
Baxter's urge to dominate. But this was more than that.

Not that Baxter was a reformed character. Like most men he
expected his women to be loyal to him, but that was as far as it
went. He felt no obligation to be loyal to Vicky at the expense
of womankind. If a woman asked a man to her bed, it was a sin
to say no. That was Baxter Merrill's philosophy.

He was thinking that way as he put on his jacket for the short
stroll down from his home at 185 Longhill and across onto
Sumner. A little early winter snow lay crisp on the ground, its

virgin whiteness decorated rather than marred by the near random imprint of passing dog and deer. The sun crisped snow a backdrop to the occasional visitations of seeming flocks of chickadee to the bird feeders, small with their lemon and white tummies, and little red shouldered finches, and pretty gray white titmouse with a bit of yellow on their side and black tufts on their heads. All these along with a solitary brilliant red-crested male cardinal, the best of birds. As he stepped outside his home he looked up to examine the flagpole. It carried the Stars and Stripes limp in the stillness. The trees bare naked now; the not-so-distant Longhill traffic part shielded by evergreen rhododendrons, already becoming limp for lack of water in the unforgiving close to frozen ground.

The Sumner Elementary School was just across the road from OLPH in a pleasant part of the city. In this West end of town, Sumner is a broad, four-lane, tree-lined avenue with comfortable sidewalks slicing through wide, neatly mown double grass verges, now sprinkled with snow but still impressive enough to put a Paris boulevard to shame. The walk took less than ten minutes. More like five. It was almost an almost balmy afternoon—less cold than it had been. The traffic was pretty busy, picking up for rush hour.

Baxter was stepping into the road to cross Sumner, dodging cars, when the white-hot stab of pain lanced into his left side below the ribs. He heard the echoed crack of the gunshot a millisecond later. The pain came first.

Unfortunately for Baxter, he was already in the road. The searing pain stopped him in his tracks and the approaching FedEx delivery truck couldn't brake in time. It hit him square on. On the plus side, fortunately for Baxter, it wasn't traveling that fast. Get hit by a car at 20 mph and you have a 97% chance of survival. Get hit at 40 mph and you have a 90% probability of death. The FedEx hit Baxter at 25. He had a second or two to gather his thoughts before unconsciousness rushed in like an oncoming dark tunnel.

And he thought of Vicky.

"I must love the girl," he mouthed mutely to himself. But nobody heard him.

4.

Better is a dinner of herbs where love is, than a stalled ox and hatred therewith.

Proverbs 15:17

Tuesday 4th December: The private room at the Bay State Medical Center was filled with flowers. Vicky Walters had seen to that. It was also filled with people, and Baxter Merrill had seen to that. When Vicky had said he had too many visitors he'd browbeaten her, as well as the head duty nurse. Which of itself was an achievement for a man who had come as close as a man could to death.

But Baxter liked being the center of attention, and he wasn't going to lose his moment in the sun. The Springfield "Republican" reporter had just left the room with his story for the Wednesday edition. Vicky was there, of course, her pregnancy too early to show. Though everyone knew. She had told them. She was proud now that Baxter was standing by her. But her eyes were red-rimmed. This was too much. Hanlin was bringing in an extra chair for her. He'd brought the two wives, Marilyn Bryer and his own wife Jane, both of whom had insisted on visiting when they'd heard the news.

The family physician, Dr Paolo, was there as well, making suitably concerned noises and explaining that Baxter would need to rest for a month. Which was when Father Seb and Alicia White came in. They had arrived at the same time. Seb had brought grapes, which was useful, if unoriginal. Alicia had brought more flowers, which was kind but unnecessary.

They were both about to beat a hasty retreat given the number of people in the room but the convalescent waved them in. "The more the merrier," said Baxter.

"How did you manage this then Baxter?" Hanlin's comment

was made when the room had readjusted itself to accommodate the newcomers.

"Some'n to do with the death of that frigging Chicano bitch."

"Baxter!" Vicky's outrage was genuine.

"Sorry, shouldn't swear. But you haven't been shot and run down all in one day."

"Baxter Merrill, you can swear as much as you like. But don't say that. It's racist."

"What, Chicano?"

"Precisely. And while we're at it, you don't call a woman— any woman—a bitch."

"OK, Vicky." Baxter paused, reflected and bit back, "What's wrong with saying 'Chicano' anyway? That's what she is after all."

"And that's why people always jump to the conclusion that they're culpable of every serious crime."

"Well they are, aren't they? Mostly? Nine times out of ten. And anyhow, Chicanos aren't indigenous. Redskins are."

Vicky's response was affable with an edge born of her new-found confidence. She was unabashed by the presence of the others in the room, and she was not going to drop the point. "Native Americans—not Redskins —not Red Indians either for that matter. Be respectful Baxter. I don't care how badly wounded you are. Respect costs nothing."

axter looked shamefaced. Seb and Hanlin exchanged a smile. "What would you call this Father Seb? The reverse of 'The Taming of the Shrew?'"

Seb laughed. "The Subjugation of the Redneck," he replied. But the words were spoken with such affable good humor and affection that Baxter didn't take offence. He did respond though.

"My manners apart. This could well have something to do with Anna's killing. Your daughter questioned me, Alicia. Along with that detective guy, Muse. And they weren't as friendly as a man has a right to expect."

Alicia looked surprised. "Really?"

"Yeh, you'd better believe it. And I wouldn't put it past that Chicano boyfriend of hers ..."

Vicky winced and was about to say something but Baxter continued, "Sorry, Mexican boyfriend—He could have got it into his head that I'd killed Anna and come after me."

Hanlin scratched his neck, "Why would he think that you'd killed Anna ?"

"God only knows," Baxter lied, his languid brown eyes as innocent as the day was long. He wasn't going to confess to having harassed her.

"Well, there's one good thing about this from your point of view," announced Hanlin.

"Which is?"

"Which is that it puts you way into left field as a suspect in the Bob Young killing."

Baxter's eyes widened. "I didn't think I ever was a suspect. They've nailed pretty little Trish Hartnett for that one."

Alicia White was shaking her head. "She's not convicted yet. And I for one view her as innocent."

Seb interrupted, "That's great news, Alicia. But does that really mean that Baxter is a suspect?"

Hanlin smiled. "We all are Seb. We all sure are."

5.

Doth a fountain send forth at the same place sweet water and bitter?

James 3:11

Wednesday 5th December: Hanlin knew the place well. It was just across the parking lot from L.A. Fitness where he was in the habit of training once a week, the same place patronized pretty regularly by Sean Hartnett. The bar she'd specified had music playing outside and a small group of girls, decked out and dancing on the sidewalk, whilst a few boys sat at nearby tables and pretended not to be looking at them. "Provincial America at its most charming," thought Hanlin. He dodged the dancers and moved back into the recessed safety of the bar beyond to wait for her. He didn't have to wait long.

"Well now. An assignation with not one but two ladies. A truly unexpected pleasure. You will have?"

"A glass of white wine. Anything as long as it's cold."

"I'll just have a tonic water, with a slice of lime."

Hanlin waved the order at the girl behind the bar before focusing his attention on his interlocutors. The contrast between the two women could not have been more complete.

Vicky Walters carried her long brown hair like a badge of honor. She had been thinking about cutting it short like Trish Hartnett had suggested but so far had failed to screw up the courage. Still, she had shed much of her latter-day hippy persona. There was just the faintest sign of her pregnancy, that early slightest of the slight rounding of the belly and thickening of the ankles that is only noticeable to the practiced eye. She was power dressing in a figure-hugging black number that was more the badge of the femme fatale than the mother-to-be. Her dark hazel eyes glistened wide as they focused their attention on Hanlin in the comfortable seats of Pazzo's spacious bar at the Basketball Hall of Fame.

Contrast the other girl, Lisa, the sometime barmaid at Pazzo's. Off duty now, she had two years on her friend Vicky. Two years and another world. From the wrong side of the tracks, Lisa, bejeweled and well bosomed, her hair pulled back in a ponytail, was every bit the rough diamond. But the two girls were friends.

The drinks were delivered.

"So ladies, what can I do for you?" Hanlin sipped his Beefeater dirty martini.

They were silent a moment and exchanged a glance.

"Tell him, Lisa."

"Better if you tell him Vicky. I don't want us to argue."

"Tell me what?"

Vicky Walters tossed and swung her head so that her long brown hair fell neatly behind her shoulders, like a filly readying herself for a race. "OK," she said. "It's about Manny." She pronounced his name in the familiar colloquial manner.

"Who's Manny?"

"Anna's boyfriend."

Hanlin nodded and sipped his martini. "Go on."

"He told Lisa that his Anna told him that my Baxter tried to rape her." The words tumbled out breathlessly, all in a run. "Which is nonsense of course. My Baxter is a man, and if that slut Anna tried to seduce him, he might have weakened. I can believe that men are like that." She dropped her gaze, flushing, embarrassed. "But my Baxter would never rape anyone. He doesn't need to. He can have any woman he wants. Just has to snap his fingers." She looked up defiantly, daring either Hanlin or Lisa to contradict her.

"So what you are saying, in so many words, is that this Manny character had a reason to try and kill Baxter and you want him stopped."

"Something like that."

"So why," Hanlin turned his attention to the other woman. "Why didn't you just go to the police, Lisa?"

6.

The king's heart is in the hand of the LORD, as the rivers of water: he turneth it whithersoever he will.

Proverbs 21:1

Thursday 6th December: Trish had told him to come round for coffee when he'd phoned. Seemed the right thing to do. Sean would be at work, and the thing with Baxter needed ending.

She'd been tidying up, cleaning around the house; not that Sean cared. Perhaps she was hoping to wash away her need for him. Perhaps she was just doing it all for the sake of it, just for something to do.

"Why am I so weak?" she was thinking. "I've been like this ever since I laid my soul bare for Sean. And now it hangs by a thread, getting battered and broken, and I can't seem to wrap it up and put it away. So I cry myself to sleep, because I know things will never be the same. But I still love Sean, even though he's been hurting me. The more he hurts me, the more I love him; until I feel helpless, unable to cope with any more crying."

She was trying hard to be patient. Her situation had changed. She felt better but she couldn't help thinking, "Now that Sean has come back to me, I still have to look him in the eyes and know that I was caused so much pain and tears because of him."

"Fuck him," she thought.

And then Baxter came round. Baxter Merrill wore a loose shirt and sports jacket with white, out-of-style slacks and black penny loafers.

"Those are summer clothes, Baxter," were her fist words when he had sat down. Actually Trish subscribed to the Paris Hilton maxim, 'Dress cute wherever you go, life is too short to blend in.' But at the end of the day there had to be limits—and in any case, that applied to girls, not boys. Trish liked her men conventional.

Baxter shrugged. "Suits me anyhow."

"That's as may be, but still they're wrong. Wan' some cawffee?"

"Thanks."

She brought a cake from the pantry, and she cut him a slice without asking whether he wanted any. It was her way.

They talked a while, the conversation coy, almost childlike. They didn't ever mention the murder charge against Trish. The one thing of substance that was said between them was that their affair was over almost before it had started.

"You sure you're OK Baxter?"

"What, with this?" He pulled his shirt button open to show his bandaged chest.

"Yes, that," she said, though that wasn't what she'd meant.

Baxter smiled. "It hurts some. But they don't want you hanging about in hospital these days."

He hesitated. "You OK, Trish?"

She smiled. "Yes. OK with Sean anyway." Then she laughed. "And I've been away from my work which has given me time to develop my website. Want to see?"

Baxter didn't, but he nodded that 'yes, he did'.

She led him over to the computer and sat him in the chair, kneeling at his side and manipulating the mouse. As she did so her breast brushed against his forearm.

Baxter felt the old hollow feeling in the pit of his stomach. Had she done that deliberately? He looked down at her, reaching for her with his hand. She held back. "It's over Baxter. I'm back with Sean."

"And I'm back with Vicky. Of course it's over." He caressed her hair as he spoke. "But what the eye doesn't see the heart doesn't grieve," she heard him say as he stooped to kiss her. And she found herself thinking, "Oh hell, one more time for the road," as she let him.

She made one lame attempt to forestall the inevitable as she felt his hand move up under the baby doll dress she was wearing. "Baxter, what about your wound?"

She saw him wince then and realized it was hurting him. But he just growled, "What wound?" as he pushed her toward the bedroom and threw her onto the bed. Then he undressed mechanically as he stood there, and she followed suit, surrendering to the moment.

It was an hour before he finally moved to leave her, then he dressed swiftly as she did her best to keep up with him. Her lips felt bruised in the aftermath of his onslaught, and she had an irrational fear Sean might notice. Her thirst for vengeance was long slaked. This was a sort of closure. Both she and Baxter knew that this was the last time. She led him to the door.

The house was dressed for the approaching Christmas season, a wreath on the glass-fronted door, electric candles in every window. Baxter kissed her briefly and perfunctorily.

Then the glass in the part open door was shattered as the bullet slammed between them.

7.

For whom the Lord loveth he chasteneth, and scourgeth every son whom he receiveth.

Hebrews 12:6

Friday 7th December: Muse felt guilty in his way about hauling the boy straight into the Springfield Police Headquarters up on Pearl Street. They'd come to Mrs Hartnett to question her, not brought her to them, not hauled her in—not at least until she'd been arrested. Same with Merrill. Was this racism then? Now that they were hauling in the Chicano.

More expediency than racism he mused. The Chicano boy was less likely to kick up a fuss, haul in a lawyer, and the rest of the whole nine yards.

So Manny stood there like a lemon.

Muse didn't think of himself as harsh. He had a lot of sympathy for the inner city people. The kids who'd only ever been shown any love by older gang members. The lads who, by fourteen, were robbing convenience stores just to prove themselves. Genuinely he felt sorry for them. What chance did they have in life? But the frequent fliers in their thirties and forties he had no sympathy for. He was sickened by the way so many of them pretended to be broke until it came to finding bail money. They deserved everything they got.

Now this lad, Manny, he had time for.

"Your full name is Manuel Sanchez?" Muse asked, pronouncing his name in the American fashion.

"Manuel Ernesto Sanchez-Rivera," he replied, reciting his full, given name. "Most people call me Manny."

"Manuel, Manny, whatever. We are here to discuss the death of

Anna Gonzalez." This was Donna White talking. She recognized her own bad mood and put it down to PMT.

Like the rest of them, Muse was tired. The vast majority of murders were drug related, gang related, or domestic and this felt like the latter. Muse wanted to get to the point. "Did you kill her?"

Manny was stunned, or at least looked the part. He unslumped his shoulders and looked up. "Santa Maria, Madre de Dios," he said.

Muse smiled. "I take it from that the answer is a 'no'?"

Manny shook his head vigorously. "She was my geerlfriend man."

Again Muse smiled. He turned to Donna. "Only once in my whole career did I ever hear a guy plead guilty to first degree murder." He looked back at Manny. "I'll ask you again. Did you kill her?"

This time Manny hung his head. "She was my geerlfriend. You understan'? I was going to marry her."

Muse nodded his head to indicate that he understood. "You own a gun Manny?"

"No. Why sh'd I?"

Donna White interjected. "To shoot Baxter Merrill."

"That Baxter killed my Anna."

"You can prove that?"

"He gave her trouble."

"That doesn't mean he killed her," Donna mused. "But you tried to kill him, didn't you?"

"Naw." Manny's tone was sullen. He thought his answer didn't matter. They'd believe what they wanted to believe.

"Naw?" Muse doubted this Chicano had it in him. But maybe that assumption was itself racist, he found himself thinking. "Yes or naw—from now on you keep your hands clean, understand me?"

And Manny nodded and rubbed his hands together. "Sure thing," he said. "Sure thing."

8.

For in much wisdom is much grief: and he that increaseth knowledge increaseth sorrow.

Ecclesiastes 1:18

Friday 7th December: Lawyer Fieldson was asking her to waive her Rule 36 rights, under the terms of which a defendant has to be brought to trial within one year. She was having none of it. He hadn't let up there either. He wanted to work on getting the charge reduced to second degree murder which carries a term of fifteen years to life. First degree murder means no parole. Life means life as in, "for and during the rest of your natural life." Where was the man coming from? Didn't he believe she was innocent?

"Well at least with first degree murder you get an automatic appeal," Fieldson was saying.

The lawyer just did not seem to get it, to understand the basics. Trish wondered if she could shock some sense into him so that he really appreciated her position. She tried honesty. "My husband told me last night that he didn't feel any real empathy for Bishop O'Malley. He said they were friends, but that something was always missing, that they came from different worlds. The one thing I do know is that when he came home, that thing wasn't missing anymore.

"He told me he took Bishop O'Malley to Pazzo's Bar. That really upset me 'cause it's a place we sometimes go to, him and I; a place where we're known. He tried to kiss me and make me feel better. Then he told me that he liked the Bishop and said he's a nice man. That made me angry. I said that I was so fucking tired of hearing that everyone else thinks the Bishop is so fucking great. Then go fucking be with him.

"God, I wish I could make my husband understand I want to

share the bad times with him as well as the good. Whatever life throws our way: Sickness, disappointment, and death, whatever. There's no one else I want to help me through those times. He's the best thing since sliced bread. I'm not willing to give him up. He can hold me up when I need it.

"I want my husband to be mine and only mine. But I have to struggle to remember the good times and forget the bad. It's not so much that you live for the moment, but that you let the moment live forever in your memory.

"But none of this helps because on top of everything else I am accused of murder. And even my husband believes I did it."

"I'm sure that's not true, Mrs Hartnett."

Trish tossed her head like a petulant child and grunted her amusement with a "Huh" that was more sneer than laugh. "Why don't you save that silver-tongued bullshit for the jury," she said. "How much am I paying you?" she added.

Lawyer Fieldson winced. This was going to be a good five figure, maybe even a low six figure, case. "A great deal Mrs Hartnett, and I assure you it is money well spent."

Fieldson meant it too. Most murder cases in Massachusetts are 85% paid for by the state. Which means that the defense attorneys may not be the best available. Pay for your own lawyer and it'll generally cost you between fifty and a hundred thousand dollars but you'll get off scot free nine times in ten. It just requires one person to have doubt. And money buys good lawyers. And a good lawyer can usually swing it. One scintilla of doubt will do the trick.

David Fieldson, Esq. was a class act, and he knew it. Slightly built with a square face and blond hair, he was far from intimidating at first glance. Combine the above with a taste for the effete in dress, expressed in a particular penchant for breast pocket handkerchiefs to match his shirts, and bright bow ties for contrast. Plus a lightness of tone in his conversation; people generally underestimated him.

But give him a hostile prosecution witness, and he was in his element. Add a brief so hopeless it would tax the patience of Job, and you were getting somewhere. He'd always been amused by the fact that the Springfield Police Department had Jude as its patron saint; Jude who was renowned as having a predisposition for hopeless causes.

Nonetheless Fieldson was by no means heartless. He didn't like the way there was a mandatory minimum sentence for so many crimes in Massachusetts, Murder One included. County Clerk Lees and he had shared a double martini lunch earlier and agreed as much. Brian Lees had helped push through mandatory minimums as Senate Minority Leader in a previous incarnation. He lamented it now. "Judges should be given more discretion," he said. "And Springfield D.A. Bill Barnett needs good funding to get good people to prosecute, to send the right signal to the community."

Fieldson agreed.

Fieldson prided himself on making sure they didn't take the defense for granted. And not for the first time he was hopeful that he was about to go head to head with the Hampden County District Attorney or, at the very least—his principal assistant— in a case that was going to be front page news regardless.

In the Commonwealth of Massachusetts, murder committed with deliberate premeditated malice aforethought, or with extreme atrocity or cruelty, is murder in the first degree. Murder which does not appear to be in the first degree is murder in the second degree. The degree of murder shall be found by the jury.

Lawyer Fieldson cut to the chase, "This business started with Mary Young's suicide, did it not?"

"So?"

"Mr. Young's murder could be unrelated, but I doubt it. The likelihood is that we are dealing with one killer."

"And is the Pope a Catholic? You sure know how to state the obvious." Then she paused, confused. "But Mary Young killed herself."

"That's a maybe Mrs Hartnett. Are you so sure we can be certain that Mary Young's death was suicide?"

"You can't be serious? The DA and the police finally had concluded it was."

"Oh but I'm not so certain. We have to be on the watch for police and prosecutional misconduct too by the way. We must dispense with all our past thinking if we are to prove you innocent."

"And you believe I am innocent?"

He managed not to look offended by her audacity. "That is scarcely the point at issue."

"It is very much the point at issue, Lawyer Fieldson."

"It matters to you what I believe? I am not the jury, Mrs Hartnett."

Trish Hartnett narrowed her green-gray eyes, the effect both intimidating and charming, like a poodle at bay. "Yes, Mr Fieldson, it matters."

David Fieldson didn't hesitate. This was ground he had travelled before with many a client. He had learnt long ago it was best to tell them what they wanted to hear.

"Very well, Mrs Hartnett. Since it matters. Yes, of course, I believe you are innocent." The lie slid easily off his tongue. He was a good lawyer after all.

PART TWO
one year later

Chapter Six: December

Prove all things; hold fast that which is good.

1 Thessalonians 5:21

Saturday 8th December: "Yes, I guess. You have to confide in someone. But why me?"

"Men find friends where they can. Christ's friends were sinners."

Baxter Merrill threw back his head and laughed. "I've got to hand it to you Bish. You sure know how to charm. There's an old proverb that goes: Where flowers and thorns are placed together, it's the thorns you feel." Baxter took a generous slug of his Johnny Walker Black Label, with its splash of soda water. They sat in the den at 185 Longhill. Both men were relaxed. "So you play Christ, and I play the sinner?"

The Bishop raised an eyebrow. "Is that what I implied? Could be *vice versa* of course."

"Somehow I doubt that. Haven't you guys got confessors for this sort of thing?"

"My confessor is Father Sebastian."

Baxter laughed again. This time, if anything, louder. "The priest that's screwing my Angie?"

The Bishop smiled in turn. "The priest that had a relationship with your wife. To the best of my knowledge he doesn't any longer."

"Really?" Baxter Merrill sat up in his chair. "Poor Angie. She sure can pick 'em."

"Huh?"

"Well first me, then a priest. And we both treat her bad."

"Did you? Treat her bad I mean."

"Used to knock her about. Does that offend you Bishop?"

The Bishop was surprised, a little shocked even, but he said what was expected. "Nothing offends me."

Baxter raised an incredulous eyebrow but didn't pursue it. Instead he asked, "Want to know why I used to knock her about?"

"Why?"

"She was too bloody perfect. Too long suffering. No real fight in her."

The Bishop winced but didn't show it. "And Vicky?"

"Vicky's carrying my child. Angie and I never had children."

"That makes a difference?"

"Maybe." Baxter hesitated. "No, I don't s'pose it does."

The Bishop smiled his concern but his concern was genuine, perhaps for Vicky more than for Baxter. "Maybe you should have counseling."

Baxter shrugged. "Perhaps. But we're not here to talk about me, are we?"

"No."

"So?"

"So. The lawyer in the Trish Hartnett case has notified me that he'll call me as a witness for the defense."

"That's neat. I always wanted to go on the witness stand," Baxter mused. Then more seriously, "She's got that prick, David Fieldson, as her lawyer." He took another generous slug of his scotch. "I don't like the man."

"I have considered suicide," said the Bishop.

"That bad eh?"

The Bishop nodded. "Not that I contemplate suicide as an option for my own benefit. Not for myself you understand. But it would save others embarrassment. The church. My friends."

"And what of your immortal soul?"

The Bishop smiled. "I've lost that already."

"Really, you think?"

"Yes, I think. The Calvinists developed this extension of the idea of predestination. You understand predestination I presume?"

"Of course, the idea that God already knows who will be saved."

"Well the Calvinists suggested that, unless that meant that God had determined that all mankind was, ultimately, to be saved, the consequence was that those not preordained to be saved were predestined to be damned. They called the concept double predestination."

"Stupid fuckers."

"Well to be fair, it's not so much that the Calvinists believe that God damns the nonelect but rather that he ignores them. He doesn't exactly preelect people to go to hell."

"Like Judas."

"Yes. I guess they distinguish between preordination, which would be God makes no choice because it's inevitable and predestination, where the choice is God's and he can save sinners if he wishes."

"So there's hope for you."

"I doubt it somehow. Omnipotent God is all knowing of course. But I doubt it. Which is why suicide is tempting. I dislike uncertainty. It would resolve everything."

"Well," reflected Baxter with a twinkle in his eye. "It would be kind of neat. This thing began with a suicide. It could end the same way."

"So you subscribe to the idea that all these killings are linked to Mary Young's death?"

"Seems a reasonable hypothesis, don't you think?"

"Perhaps. You haven't asked what my problem is."

"Don't want to pry, Bishop. You'll tell me if you wish to."

"It's Patrick, and yes I'll tell you."

"Go on."

Bishop O'Malley gazed at the floor, nursing his drink as he spoke. "Sean Hartnett was my lover."

"You're gay?"

"Evidently." The Bishop smiled. "Gay is almost too small a word. I don't like the expression. Too much of a cliché. But yes, I'm what's commonly called a fag—a fag with a crush on a gym bunny."

Baxter was unfazed. "You got Aids then?"

"You don't understand?" The Bishop raised an eyebrow. "All this stuff about Sean will come out in open court."

Baxter wasn't that easily deflected. He went on like a dog with a bone. "You got Aids then?"

"I don't know. Does that matter?"

It was Baxter's turn to raise an eyebrow. "It matters. Get it checked out."

"What about being exposed in the courtroom?"

"Exposed? That's an insubstantial here today, gone tomorrow thing. What if you exposed me to the world as a wife beater? It'd be a storm I could weather with gravitas and endurance, plus display a smidgen of repentance. These are mere phantoms. Now talk to me of Aids or bankruptcy and you mention real demons.

"No. The worst of it would be the hurt to your pride. And it does us good to tear away that particular veneer. So many of us are virtually crippled with pride. We are better without it." Baxter stirred his drink with his finger in an absentminded way.

Then setting it aside he looked at the Bishop with his soulful, languid brown eyes. "The substantial—that frightens me," he said. "Not mere tittle-tattle and gossip. Sticks and stones may break my bones but words ..."

And the Bishop looked again at his new friend. "You genuinely believe that?"

"Sure I do. Take the fifth. The Martin Luther King option. Remain silent and imitate Christ for once."

"The Martin Luther King option? What's that?"

"They say he screwed around. He would never defend himself though. He gave his life to defend others. Not himself. Never himself. So go figure."

And Bishop Patrick O'Malley felt easier, for the first time in days. "Thank you Baxter," he said. "Really thank you very much."

2.

Be not rash with thy mouth, and let not thine heart be hasty to utter any thing before God: for God is in heaven, and thou upon earth: therefore let thy words be few.

Ecclesiastes 5:2

Sunday 9th December: "You're joking."

"I'm not. It's right here."

Jane Hanlin was sitting at a breakfast of bacon, pancakes, and maple syrup. Mike Hanlin was confined to toast and grapefruit. They both drank coffee like true Americans. It was the Springfield "Sunday Republican" that Jane Hanlin was reading, the "Cries and Whispers" column.

Mike Hanlin set aside his toast and finished his mouthful. "Read it out," he demanded before picking up his coffee.

Jane folded the paper down to the article. Then obeyed.

"Which potentate of the Springfield Church will be called as a witness for the prosecution in the Bob Young murder case? As readers will know, one-time Springfield Classical High homecoming queen, Trish Hartnett, stands accused of the murder of Springfield Schools Superintendent, Bob Young. The case is due to go to trial later this week.

"And the whisper is that a Springfield Church leader will be called as a hostile defense witness. And we are not talking of any mere Parish priest but rather one who wears the purple so they say.

"Why hostile? Well, the nature of this high cleric's testimony is unclear except and in so much as it will, we understand, expose in the process the sexual shenanigans of said pillar of the church. Remember: You heard it first in 'Crys and Whispers'."

Jane Hanlin set the newspaper aside and picked up a trim slice of crisp bacon and held it delicately between thumb and forefinger. She looked at her husband, the bacon poised in mid-air like a conductress' baton. She pointed the slice at her husband. "So, dear, what do you think?"

Hanlin put down his coffee cup. He saw the funny side of the whole business, despite which, or maybe because of which, his face was grim. "What I think is that I'll be calling on Bishop Patrick this afternoon." He shook his head in exasperation. "The poor man needs every friend he can muster."

3.

But if ye bite and devour one another, take heed that ye be not consumed one of another.

Galatians 5:15

Monday 10th December: The last execution in Massa-chusetts was by hanging and took place on 30th December 1898. The criminal was Dominick Kathofski. He was executed in Hampden County Jail for killing his stepdaughter Victoria Pinkos. Since when they just imprisoned their murderers. But in Massachusetts life means life, which bothered Trish Hartnett. "I've burned a lot of bridges this past year. The person I've become is someone I don't recognize anymore. Somewhere along the road, I lost my way, lost the person I once was," or so thought Trish Hartnett. She sat with her lawyer. "I'm not going to blame that on others," she thought.

And she said as much to Lawyer Fieldson. Then added, "I've become so proud, so selfish; it's made me realize that I am not the person I want to be in this life.

"I know that I have pushed things too far. I have no reason to expect that anyone should believe a word I say. I have been angry and unapproachable.

"I've lost most of my friends. Best friends who have been there for years. I took them for granted. Over the past few months, I've had some bitter lessons in pride and in patience. I must start being responsible for the things I say and do. I've hidden my feelings far too long."

Lawyer Fieldson thought this was all too self-indulgent. He subscribed to the sentiments expressed by Mark Twain when he wrote, "There's nothing sadder than a young pessimist except an old pessimist."

"The woman has her head way up her own backside," he thought. But he didn't say so. Instead he expressed his own suspicions as to who was really culpable in the Bob Young murder case.

"What?"

"It makes perfect sense."

Trish stared at her lawyer in silence for the longest time, her mind turning like the tumblers of a slot machine searching for an elusive jackpot. Then it connected.

"You think it could be true?" said Trish with a slight trembling in her voice.

"It's not a question of what's true, Mrs Hartnett. It's possible and we need to explore possibilities."

Trish tried to disguise the growing sense of exhilaration she was feeling. It just was so possible. Not likely but possible. And if it were possible, however improbable, it meant that there was reasonable doubt as to her own guilt.

"Think about it Mrs Hartnett. He has been with you through this. This seems to speak to me really loudly. He could, indeed would, have a copy of your signature. Could have borrowed your driver's license. Could steal your card and other personal items."

"But the woman they say was me who hired the vehicle."

Lawyer Fieldson pulled his glasses to the end of his nose, peered over them at Trish, raising his eyebrows in the process. "Easy," he said. "Hire any good call girl. Pay her a few thousand dollars. Don't tell her what this is about or who you are. Just school her in this, some girl that vaguely resembles you and has no scruples."

"You seriously think this could have happened?"

"No, but it may have happened, and I hate to use such a cliché, but it's reasonable doubt that matters." His pale blue eyes narrowed and lawyer Fieldson almost purred. He took the glasses off his nose and prodded the air with them for emphasis. "Michael Hanlin is a Hummer freak. He's in on everything in this. Too good a chance to miss. The world has changed."

4.

For [there is] not a just man upon earth, that doeth good, and sinneth not.

Ecclesiastes 7:20

Tuesday 11th December: Trish shivered. Not because she was cold. The Hanlin's house was like an oven; the fire roaring in the grate kept the Springfield near winter-like weather well and truly at bay. In the corner there was a massive Christmas tree, one of several scattered throughout the large house, decked in so many tiny white lights that it dazzled like thousands of small, polished diamonds.

Trish shivered because she was nervous. One of those a-goose-walked-over-my-grave type shivers. She was nervous because lawyer Fieldson fully intended to go for Hanlin's jugular, and Hanlin didn't know, and Hanlin had called her over to help her. She felt a mix of emotions in which shame vied with hope, fear with excitement. So she shivered.

But no one noticed. They were seated in the living room, Trish and Hanlin with Bryer, Seb, and Baxter. And they were talking about the Bishop.

"What does your defense team expect to gain by questioning the Bishop?"

"My defense team?" Trish snorted. "Together they can just about manage a complete thought."

Trish's sharp eyes focused on Hanlin. "I've told them not to question the Bishop. Not, that is, unless it's a last resort."

"And will they call on him?"

Trish gave one of those helpless little girl shrugs.

"So what can they possibly gain?"

Trish's mouth set in a grim smile. "Do I have to spell it out?"

Baxter reached out a reassuring arm. "No, Trish, you don't." He looked squarely at Hanlin. "In theory, however unlikely it may seem, the Bishop could well have had a motive to get Trish out of the way. A reason to implicate Trish."

"Ah, Sean, you mean," muttered Mike Hanlin, looking anxiously at Trish.

Trish's pretty face contorted into a grimace. "Yes, my Sean. I hope that won't have to be thrashed over in open court." She stood up, pushing her chair away behind her. "Not that I wouldn't like to see that fucking faggot, Bishop bloody O'Malley, squirm."

She looked down at the three men like she was addressing an audience. They had all been too surprised by her sudden change in manner to haul themselves to their feet in turn, as traditional American etiquette demanded.

"He's the same as the rest of them, the pope included. His Holiness is soft on gays. His attitude stinks. On the environment he has my vote."

Hanlin intervened. "I know you're feeling wounded but that's a bit strong, Trish."

"Bloody right I'm feeling wounded. None of those priests can keep their hands off the altar boys. And now the Bishop's messing with my Sean. OK, OK. Maybe if Sean wasn't married to me perhaps I wouldn't give a damn. But he is and I care. You know what the fucking Bishop had the audacity to do the other day?" The question was rhetorical, she didn't pause. "He preached a sermon backing up the Pope's misogynist views on women priests. A sin His Holiness says. A fucking grave sin to be a woman priest. And Bishop bloody O'Malley backs him up. Yuck."

She took a couple of steps away from them. She was still talking. "I know that Sean's behavior over the past year hasn't only affected me. It affected all my friends, and my relationships with them. And if I can't repair them now, at least if I can say what needs to be said, I'll feel a little better, but not much.

"I realized it last night, when I was lying on my bed. I just wish Sean would admit to himself that he loves my company, and that I really do make him happy.

"He's so afraid to spend time with me. I don't blame him. It's my fault. I've been so angry about what he did. And now it's like he's holding out his heart to me and when I reach for it, he snatches it back. I am trying so hard to be patient and not to push. I just want to make him feel better."

Trish walked out of the room then, embarrassed by her own outburst. Baxter got up to follow her. Which left Hanlin, Seb, and Bryer.

The three men glanced at one another, exasperated.

"Doesn't make much sense though."

"How so?"

"If the Bishop wanted Trish out of the way so he could mess about with Sean, why not kill her? Bob Young makes no sense as a victim."

Seb looked up then. "Maybe killing her was too obvious."

"Why?"

Seb hesitated. Hanlin had just walked back into the room. He provided the answer. "She was blackmailing him. If he'd killed her, he'd be suspect number one."

Bryer was too astonished to speak. Hanlin continued. "Mind you, having a motive doesn't prove a thing. You don't have to be a murderer to have a motive, just like you don't have to be a virgin to go to the Virgin Islands. The number of people I've got good reason to kill is nobody's business."

Bryer laughed. Hanlin moved across the room to fix the drinks.

"How well do you know Sean Hartnett?" asked Seb, his eyes on Baxter, who'd just reentered the room having left Trish in the kitchen where she was being ministered to by Hanlin's wife Jane.

"Well enough. We sometimes play a round or two of golf. He's good."

Seb sighed. "Golf. Not a game I'm much enamored with."

Baxter laughed. "Golf is like the Catholic Church."

"How's that?"

"Full of rules that can't be obeyed and a firm belief that it will deteriorate if women are admitted to full membership."

5.

Stand fast therefore in the liberty wherewith Christ hath made us free, and be not entangled again with the yoke of bondage.

Galatians 5:1

Wednesday 12th December: "Remain standing. Do you swear to tell the truth, the whole truth, and nothing but the truth, so help you God? ..."

Bishop Patrick O'Malley looked around the faces in the packed courthouse. He recognized a number of church members but few friends. Seb was there, he noted.

He answered the clerk to the court in the anticipated fashion. "I do."

Then he sat.

Bishop Patrick had thought long and hard about this moment and had dreaded it. Wide eyed with worry and trembling just a little, he felt like a bullock in the slaughter pen.

Indeed as you enter the modern concrete block which is the Hampden County Hall of Justice, there's a sign above the door that reads, "Obedience to Law is Liberty." It was meant to reassure but Bishop Patrick was reminded more of the "Work Shall Set You Free" motto above the gates to Auschwitz. This thought disturbed him.

He tried to calm himself, to depend on his savior, on his God. What else was there? "God looks after every sparrow that falls, how much more does he love me?" So he told himself and found fleeting comfort, until he reflected again on his own sins, and the despair closed in and threatened to overwhelm him.

The Bishop glanced at Trish Hartnett in the dock. She wore

a plain black dress. No jewelry. No accessories. Just the dress. The lawyers had probably told her to dress down. There were the women on the jury to consider.

But the lawyers had been sorely deluded if they thought for one moment that Trish would cut a more sympathetic figure in a little black dress. Trish's mane of auburn hair, her green-gray eyes, her ice cool expression, all in stark contrast to the black dress. Black looked good on any woman but, "With Trish in her fiery mood," thought the Bishop, "I could be looking at the Goddess Kali in the flesh."

Lawyer Fieldson got to his feet. Trish Hartnett bit her lip like a schoolgirl. The Bishop tore his gaze from the mesmeric figure of the accused. The lawyer was saying something.

"Bishop, I am right in supposing that you know the defendant?"

The Bishop nodded. "Yes. I do indeed know Mrs Hartnett."

"You also know, or rather knew, the deceased, Mr Robert Young?"

Again the Bishop nodded. "Yes. I did."

Fieldson's eyes swept the courtroom and settled gently, almost absentmindedly, on the jury.

"And would you, Bishop, have reason to implicate the accused, Mrs Hartnett, in the murder of Mr Young?"

The lawyer's slight unprepossessing frame made him appear benign, his tone almost diffident. But his pale eyes told another tale. His eyes were ice cold and distant.

The Bishop's sense of foreboding was now well honed.

The Assistant District Attorney climbed to his feet almost casually, as if there were all the time in the world. "Object, Your Honor."

Bishop Patrick shifted his head slightly to look at the defendant. Trish Hartnett was fHartnett was flanked by the Stars and Stripes and the flag of the Commonwealth of Massachusetts on one side and lawyer Fieldson on the other. She was looking confident. Her eyes were fixed on the judge as if willing him to support her. The Bishop allowed his gaze to pan across the paneled wood and brick of Courtroom Number Two. The judge sits high in a Massachusetts courtroom. At his or her back a phalanx of law books are shelved for reference. General legal books bound in green leather, Massachusetts state legal records in brown leather, making for an impressive duotone wall. Judge Wilkinson was a thin but sinewy man, lanky and reflective, like some latter day Abe Lincoln. "Sustained," he said.

Lawyer Fieldson wrung his hands in contrition like Uriah Heap reborn, and bowed his head.

"Of course. I beg your pardon Your Honor." He snapped his gaze back to the Bishop like a pointer on the scent. "Bishop O'Malley, do you also know the husband of the accused, Mr Sean Hartnett."

"I do," The Bishop nodded, his calm demeanor masking a cacophony of emotion.

"Of course you do Bishop. How well precisely?"

The Bishop grew pale and wiped small beads of perspiration from his forehead. "Very well."

"Very well indeed perhaps. You were lovers?"

If there was anyone in the crowded courthouse who hadn't been paying attention, they were now. You could have heard a pin drop. The Bishop knew well enough that he could lie or remain silent. The last thing he wanted to do was to hurt Sean.

The Bishop fought the instinct to hold his head between his hands. "We were good friends," he said as defiantly as he could manage, given his dejected state of mind.

Judge Wilkinson leaned forward, his deep blue eyes sympathetic. "You may plead the fifth amendment, Bishop O'Malley. But if you do not, you must answer the question."

Lawyer Fieldson interrupted. "It's all right, Your Honor. I withdraw the question."

The judge looked surprised. But not for long. He understood full well what was going on. Fieldson was no fool. Fieldson had established that the Bishop was gay without hounding him more than absolutely necessary which might have alienated the jury. Judge Wilkinson called the attorneys side bar and leant across to whisper, as was the practice in Massachusetts. "Be very careful, Mr Fieldson. You are trying the patience of this court." Fieldson stroked his fingers back through his hair, his manner absentminded, almost distracted. "I apologize, Your Honor," he said.

The judge nodded and Fieldson returned to his place, then his questions came in sharp staccato bursts.

"Bishop O'Malley. Would you describe your relationship with the defendant, Trish Hartnett, as cordial?"

"No, I can't say I would," the Bishop answered in a weak voice, fighting to hold back tears as large as sorrow.

"You were enemies?"

With an effort, the Bishop regained his composure. "I didn't say that."

"Friends?"

"No, I didn't say that either."

"Had Mrs Hartnett asked you to stop meeting her husband, Sean Hartnett?"

"Yes but I don't see ..."

"Don't you?" Lawyer Fieldson preened himself, his head up and his breast full, like a cock robin.

"I have no further questions at this time, Your Honor."

6.

*For man also knoweth not his time: as the fishes that are
taken in an evil net, and as the birds that are caught in the
snare; so are the sons of men snared in an evil time, when it
falleth suddenly upon them.*

Ecclesiastes 9:12

Thursday 13th December: Hanlin and Bryer sat in the glassed-in
porch overlooking the Connecticut River, bathed in the pale
warmth of the late morning, early winter sun like toads on a
mudbank. Bryer nursing a BBC Steel Rail and Hanlin a whisky. He was experimenting with a new Glenmorangie, matured
in Madeira casks, that quite frankly did not impress him very
much.

The women were in the kitchen fixing soup for lunch. As with
most of modern America, this was no politically correct home.
When it comes to twenty-first century female emancipation,
the USA lags far behind Western Europe.

Having said which, both men felt they deserved the drinks.
They'd just finished joining Bart the dog in chasing the deer
away from Jane Hanlin's prized rose bushes, now resting under
a blanket of snow for the winter. She'd tried everything, right
down to putting bars of Irish Spring soap on ribbons and hanging them from the bushes on the premise that the creatures dis-
liked the smell. In the end, good old-fashioned standing guard
and hollering had proved the only truly effective defense against
the ever-determined Bambi.

But now they are inside whilst outside the fresh snow lays damp
heavy on the firs and now and again falls from the branches
to the ground as if wearied. The light breeze lifts and unfurls
the American flag that stands high on its gold-crested pole. In
the middle distance cars from Agawam side roll gentle on the
slush damp highway across South End Bridge, their thrum and

rumble caressing the winter air. There is a laziness about the place, reflected by the easy traffic on this late still bright white morning.

Bryer stretched, flexing his arms without letting go of his beer. He broke the silence. "Assistant D.A. seems to have been wrong-footed by David Fieldson."

"Fieldson's a smarmy lawyer. Can't say I like him."

"Springfield's best though. Trish Hartnett's lucky to have him."

Hanlin wrinkled his nose. "He's lucky to have Trish Hartnett. She'll be a rich woman no longer by the time he's finished with her."

"Innocent you reckon?"

Hanlin shrugged as he reached toward his Glenmorangie. "God knows. But it just doesn't fit does it? I mean, all that hands on violence. Knifing Father Seb. Running down Bob Young. Slitting poor Anna's throat." He shuddered. "None of it's very feminine."

"She sure has you on her side," Bryer laughed. "Women are as capable of calculated violence as men ever were. There's more to this world than the testosterone thing. And remember how in-expert that attack on Seb was. Could easily have been a woman."

Hanlin refused to be diverted. Like a dog with a bone he was determined to hold to his course. "So the incident with the bullet, when she and Baxter were shot at the other day. She did that to herself, did she?"

Bryer smiled with genuine amusement. "No. I confess that would be something. But maybe that's not directly related. A third party. Anna's boyfriend, perhaps. If he thought that Baxter had been forcing his way into Anna's affections —he could have done that."

Hanlin conceded that point, albeit grudgingly, with a shrug that would have done credit to a cowboy. But he wasn't done. "Could've been the boyfriend that killed Anna, wouldn't you think?" he drawled.

Bryer sighed and put his glass down. "I still reckon Trish Hartnett is guilty of the Bob Young murder. At least it seems likely."

Hanlin stared out of the window. "Anything's possible," he answered. "But don't hold your breath if you expect me to subscribe to the theory you're now expounding."

"You have something better to offer?"

Hanlin raised an eyebrow. He was thinking, "Give me time. I'm getting there." But aloud he was more equivocal. "Not really," he said. Then again in acquiescence, "Not really. No."

7.

Submit yourselves therefore to God. Resist the devil, and he will flee from you.

James 4:7

Friday 14th December: Donna White sipped her coffee. It was early afternoon. Partners Diner in Agawam was quiet. She looked across at Father Seb. She felt easier with him now. He wore the half-smock of a postulant Franciscan. He'd atoned she thought. He deserved her compassion. Judge not, the Bible said. And what did she do all day every day but judge people. It was her job after all. Being a cop. Donna had an old-fashioned attitude to Catholicism. She'd once been asked why Catholics went to church and she'd replied glibly but with some honesty, "The purpose for us is not social. The purpose is redemption in 45 minutes or less."

She watched as Seb talked. She always found she made more progress if she let people talk. He was speaking of Mary Young.

"Why did she marry him in the first place?"

"She loved him," she answered easily.

"Bob Young was not the most charismatic of men."

Donna laughed. "Shame on you, Father Seb. I was just thinking we shouldn't judge one another."

Seb grimaced bravely with grim resignation. "Seems I'm not perfect."

Donna raised her eyes from her coffee. "No. You aren't, are you?" she said, and watched the hurt in him and immediately regretted her words. "But let's go with your theory. What if she had to get married because she was pregnant?"

"You're serious?"

"Why not? She had lovers later. Why not then? Her eldest child, Jenny was premature."

Father Seb was astonished. "You have been busy," he said.

"Just thorough."

"Premature equates with illegitimate?"

"If you give the doctor the wrong dates it does. So I'm guessing that's how it was. Beats me though."

Seb raised an eyebrow. "What?"

"Why not an abortion rather than marry someone you don't love?" She sipped her coffee again, then put down her cup and frowned. "Though abortions aren't so easy today with groups like the Army of God around."

"How can you be sure she didn't love him?" Seb asked. Then he frowned, "The Army of God: Who are they?"

"The people who kill doctors. They advocate 'waging war' as the only way to end abortion in the U.S. Doctors they've killed appear on their website with a line through their names."

"Sick." Seb frowned at his own emotive reaction. "Sad I mean."

"Yes, but back then it was easier perhaps. As easy anyway." Donna paused, momentarily confused. It was her turn to frown. "Oh perhaps not. I don't know really."

Seb smiled gently. "I don't imagine it was ever easy to have an abortion."

"On the other hand, if she'd not wanted an abortion, she could have been an unmarried Mom."

Seb bit his tongue, responding moderately, and wanting to mean it. "Not so easy either. People find that very tough. Bringing up a child on their own I mean."

"But they do it. The U.S. is full of single-parent families."

Seb smiled again. "I'm not arguing with you," he said. Then more incautiously, "Being a single parent is infinitely preferable to killing your unborn child."

"I beg your pardon?"

"It's a subject on which I have been studying scripture for guidance. I mean when does life begin? Psalm 22 says that we belong to God from our mothers' bellies. Isaiah says God knows us from the womb. These are living children that we abort."

Donna looked at him in silence for a moment, then something in her snapped. She slammed her coffee cup down and slapped the table with the flat of her hand. "I'll not take that from you." Her anger was a raw thing, unbidden. And she was very angry. "Those sentiments are what drive the killers in the Army of God." She was furious and felt like hurting him. "How dare you say anything? You are in no position to judge anyone given your recent behavior."

Seb sighed. "Of course. I apologize." He felt profoundly sad, as if he were drowning; he was that alone.

Donna hadn't noticed, the anger washed away from her; like emerging from a river, she felt cleansed. She spoke calmly once more. "Anyway it works as a hypothesis. A woman bound by convention. Outwardly prim and proper. Driven by an unhappy marriage entered knowingly into a series of secret affairs. A sham and vapid life which she ended of her own volition, triggering the sequence of events that has culminated in the Trish Hartnett murder trial."

Seb thought that a bit harsh, coming as it did from someone

who'd just been reprimanding him for being judgmental. But he didn't say so. Instead he nodded three or four times, his eyes focused on the table. Then, to cover his discomfort, he called for the check.

8.

If any man among you seem to be religious, and bridleth not his tongue, but deceiveth his own heart, this man's religion is vain.

James 1:26

Monday 17th December: Superior Court Number Two is the court in which murder trials are normally held in Hampden County Halls of Justice in the City of Springfield in the Commonwealth of Massachusetts. The court is ordered church-like with a central aisle. As you face front, the witness stand is center court front under the stern gaze of the portraits of former Judges Moriarty, Griffin, and Macaulay; whilst on the left wall Judges Dillon and Callahan gaze down from imperious frames. The actual trial judge dominates the court, sitting in black ministerial-type robes on a huge book-lined raised dais in the front right corner of the room. The jury of twelve good citizens plus two alternate jurors (in case of sickness and such) sits front left. The prosecution sits front of court left facing front near the jury. The defense sits with the accused, front of court right facing the judge. Set back against the right front wall, opposite the jury, are two enormous stand-alone flags. One the Stars and Stripes. The other the flag of the Commonwealth of Massachusetts, which consists of a huge cigar-store-style Red Indian Chief, in this instance on a buff yellow background and surrounded by a ribbon inscribed the state motto, Ense petit placidam sub liberate quietem, which translates, "By the sword we seek peace, but peace only under liberty."

"Do you swear to tell the truth, the whole truth, and nothing but the truth ..."

Sean Hartnett was on the witness stand in Court Number Two. He was nervous. That much was clear. He was dressed uncharacteristically, his muscled form looked cramped in the seersucker jacket he was wearing, itself utterly out of place, befitting a Louisiana summer not a Springfield winter. To add to the incongruity, he wore a stiff white-collared shirt and tartan tie. The effect was clown-like whereas the attempt had been to be dignified. Sean was frightened. Unnerved by the process to which he was being subjected. Beads of sweat pricked his forehead. Lawyer Fieldson could almost smell the fear and it delighted him. This was his kind of case. Empowering.

"You are the husband of the defendant—Mrs Patricia Hartnett?"

"Trish is my wife. Yes."

Fieldson's tongue flicked out to lick at his upper lip, like he was being presented with a delicious meal. He delivered his line rapier quick with studied indifference. "You and Mrs Hartnett were having difficulties in your marriage?"

"Object!" The Assistant District Attorney got to his feet. "Relevancy. Mr Hartnett is not on trial here."

"Your Honor, the state contends that my client is guilty, in large part, because she had a motive for killing Bob Young and no alibi. I intend to show that she is not the only person that meets those criteria."

The judge nodded his acquiescence. "Overruled. The witness is instructed to answer the question."

"We had been."

"But not anymore?"

"No, we are reconciled. We're back together."

"But at the time of the Bob Young murder you were estranged from your wife?"

"I don't understand."

"You and your wife were having marital difficulties."

"Yeh. I just said that."

"And you were not home that night. The night when Robert Young was murdered."

"Maybe. I can't exactly remember."

"There were a lot of nights you weren't home then?"

"Some."

"And where were you when you weren't home?"

"Bars. Staying with friends."

"And that night?"

"Dunno." Sean shrugged. "Sorry."

Lawyer Fieldson smiled. He pushed his advantage. "Is it even remotely conceivable that Mrs Hartnett could have traveled to Bradley International Airport in Hartford and hired a Hummer and kept and stored the vehicle without your knowledge?"

The Assistant D.A. wasn't having that. "Object. Calls for an opinion from the witness."

"Sustained."

"Have you on any occasion seen your wife in possession of a Hummer?"

"No."

"What was your wife's relationship with Mr Robert Young?"

She had none."

"And with the late Mrs Mary Young?"

"She knew her much better. She's a neighbor, or rather she was, and they did things at church together, but she had no special relationship with her either."

"So, there is nothing particular to connect you and your wife with the Youngs? On the other hand, there were those who would have been glad to implicate your wife in this murder?"

"Object. That's conjecture."

Judge Wilkinson frowned. "Keep your opinions for the summation Mr Fieldson. Objection sustained."

"Thank you, Your Honor. No further questions."

Assistant D.A. Johnson was taking a leaf out of Fieldson's book. He was in no hurry. He got slowly to his feet to cross-examine.

"You and your wife were reconciled after Mr Young's murder?"

"Well yes, but ..."

"But at the time of Mr Young's death you were absent from the house and could not provide your wife with an alibi."

"That's true but ..."

The Assistant D.A. allowed himself the slightest of smiles. "Indeed, your wife did have a motive to kill Mr Robert Young, did she not?"

"Object."

Judge Wilkinson glared at the lawyers, irritated by the number of objections which he thought undignified. It was not the way they did things in Massachusetts. He was tempted to call the men sidebar but instead he glowered the word, "Sustained."

"Though your wife may have had no relationship with Mrs Young, you were once the late Mrs Mary Young's lover, were you not?"

The hush in the court was total. Sean Hartnett looked confused. "I don't know what you mean ..."

"Careful Mr Hartnett. We can produce evidence to support this allegation. Don't be tempted to perjure yourself."

Sean used the sleeve of his jacket to wipe the perspiration from his forehead. He spoke softly. "We were friends."

"That may be so. But you were also Mrs Mary Young's lover?"

Sean Hartnett said something but he was too soft spoken to be heard in the near silent courtroom.

"Speak up please."

"Yes." The word was barely above a whisper.

"Louder please, so the jury can hear your response."

"Yes."

"Yes, you were Mrs Mary Young's lover?"

"Yes. But that wouldn't mean Trish had a reason to kill Mr Young."

"Really? Not even if Mr Young had discovered the nature of this relationship of yours and was about to cause trouble over his wife's death?"

"Object."

"Overruled. I want to see where this is going."

"No it's impossible." Sean Hartnett was clearly distressed.

"Why, Mr Hartnett? It seems more than possible to me."

"No it wasn't her."

"No further questions Your Honor."

The Assistant D.A. sat and Lawyer Fieldson almost leapt to his feet to redirect.

"With your permission Your Honor?"

The judge nodded.

"There is someone else who could have committed this crime is there not Mr Hartnett?"

"Objection."

"Overruled. Go on."

"There is someone else?"

Sean nodded, more assured now, almost defiant. He straightened his shoulders and stared Fieldson straight in the eye. "There is."

"Really. Whom, precisely do you suggest?"

The Assistant D.A. jumped to his feet. "I must object, Your Honor."

Judge Wilkinson was irritated but didn't show it. "Overruled. Please continue Mr. Fieldson."

Which Fieldson did, almost snarling his repeated question. "Whom?"

Sean Hartnett cupped his face in his hands like a schoolboy, composing himself for a moment. Then he looked up, his eyes red, not with tears but with anger. "Trish had nothing to do with it," he said. "I killed him."

9.

Seek ye the LORD, all ye meek of the earth, which have wrought his judgment; seek righteousness, seek meekness: it may be ye shall be hid in the day of the LORD's anger.

Zephaniah 2:3

Tuesday 18ᵗʰ December: There was a sort of inevitability about the chain of events that led to Lisa, the well-bosomed, well-adorned, twenty-four-year-old barmaid from Pazzo's moving into the carriage house at 195 Longhill.

Point one. Vicky Walters was her friend.

Point two. Michael Hanlin had met Lisa and knew Vicky well.

Point three. The Hanlin's carriage house was empty and Lisa needed somewhere to sleep because her landlord had discovered she was an illegal and had decided to up the rent. She'd stormed out on him before she'd thought about where she was heading.

She'd come to Vicky for help and hence to Jane Hanlin. She could have gone to the former ambassador for the same favor, but it's always best to go to the top in any chain of command, and when it came to matters of the home, Jane ruled. America is a conservative place, possibly one of the most matriarchal societies in the Western World.

What was less predictable was what happened next. Sure the Hanlins had known Anna. As did Vicky. But neither the Hanlins nor Lisa, nor for that matter Vicky, were on anything beyond nodding terms with Anna's boyfriend, Manuel.

But Lisa had got to talking to Manuel after church. Given the fact that they shared a language and shared a lost friend, it was far from surprising that they shared friendship in view of the commonality of their grief.

It was obvious the way it happened in the end. Almost predictable. He had offered to walk Lisa home from church. It wasn't so far from OLPH but Lisa accepted, being the big-hearted girl she was. She could see Manny wanted company and was at a loose end without Anna.

And she felt sorry for him. Which was why she invited him in for coffee. It was out of pity that she gave him lunch just as it was out of pity that she had later surrendered her bed and her body. Not that given time she'd not have slept with the boy. Just not that quickly had he not seemed so vulnerable.

Their conversation on the way back from church ran as follows.

"Amazing Mr Hartnett confessing to the Robert Young murder. Would you do that Manny? Confess to something you didn't do to save someone you loved?"

Manny grimaced. "Who says he didn't do it?"

"Well they're still going on with the murder trial—of Mrs Hartnett I mean."

"That doesn't mean he's innocent."

"Maybe not but would you? Confess to save a lover I mean? If it meant you'd be executed?"

Manny pondered for little more than a moment. But his Latin blood was as ever to the fore. Manny knew there was no death sentence in Massachusetts but that was scarcely the point. "Of course. I would be ashamed not to."

Lisa pursed her lips approvingly and nodded her head. "Yes of course, indeed of course. So would I." She broke step and looked squarely at Manuel, forcing him to break stride in turn. "But she couldn't have killed Anna." Then she flushed, her cheeks burning with embarrassment. "Sorry Manny."

He shrugged. "No problem. No, she had no reason to. That was Baxter Merrill."

"You so sure of that?"

Manny snarled his response, contorting his face to do so. "Sure I'm sure. And he'll pay."

"Seems he's paying already."

"No," spit out Manuel. "Not enough," he said. "Not nearly enough."

10.

Confess your faults one to another, and pray one for another, that ye may be healed. The effectual fervent prayer of a righteous man availeth much.

James 5:16

Wednesday 19th December: Jennie Moore was a superb pianist with the highly regarded Springfield Symphony orchestra whose young maestro had brought new verve and interest in the classics throughout the valley. Jennie also played for the annual Springfield Holiday Festival, when the glitterati of the New York opera headed north to do their stuff in the 'provinces.'

A small troupe from the Met was now in town for their annual performance at Springfield's Symphony Hall. Organizing this event was Angie Merrill's contribution to the festival.

"He's a rat, dear." Jennie's comment was vis-a-vis Father Seb.

"Whatever doesn't kill you makes you stronger," Angie said, not looking as if she meant it.

Jennie smiled at her sympathetically. "They are all the same." She sipped her coffee. "Men I mean."

The contrast between the two women could not have been greater. Almost any man would find Angie attractive, that despite the fact that she'd put on at least ten pounds since she'd split with Seb. Angie was sanguine enough to realize the 'ultra thin is attractive' equation is more a woman thing than a man thing. Angie always assumed that people were good. Her problem was that she assumed that people would be as good to her as she was to them, or that they would accept her the way she was as she accepted them, or that they would respect her right to be different as she respected their right to be different.

Angie was not getting any younger either, and she recognised that now she would never have children. This year she would become 36, and looking back at her life, she felt that for the past 12 years, she had been going around in pointless circles.

Jennie on the other hand was no beauty. She was short, plump, pale, with a nose too large for her face and dark brown untidy shoulder-length hair. But they were close, Angie and Jennie. As close as two friends could be without being lovers. Which was what they would have been had Jennie had her way. Jennie was gay.

They were at Jennie's place. Angie looked up at the mantle shelf, where Jennie had set lit candles. "What is it with Lesbians and candles?" Angie asked, despite the tears that were clouding her eyes.

Jennie laughed and shrugged.

"They say you should forgive everyone everything." Angie brushed aside another tear. "He's joining a monastery now."

"I thought you said a seminary?"

Angie shook her head. "That was the idea, but he's changed his mind. He's going to be a postulant."

"What's that?"

"The trial period when you think about being a novice."

"And what's a novice?"

"A sort of trainee monk. You're a postulant for three months or thereabouts. Then a novice for three years. Then you take your final vows."

"What's the point of that?"

Angie looked up red-eyed. "No point. No point at all. He's just running away from me." And the tears came unbidden. "What did I do wrong?"

Jennie moved to put down her coffee. "All that truly matters in the end is that you loved." She hesitated a moment as Angie looked up at her. Angie knew what was coming. Jennie had tried this before. In the past Angie had rejected her kindly, and she would do so now.

But she was so very tired.

"It's all right dear," Jennie was saying. "The best is yet to come. No matter how you feel, get up, dress up, and show up. You always have me. Friends are the family we choose for ourselves."

It wasn't that Jennie was calculating. Her heart bled for her friend. But Angie was so very lovely and Jennie knew she'd never have a better chance. The girl was on the rebound and vulnerable. Jennie was completely aware of that and completely capable of taking advantage of the fact. She steeled herself for the inevitable rejection. She reached an arm round her friend's shoulders and stroked her cheek to still her crying.

She felt Angie stiffen, momentarily. "Life is too short to waste time hating anyone," she said gently.

Then it was as if for Jennie all her Christmases had come at once in one glorious epiphany as Angie Merrill softened and let her friend kiss the tears away from her cheeks, their mutual vulnerability so acute that they were both trembling as Angie turned her face to allow Jennie's lips to brush hers in the first of many gentle kisses.

11.

But I say unto you, That whosoever is angry with his brother without a cause shall be in danger of the judgment: and whosoever shall say to his brother, Raca, shall be in danger of the council: but whosoever shall say, Thou fool, shall be in danger of hell fire.

Matthew 5:22

Wednesday 19th December: Trish Hartnett was on the stand. She looked every inch the girl who was once the Springfield Classical homecoming queen. The black, figure-hugging dress had been replaced by a red, figure-hugging dress. She'd cut her auburn hair shorter, bobbed back around her head. She looked good.

Assistant D.A. Mark Johnson was a stocky, Perry Mason type man. He had short legs, a barrel chest, and a craggy face. Think Perry Mason but shorter with the low gravelly voice of a Henry Kissinger and you'd be close. Many people saw Johnson as a shoo-in as the next D.A.

"I have never had much time for Bob Young. That doesn't mean I killed him," Trish was saying. She was standing akimbo, her hands clenching her hips in exasperation. The pose confrontational.

"You may sit down Mrs Hartnett."

She did.

"Witnesses say a woman answering your description hired a Hummer at Bradley on the day before the murder." The Assistant D.A. was referring to a sheath of papers in his hand. "Any idea how the killer could have acquired your credit card to use for the transaction?"

Trish lifted her eyes heavenward, her exasperation complete.

"I don't know. I use my credit cards a lot. Maybe she just got lucky."

"Maybe. The vehicle used to kill Bob Young was of course identical to the one hired with your credit card by a person answering your description."

Trish Hartnett dropped her jaw in apparent frustration. "Oh come on, I can't believe this. Can't you see that this is a frame?"

"Miss Hartnett, I'm afraid we see it more like an airtight case."

"Object!"

"Sustained." Judge Wilkinson frowned a 'you-should-know-better frown' at the Assistant D.A.

"I apologize Your Honor." Assistant D. A. Johnson turned back to Trish. "You are, no doubt, aware that the late Mrs Mary Young had been involved with another man?"

"What has that got to do with anything?"

"Possibly everything. Can you explain, Mrs Hartnett, where you were on the late evening of 26th October at the time of the murder?"

"I was at home in bed."

"But there is no one who can vouch for that. You were alone?"

"Yes. Alone."

"I call your attention to State's exhibit B. This is your powder compact?"

"Yes."

The Assistant D.A. growled his next question. "You are aware it was found in the driver's side pocket of the Hummer discovered in the parking lot of the LA Fitness Center?"

"Yes."

"The same Hummer allegedly hired by a woman answering your description?"

"Your witnesses say the woman who hired the Hummer in my name wore a headscarf and dark glasses. It could have been an escort service girl pretending to be me."

"Yes Mrs Hartnett. It could have been. But even at the time of the car rental, you have an alibi which can't be corroborated?"

"I was at the movies."

"But there is no evidence to that effect." Assistant D.A. Johnson allowed himself a wry smile. Perhaps you were twenty miles away, hiring the vehicle used to kill Mr Young. Is that what you were doing?"

"No. I wasn't hiring a vehicle. I was at the movies. I'm sure if the Police Department had sent someone down there they'd've found someone who could've said they'd seen me. Anyone could have stolen my credit card and driver's license and used them to hire the Hummer."

Judge Wilkinson intervened. "I'm confident the Police Department did everything they could at the time Mrs Hartnett." He nodded to the Assistant D.A. to continue.

"We have heard about Mr Hartnett's close relationship with Bishop O'Malley alluded to in this context. You have been under a great deal of strain, have you not?"

"Yes I have."

"You loved your husband?"

"I still love him."

"And your husband was elsewhere at the time of the murder— or you'd have the alibi you need?"

"I have said that."

Lawyer Fieldson had had enough. He rose to his feet to interrupt.

"Your Honor, I fail to see the point of this line of questioning. This has been discussed already. The Assistant District Attorney is wasting the court's time."

But the Assistant D.A. had made his point. "No further questions."

"No questions. Your honor, I reserve the right to recall Mrs Hartnett, and now the defense calls the Police Detective in charge of the investigation." Lawyer Fieldson pulled himself erect and stared front center as he made the customary announcement. "Call Robert Muse."

Trish stood down, and Muse took the stand, and the usual formalities were conducted. Fieldson was taking a calculated risk calling the detective in the case, but he knew the Assistant D.A. would do so otherwise and he wanted the bad news out of the way.

"Did you examine the Hummer identified as the one hired by a person using a credit card in the name of Mrs Hartnett?"

"We examined it for fingerprints."

"And you discovered?"

"We took only the full and partial prints that could be found on the vehicle and the contents of the said vehicle. All of which had been wiped clean except for a set of prints on an empty Diet Coke can that appeared to have been overlooked in the well behind the driver's seat."

"Were you able to identify those prints?"

"The matched prints belonged to Mrs Patricia Hartnett."

"You see what I'm getting at. How can you be sure that Coke can was not planted?"

"You really think we'd do something that low just to make our solve rate go up?" Detective Muse looked at Lawyer Fieldson with thinly veiled contempt. "We found what we found and those prints belonged to Mrs Hartnett."

David Fieldson smoothed back his hair. It was thinning prematurely and that depressed him. He'd have to get something done about it. It was the one thing he had in common with Detective Muse. Pretty much the only thing. But the lawyer and the cop had business. Fieldson was talking. It was now time to use this witness to his client's advantage.

"Detective, this was a terrible crime. A decent hardworking man murdered as he walked back to his own house. All of us present in this courtroom wish to see Mr Robert Young and his family given justice here today." He paused, taking a moment to look at the jury. My client is concerned that you may not be investigating other suspects as you should. What, she would like to know, have you done to investigate Ambassador Hanlin?"

The Assistant D.A. looked outraged. "Object!"

The judge frowned and called the attorneys sidebar for a whispered private conversation. "Gentlemen; I find these constant objections damage the dignity and authority of the court. Please restrain yourselves." He rested his eye on Lawyer Fieldson. This is not the summation Mr Fieldson. Can you justify the line you are taking?"

"I wish to show the jury that any number of people could have committed this crime, Your Honor."

"Proceed then, but with caution Mr Fieldson."

"Thank you, Your Honor," and he barely gave the Assistant D.A. time to get back to his place before he continued as he turned to Muse, "Detective Muse, what made you so sure that Mrs Patricia Hartnett was guilty?"

"What apart from her credit card having been used to hire the murder vehicle?" Muse turned his head to address the judge. "I guess it was on account of her prints being in the vehicle Your Honor."

"Have you investigated Ambassador Hanlin?"

Again Muse addressed the judge, "What motive could he possibly have Your Honor?"

Unfazed, Fieldson continued. "Perhaps he was Mary Young's secret lover. It is possible. These are murky waters and no one can be sure of anything, least of all that my client, Mrs Patricia Hartnett, has any motive to have conducted this killing. However, the point is that Ambassador Hanlin had the opportunity. He owns a Hummer does he not? He could be the killer."

"He could," acknowledged Muse, "I'm not denying that."

"So have you checked his whereabouts on the night in question?"

"He says he was in New York."

"And, you have proof of that?"

"Well, not exactly. We have been unable to find any record of his having traveled to New York. Plus no one can remember him in the bar where he says he ate supper. Plus he no longer has the parking stub for the hotel parking lot he says he used."

Fieldson beamed from ear to ear. He actually rubbed his hands together in his excitement. "Excellent," he said. "That's just excellent. No further questions."

The Assistant D.A. decided to keep his powder dry to see if Fieldson dug his own grave. "No questions."

Lawyer Fieldson drew himself up to his full height. "Your Honor, the defense calls Ambassador Michael Hanlin to the stand."

Hanlin had been expecting this. He brushed his black hair away from his blue-gray eyes and stepped forward, taking the book in his right hand and going through the customary ritual.

David Fieldson contemplated his victim. He relished moments like this. They were what he lived for.

"Ambassador Hanlin, is it true that you were having an illicit relationship with Mrs Mary Young prior to her death? To be precise you were having an affair?"

Hanlin was astounded and would have said so but Assistant D.A. Johnston got to his feet and intervened. "Your Honor, I object. This is pure conjecture on the Defense Attorney's part."

Judge Wilkinson looked down on Fieldson. He genuinely did not like the constant objections. In his view they confused the jury as to the probity of the witnesses in a prejudicial manner. He frowned. "I'll see you sidebar," he said. Fieldson came forward and the judge leaned over. "I trust you are going somewhere constructive with this?"

Fieldson nodded. "Yes, Your Honor."

Judge Wilkinson again frowned his displeasure. "You had better be sure of that. But very well. You may proceed." The judge turned back to the court, drawing his black robe around himself as he resumed his position, then he raised his voice from the near whisper he'd been using. "Objection overruled. Answer the question please, Ambassador Hanlin."

Hanlin drew himself up and tilted his head back slightly. He was a full head taller than Fieldson, and he lifted himself off the chair, his hands grasping the edge of the witness box in something approaching white-knuckled anger, but his voice remained calm and measured. "No. Most certainly not."

Fieldson was unfazed. His pale blue eyes locked with Hanlin's. The atmosphere in the court was electric.

"But you had been lovers had you not?" He paused. "Consider your answer most carefully Ambassador Hanlin."

"Sure, we dated at college, but that was more than forty years ago."

"And it was because of Mary Young that you moved to Springfield in the first place?"

"That's nonsense."

"Whom did you know in Springfield, apart from Mrs Mary Young, when you decided to settle in this city?"

"My friends Dick Bryer and his wife, but that's beside the point. It was also a convenient place to live."

"Convenient for what Ambassador? For Washington? For New York? Or for Mrs Young?"

Hanlin, a normally phlegmatic man, almost failed to suppress his anger. "This is ludicrous."

"Ludicrous Ambassador? Please tell the court. Do you own an H3 Hummer?"

"Yes I do. But so do others."

Lawyer Fieldson's lank form seemed almost to preen like a budgerigar. "Not within Springfield City limits Ambassador. Yours is the only vehicle of that kind registered within the metropolis."

"There're three I've noticed in the greater Springfield area. But anyways. Are you seriously suggesting that I killed Bob Young that night?"

Lawyer Fieldson's normally stooped shoulders unfurled like a peacock protruding its chest, about to display. "You have to admit, Ambassador," he said, "That it is a possibility." Then he turned to the judge. "The defense rests, Your Honor."

Assistant D.A. Mark Johnson almost leapt to his feet. "Your vehicle was where exactly that night, between 1 and 3 a.m. on 27th October, when Mr Young was killed?"

"On the road from New York to Springfield."

"With whom?"

"I was alone. I'd gone to New York earlier the previous day, Friday. Usually, I take the train, but on this occasion I drove. I parked my car at a mid-town hotel lot where I usually stay when I'm in the city, met with friends until after nine o'clock. Then I took a late supper alone, paid cash, and watched some sports on the TV in the bar, and left for Springfield well after midnight."

"So you cannot prove what time you left New York and consequently you cannot prove what time you arrived in Springfield?"

"No, not precisely. Of course, I woke my wife and was greeted by the dog when I finally returned home." said Hanlin.

Judge Wilkinson smiled indulgently at the young Assistant D.A. "Are you prosecuting or defending sir?"

"Forgive me Your Honor, but when the Defense Attorney informed me he'd be calling Ambassador Hanlin as a witness, I realized the direction his case might be taking. I asked the NYPD for assistance. The Springfield Police Department has just handed me this videotape which I enter as people's exhibit G. It is the CCTV camera tape from a parking lot at the

Holiday Inn on West 57th Street in mid-town Manhattan. It shows Ambassador Hanlin removing his Hummer at 12:50 a.m. on the morning of Saturday, October 27th. It might have been technically possible for him to have reached Springfield in time to murder Bob Young. But it is extremely unlikely unless he drove the whole way at 90 mph."

Trish Hartnett's sigh was the only sound audible in the silence that followed. A major plank in the defense case had just crumbled.

12.

These are the things that ye shall do; Speak ye every man the truth to his neighbour; execute the judgment of truth and peace in your gates:

Zechariah 8:16

Saturday 22ⁿᵈ December: The tension in Hanlin's living room was of that acute depressive kind that you get amongst the losing camp at a political recount. The mood was dour, subdued, and electric.

Most of them were there.

Donna White stood alongside Michael Hanlin in front of the fireplace. Ranged before them clutching an assortment of drinks, slumped in chairs and armchairs, were, in an arc from the window to the door: Dick Bryer, Father Seb, Angie Merrill, Vicky Walters, Sean Hartnett, and the Bishop. The wives, Jane and Marilyn, were once more in the kitchen with Kate, the Hanlin's new part-time housekeeper, preparing refreshments.

Most of the people in the room were still reeling from the grim events of the past twenty-four hours. Twenty-four hours in which Baxter Merrill had been arrested on suspicion of murder with regard to the death of Anna Gonzalez; and in which a jury of her peers had found Trish Hartnett guilty on one count of murder one in the Bob Young case. Both had been jailed. And Trish was by now at Cedar Junction for processing. Next stop Framingham Women's facility, constructed 1898, in maximum security for the rest of her natural life.

Hanlin caught himself thinking she was lucky. If this was Florida or Texas, they'd be setting themselves up to fry her pretty little ass like a steak on a barbecue. But it wasn't and he was glad that was so. He shrugged away the thought and paid attention to his guests. Vicky Walters was tearful. Sean

Hartnett morose. They sat alongside one another. Vicky started to talk about Baxter.

"He didn't do it. He couldn't have."

Hanlin stepped across to her, reaching his hand out, but she leaned back and flinched, looking him in the eyes. "He didn't do it," she said again.

Hanlin seemed to tower above the young woman. He shook his head to indicate his agreement. "Bothered me that an anonymous letter led to the recovery of the knife."

"Bothers me, too." This from Donna White. "The way we were tipped off by that anonymous note. No saliva on the envelope. So no DNA sample. So carefully done."

"The same letters. By which I mean the same author, for the correspondence in both murder cases?" Hanlin observed. It was more of a comment than a question.

Donna nodded her agreement.

Sean Hartnett looked up. "Could have been anyone who hid that knife in the woodpile at the Merrill home." He looked at Vicky. "Even you," he said.

Vicky jerked her head back as if she'd been slapped. "What did you say?"

"I said it could have been you." Sean replied.

Hanlin thought he'd best try and calm the atmosphere. "Let's not fight amongst ourselves," he started to say.

Sean's response was sharp, edged with anger. "No let's. Time we all faced a few home truths. Vicky could have murdered Anna. That's at least as likely as Baxter doing it."

Hanlin was genuinely perplexed. "Why?"

"Lots of reasons. Could be Anna was giving Baxter a hard time what with Baxter having hit on her. Maybe she was threatening to go to the police."

"Then Baxter would be implicated."

"Maybe." Sean's face was grim. "Or just maybe Vicky decided to defend her man."

Curiously it was left to Angie Merrill to defend her ex-husband's lover. Her golden hair bobbed as she startled the room by jumping to her feet. Her mouth pursed in defiance, her slate-blue eyes scanning the others present as if daring anyone to contradict her as she marched over to Vicky Walters' side and placed a firm hand, almost possessively, on the shoulders of the now weeping woman. Then she spoke, her words calm but confident and measured.

"You can all stop that now," she said, looking first at the others in the room and then down at Vicky. "There's no way Vicky could have been involved in Anna's death."

Hanlin smiled gratefully. "Well for one thing no woman would kill anyone like that."

Sean wasn't going to let that go. "Perhaps not but, still, women have committed brutal crimes in the past."

But Angie hadn't finished. "She couldn't have done it. She was with me."

"How can you be so sure?"

"Because though Baxter and I have split up, I still care for him, regardless of how he treated me." She again stared around the room. "And I've taken enough interest in this case to find out the time the medical examiner provided for Anna's death. It is my ex-husband we are talking about here."

"So."

"So, I may not be able to provide an alibi for Baxter—though as sure as hell I know he didn't do it. But I can provide Vicky with an alibi. She was teaching at Sumner when Anna died. And straight after school that day, by 3 p.m., she met me at Pazzo's bar."

"She met you?"

"Sure. You think I wasn't going to take an interest in the other woman in my Baxter's life?" Angie smiled her best smile, "We had a good long heart to heart. Vicky didn't do it. She couldn't have."

Hanlin smiled in turn. "Well that seems to settle that." Then he scanned the room. "But that still leaves us nowhere. Let's try and nail this business. We are gathered here to see if there is anything we can do to help our friends, Trish and Baxter. The first thing we should do is establish that none of us could have committed these crimes. We are, or at least were, all potential suspects. Isn't that right Donna?"

Donna nodded. "I guess that's definitely right. We have considered most of you suspects," Donna paused. "Even you Mr Hanlin."

"Moi?" Hanlin smiled. "Yes I suppose I was right in the frame for the Bob Young killing, as the owner of a Hummer. At least until the Assistant D.A. came to my rescue."

Bryer spoke up. "You also have your own wife to vouch for you anyway. Jane will confirm you were home in bed."

Again Hanlin smiled. "Very loyal of you, dear friend. And your glass is empty. Let me deal with that." He reached for another BBC Steel Rail. "But a wife's testimony is scarcely impartial." He took Bryer's glass and topped it up for him. "So I am in the frame again."

"You have no motive."

"Perhaps. Let's leave that on the table for a moment. Who else could be a suspect in any of these killings?"

There was silence. Hanlin looked around the room. "You, for instance, Sean."

Sean turned his head to look up at Hanlin. "I tried to say I killed Bob Young. The Assistant D.A. wouldn't have it."

"No, he wouldn't, would he? The circumstantial evidence against Trish was too strong." Hanlin paused. "But what about you being in the frame for the Anna killing?"

"Anna?" Sean looked genuinely stunned. "Why would I have killed Anna?"

"Let's leave the why aside for a moment. Could you have done it?"

Now Bishop O'Malley intervened. "He didn't."

"How come?" This from Bryer.

"Because he was with me."

Hanlin almost winced. "The alibis are flowing thick and fast," he thought. Aloud he said, "Very loyal. And you'd swear to that?"

The Bishop seemed to hesitate but nodded. "Yes I'd swear to that."

Hanlin smiled again. "Excuse me for this, Bishop, but given the nature of this case, we are all aware that your friendship with Sean was more than merely platonic. You were very close. Which puts your evidence for Sean in the same class as Jane's for me ... slightly partial."

Donna broke in. "When was he with you?"

"When Anna was killed."

"When was that?"

The Bishop looked confused. "I can't exactly remember, but I remember being told and I remember working out that he was with me."

Donna gave the Bishop a withering glance. "Noble but misguided Bishop. When you can't even rely on the church to tell the truth you are truly up a creek without a paddle."

Bishop O'Malley blushed red but said nothing. Bryer eyed O'Malley then Hanlin. "You expect to solve this case today?"

Hanlin smiled pursing his lips and raising his eyebrows. "I don't see why not," he said. "I work on the premise that when violence impacts the lives of a small group of friends: a) the violent incidents are related and b) the probability is that a member of that group is the culprit." He paused.

"The problem is that we fail to acknowledge where this all started."

"Which is?" asked Donna.

"With Mary Young's suicide." Hanlin took a lingering sip of his Balvenie whisky, savoring the complex, spicy flavor of his favorite single malt Scotch. "There is something that can remain unsaid no longer." Hanlin hesitated. Every eye in the room was watching him now. "Bob Young was not the father of Mary's daughter, Jenny."

There was an embarrassed silence.

"But does that alter anything?" asked Vicky Walters.

"I believe so. Take things in chronological order. After Mary's suicide, Bob Young attacked Father Seb, thinking perhaps that Seb could have prevented Mary's death. Thinking he knew what strain Mary was under but had done nothing rather than betray the confidence of the confessional. Perhaps even, in some twisted way, thinking Seb was having an affair with Mary. Right Seb?"

Seb nodded. "He thought I'd met Mary in secret. Whereas the meeting I'd had was with Angie."

Hanlin nodded like a schoolmaster with a clever pupil. "Then you were attacked again. More violently on this occasion. The natural conclusion is that your attacker this second time was Bob Young. But what if you were attacked by the person who was subsequently to kill Bob."

"Why?" asked Donna.

Hanlin turned to look at the young police officer. "The same reason as that which motivated the attack by Bob. The killer thought that Seb was the only person that knew the true identity of the father of Mary's child." Hanlin switched his attention to Seb. "Did you know the name of the father? You could save us all a lot of time."

Seb shook his head. "No."

"No. Exactly. But the killer didn't know that. And about that time we had the first of the poison pen letters implicating Trish Hartnett." Hanlin ran his fingers back through his lank black hair. "Those letters could have been sent by the real killer, to distract us."

Donna nodded. "A fact that didn't escape us but they could equally well have been telling the truth. Trish Hartnett could have been the killer. Especially if Sean had been Mary's secret lover."

Sean flinched. "Ridiculous," he muttered. Then louder.

"Ridiculous. She was old enough to be my mother."

"That hasn't stopped people before. Books have been written in praise of cougars." Hanlin smiled. "And as many a pubescent boy has discovered, 'Old chickens make the best soup'."

"That's enough, Mr Hanlin," Donna White winced. "But what I don't get is what triggered all this in the first place. Why did Mary think her lover's identity was about to be exposed?"

"I'm not sure, but I have a theory about that."

"Which is?"

"Well her daughter was engaged to be married."

"So?"

"So Massachusetts was one of the last states in the Union to abolish blood tests before marriage."

"But they've been abolished. And they were only for STDs and Rubella anyway, not blood type."

"Yup. But Mary Young may not have realized that."

"Doesn't seem very likely."

"Perhaps," Hanlin nodded. "Let's come back to that," he said. "After Kate's refilled your glasses."

13.

There is one lawgiver, who is able to save and to destroy: who art thou that judgest another?

James 4:12

Saturday 22nd December: "So. If you are all sitting comfortably ..." Hanlin and White retained their positions near the mantelpiece. Hanlin smiled.

"Bob Young was killed just a few hundred yards from here, and pretty late at night at a time when no self-respecting person would be marching the streets."

"Which means?" asked Donna. She was enjoying this.

"Which means that his killer knew he'd be there. Let's make an assumption. Let's assume that Bob had worked out whom it was that had been his wife's lover."

"Or been told," interrupted Donna.

"Yes, or been told." Hanlin's face took on an uncharacteristically grim mien. "Let's examine the possibilities."

"Bishop, you could have been the killer." Hanlin raised a hand to stop the Bishop interrupting. "If you knew your boyfriend, Sean, was two-timing it with Mary Young and was being threatened by Bob Young with exposure or worse, physical harm, you may have wished to protect him."

"That's nonsense. I'd have to be a psychopath."

Mike Hanlin shook his head. "It's not nonsense Bishop. And, with respect, you could be a psychopath for all we know." As he said this Hanlin knew full well the idea was nonsense. The Bishop may have had two of the three classic personality traits of a psychopath, a lack of inhibitions and a lack of fear, but the third, a lack of empathy, was not part of the Bishop's universe. In Hanlin's eyes the Bishop was 'a real softy.'

He circled round and picked out young Vicky Walters. Her pregnancy was well advanced now, and it was beginning to show. "Could equally have been you, Vicky, and for similar motives, if your Baxter had been the one who'd fathered Mary's child."

He gave Vicky no chance to respond. Moving swiftly on he added, "Or I could have killed Bob."

Donna laughed. "You sure could. Being a Hummer owner. You were a prime suspect."

"Yes. We'll assume for a moment that I was Mary Young's lover."

Bryer looked up. "It's a good thing that Jane and Marilyn are in the kitchen's all I can say."

"True," smiled Hanlin. "But assume I fathered the child and Bob found out, and he'd phoned to say he was coming round here. Then I might have killed him."

"Yeh," said Bryer, "Or Sean could have been the killer," he said pointing with his finger. "Just as likely as Sean's wife Trish." He lowered his finger and relaxed his hand, "Or Baxter could have been having the affair with Mary, and he could have killed Bob. As could Angie out of some misguided sense of latent loyalty." He swung round and pointed at Angie.

Angie raised an eyebrow, "Or Mike could be wrong," she said. "This could have nothing to do with Mary Young."

Donna White felt like she was swimming in porridge. This was going nowhere. "And it could well have nothing to do with Anna."

Hanlin turned to look at his interlocutor and stabbed at her with his whisky glass. "Not so sure about that. Could have had everything to do with Anna."

"How so?"

"Anna had something on Baxter. Something she used on him when he tried it on with her."

Vicky was not amused. "He never tried it on ..."

But Hanlin held up his hand to silence her. "We're just looking at possibilities here. So let's assume for a moment that Baxter had had an affair with Mary Young. Perhaps was still having an affair with her right up to the time of her death. Who knows? There are stranger things. Let's assume that Anna knew this and was using the information. Then Baxter might have killed her."

"Which lets me off the hook," said Sean. "Anna was never our housemaid."

Hanlin smiled. "And there was me thinking you wanted to be a suspect. Or what was the point of that dramatic confession from the witness box?"

"The point was that the Assistant D.A. wouldn't listen. But I wanted to help Trish."

"And perhaps you still can." Hanlin smiled. "Let's go back to the beginning."

Someone groaned, but it didn't stop Hanlin. Jane and Marilyn had come into the room carrying little trays with Jane's usual display of exotic hors d'oeuvres. It eased the tension. Though not by much.

But Angie had the bit between her teeth. She wasn't about to let him off that easily. "And all that evidence against Trish?"

"Think about it. Almost any one of us could have borrowed her credit card. Hired a woman that vaguely resembled her. A hooker down on her luck perhaps. You could have hired that Hummer in her name. It's an easy matter then to place a few pieces of hers in the vehicle to be discovered later."

"You'd need her driver's license."

"Perhaps," Hanlin grimaced. "Remember that business of the blood test?"

Everyone watched him now. "In the eighties, Illinois used to have a compulsory blood test for Aids for couples who wanted to marry."

"So?"

"Just a curiosity really. Mary Young underwent a blood test for Aids shortly before her suicide."

"What?" Angie spoke for them all.

"The results were negative. She didn't have exposure to HIV, let alone Aids." Hanlin drew himself up. Like most tall men he had a tendency to stoop. Not now." But she thought she might." He looked around at the company. He had their complete attention. "It is my belief that Baxter and Mary had an affair many years ago, the consequence of which was that Mary became pregnant. How long that affair lasted I have no idea. Years maybe. Long enough for Anna to find out about it in any case. However, I believe that in the past year Mary took another lover."

Hanlin looked squarely at Sean Hartnett. "You, Sean, were her lover. You implicated your own wife. It was you who killed Bob Young, after first trying to frame him by stabbing Father Seb. And it was you who typed and sent all of the anonymous notes. What I don't understand is why you killed Anna?"

Sean, to do him credit, remained calm. "You reach that conclusion on the assumption that Mary must have had a gay lover if she was worrying about HIV? What are you? Homophobic?

314

Why didn't you voice your suspicions earlier?"

Hanlin smiled. "It needed talking through to make it clear. But why did you kill Anna?"

Sean Hartnett scanned the room. He was clearly fighting to hold himself together. Then the fight seemed to go out of him, overwhelmed by the combined weight of their suspicion.

"It was like you said, I was Mary's lover. Just like Baxter but he had stopped seeing her. She was just lonely. People get lonely you know." His eyes roamed the group defensively then fell to the floor. "Anna didn't just see Baxter with Mary. She also overheard Baxter and me arguing over Mary. Mary had discovered that I was bisexual and had told Baxter she was afraid she might have HIV."

Sean paused. The silence in the room was now deafening, with the exception of embers of great eight-inch wide yard long splintered logs crackling away in the fire place.

It was Donna White, Detective White, who broke the silence. She stepped forward and calmly said: "Sean Hartnett, I arrest you on suspicion ..." But that was as far as she got.

Sean had reached into the inside breast pocket of his jacket. The gun he now held was one of the new polymer framed Smith and Wesson pistols. The ten rounds in the weapon were sufficient. He held the gun like he too was pointing a finger. At arm's length, the stainless steel of the slide glistening hypnotically.

Sean was far from sure what he intended to do. He started to move toward the doorway to the sun porch and didn't see Hanlin's dog, Bart, until he stumbled over the languid 80 pound beast. He only lost his bearings for a moment, however. He retained his grip on the pistol. Like all firearms of this type it was designed to be held and fired with one hand.

But that moment of disorientation had been more than enough

time for Angie. She used Sean Hartnett for the focal point for all the misandrist anger she had nursed since Father Seb's betrayal.

Angie snatched one of the heavy Arab coffee pots from the display shelf on the wall behind her. The thing was solid brass. The thud was sickening as she brought it down on Sean Hartnett's handsome head. He twisted as he fell, and she gasped as she heard the crack of the pistol and felt the hot searing pain as the bullet grazed the flesh of her forearm. But she was OK. Sean Hartnett was not. He was flat on the floor. The blow had been harsh and hard. His skull was cracked open by the force. His eyes rolled momently then froze wide like a man in shock and stared past them and moved no more. But he wasn't in shock. Not now. He was dead.

CHAPTER SEVEN: MARCH

For the priest's lips should keep knowledge, and they should seek the law at his mouth: for he is the messenger of the LORD of hosts.

Malachi 2:7

Saturday 8th March: The kitchen of Meadowview Friary's small guest house overlooked one of the smaller lakes that dotted this border area between Maine and Eastern New Hampshire. There were still a few late winter drifts of snow in amongst the pine trees and the mist was down. In the summer, the little lake would be a magnet for children and gnats, the latter in infinite number. But now all was still, almost eerie.

But the kitchen was warm and they sat round the pine breakfast table, scrubbed white from weekly applications of bleach in a ritual imitated in backwoods settlements down through the generations. It was cosy here.

Seb was drinking wine. "My first glass since Christmas," he said gleefully. It was Lent, but he felt no obligation to set aside the alcohol. "It's always Lent here," he said.

Mike Hanlin nodded. He had just had lunch with the monks and had brought a case of Excelsior Cabernet Sauvignon as a kind of 'thank you'. Lentil soup and homemade bread. Healthy, provided you weren't prone to flatulence. Hanlin liked the soup; one of his favorites from his days in the Middle East. But he wouldn't choose it for pretty much every day, which was how it was for the monks.

And these were Franciscans, the supposedly 'happy' monks.

Seb still wore the half smock of a postulant. It made him look like a nineteenth century fisherman. "I get my habit when I take my vows at Pentecost," he'd said. "Then I become a novice."

"You won't be lonely?" asked Hanlin. "Being a monk I mean." Hanlin had noticed how dysfunctional many of the monks were. Seb was an extrovert in a crowd of introverts; many of those who chose the monastic life were socially challenged.

Seb dodged the question to give himself space to think. It was an issue that troubled him, loneliness, in much the same way that younger men are troubled by death. But he wasn't going to share that particular dark night of the soul with Hanlin.

"We Franciscans are friars you know. Not monks. Monks generally hang out in one spot for much of their lives, usually a monastery. Friars can live in monasteries or purpose built friaries or even in the community at large. They get posted hither and thither like soldiers to different barracks. Generally they are more involved in the world than monks." He shook his head. "But to answer your original question, "I am not as lonely as you might think," he looked down at the floor as he continued. "No, for the first time in my life I have a family."

"You didn't have a family before?" asked Hanlin, who thought the response a little weak. Then he added a little pompously, regretting the words as soon as they were uttered, "What was your congregation, if not your children?"

"No, you misunderstand. A family of my own. I belong. A congregation is different. They are your flock. You care for them. But you never really belong to them. You are set apart. Here I belong. This is my family."

Mike Hanlin nodded. "So you'll stick with it? This monastic life I mean?"

Seb laughed. "I think so. I have three years as a novice then I get knotted."

Hanlin raised a questioning eyebrow.

"Three knots in the rope round your cassock means you're a proper monk—or in our case friar—not a mere novice." Seb smiled. "Then another three years and you take your final vows and give away all your possessions."

"Which in your case is irrelevant because you have no possessions. But at any of those points you could leave the order?"

"Yes."

"Will you?"

"Who knows? For now though, this is best for me." He paused. "What happened with Baxter and Vicky?"

"They married in indecent haste soon as Baxter's divorce could be rushed through. Everyone cooperated, Angie included." Hanlin smiled, "Strange how these things work. I hear they've asked Trish Hartnett to be Godmother, even before the birth. Baxter told me he owes her though I'm not entirely sure what he means by that."

Seb smiled in turn. "I can guess maybe. But what happened to Angie in the end?."

"You didn't hear?"

"I don't get that much time for reading papers."

"Following those sad events in my house last December, she was exonerated by the DA. Clearly, she was acting in self-defense and possibly to save any number of us."

Hanlin refilled his friend's glass with some of the red wine he had brought with him.. "Angie and Jennie Moore are lovers now. You know that?" They're living over in Jennie's splendid Cape Cod home down along the Westfield River."

The answer, when it came, was a little mechanical. "I am very happy for them."

"You don't miss her?"

"Of course I do."

"Would you go back to her?" Mike Hanlin asked, pushing at the envelope. "If you could I mean."

"And take the other path through the wood—the road less traveled?"

"No," Hanlin laughed. "The well-beaten path. This is the road less traveled."

"Not for me and my kind." Seb smiled in turn. "And the truth is I can't answer you. I was younger back then, a few short months ago. Less able to cope. I am older now. But time has shifted. She has moved on as have I. And I am happy. And I am happy for her."

Hanlin thought 'the lady doth protest too much' but didn't say so. Instead he asked, "So no might have beens?"

Seb smiled the bitter-sweet smile that comes with memories of what had been. Then shook himself like a dog shaking off the rain. "No," he said. "No might have beens." And he meant it. He had no regrets. Though in his heart he knew that of all the friends he'd ever known over all the years of his life, there'd be one face he'd hold in his mind's eye on his death bed. And that one face, the face he would see in his mind's eye as he breathed his last breath, would be that of his one and only lover, Angie Merrill.

POSTSCRIPT

For he shall have judgment without mercy, that hath shewed
no mercy; and mercy rejoiceth against judgment.

James 2:13

Tuesday 7ᵗʰ June: Springfield had been through a lot the past days. On Wednesday, June 1st a tornado struck, F3 on the Fujita scale which is calculated on the basis of damage caused. And there had been a lot of damage. Downtown Springfield, South End, Maple and Central over to Indian Planes and Eastern portions of the city had all been affected. Cathedral High was pretty much destroyed. Then the tornado continued on to Wilbraham, Monson, and Brimfield some 23 miles distant. The tornado destroyed 42,000 trees and caused $183 million worth of property damage but miraculously only three people were killed and Forest Park was spared. The authorities begged people to go pick up wood. One brave lady lost her life by lying across her daughter to save her. The force of nature is just incredible. In fifteen seconds everything you have may be gone. In some ways, for some of those listed in these pages, there was closure in that moment when the storm came, a sort of cleansing.

But here, now, Seb and the Bishop were in another world—another universe. The friary nestled in a bowl-shaped valley cut like a cirque into the hillside. Fields like rivers tumbled out of the valley into the foot hills and pastures in the adjoining semi-wooded lowlands. The sun beat down intermittently on this refuge.

They were in the garden on the roughly trimmed lawn. The little low gabled guest house with its picture book four windows and door marked one side of the square enclosure. A high beech hedge marked the South and East boundaries of the lawn, respectively, and set it apart from the cloistered friary next door. The West side of the lawn was open to the wooded hillside but for two or three yew trees brought in, no doubt, generations ago as seedlings from Europe.

And from the West the blazing rays of the afternoon sun scorched in on them, making Seb squint if he looked directly at the Bishop, who was seated on a kitchen chair Seb had set there, a small table at his side with coffee. Seb sat facing him on the grass. He wore the full dark brown habit of the novice. Though not yet with the three knots in his belt that signified a Franciscan who had taken full vows.

The other friars were at prayer. Franciscans were no enclosed order, but they still did a lot of praying. The breeze rustled gently through the nearby trees, making the same sound as waves on the shore. But it was hot for all that.

"They'll let me retire gracefully," the Bishop was saying. He was enjoying this visit to his young friend and one-time confessor. It gave him a sense of closure. "After all, it's not as if I was caught buggering the choirboys." He laughed at Seb's grimace.

"I shouldn't joke about it. But really ..." he paused for effect. "Consenting adults is quite a different thing." He sighed. "I shall go to New York. There is an apartment there gifted to the diocese some years ago. I will do a little light work for the local Cardinal, who is a good friend, but generally I shall remain in the background." He chuckled. "And I shall enjoy New York."

"And you? In yourself?" Seb asked.

The Bishop paused before answering. Then, resting back into his chair, he slowly intoned: "Loss of self in self-abnegation is one of the most direct roads to God, and therefore to Christian healing. We are, all of us, preoccupied with our own hopes, our own fears, our own pride, our own prejudice, as well as with our own righteousness, and our own sin; preoccupied with our own

322

salvation for that matter. We find it hard to surrender ourselves to God, to become his servants, willing to live for his purpose. Yet it would be far better for us if we could concern ourselves with the salvation of others, rather than with our own salvation. In so doing we would find our own salvation assured. Whoever would save his life must lose it. We truly must be more concerned about the happiness of others than we are with our own welfare. Paradoxically, it is the only way that we can ourselves find lasting happiness.

"I believe we all need to take this path of self-abnegation. So many of us are seriously bound up in ourselves to the point of self-pity. I certainly was."

The Bishop's measured tones sounded pompous, even to himself, but he continued his monologue regardless: "What are we set against the backdrop of an immense cosmos? Drops of water in an eternal ocean? Even a mere thousand years from now we will all be long forgotten. Our material ambitions are utterly and completely meaningless in the eternal scheme of things. Yet we can, nonetheless, mean something.

"We can contribute to God's plan. But only in so much as we lose ourselves and work to serve God by serving our fellow man. If we do less than this, if we concern ourselves primarily with ourselves, we become like stones cast into the ocean. The water ripples a little, and then is still once again. There is nothing, and we have meant nothing."

The Bishop paused, and as he did so, first he smiled and then he started to laugh. "But me, now, at last, I am content."

Seb laughed in turn. "I am happy for you."

The Bishop raised a questioning eyebrow toward his former pastoral colleague.

"Yes, well, I'll stay with the Franciscans for the full three years of my novitiate, since you ask so pointedly."

"And then?" asked Bishop O'Mally.

"Then perhaps I'll leave the order."

The Bishop opened his mouth in genuine surprise. "Forgive the sense of deja vu," he said.

"Well perhaps not the order. There are lay brothers with the Franciscans. But, in its way, this period is giving me time to adjust to the day when I will no longer be a priest."

The Bishop smiled. "You could always stay a priest and join the Episcopalians. I'm sure they'd be grateful."

"Perhaps they might." Seb sighed. "But, no, that would seem too much like betrayal."

Bishop O'Malley cocked his head on one side. "You intend to try to go back with Angie Merrill?" he asked.

"Heavens no. She has someone else now," he said, not without a hint of bitterness that embarrassed him. "I still think of her though, in ways that are inappropriate for a friar. Even a Franciscan. Quite inappropriate and far too often. Which is why I realize I am no longer fit for celibacy." Seb paused for a sip of his coffee. "I think I'd like to work with some of the Somali, Haitian, and Iraqi refugees back in Springfield, in a perfect world."

The Bishop thought well rather you than me but didn't say so. Instead he said, "Perhaps it is a perfect world. I have contacts in a Springfield charity that does that sort of work. I'll see what I can do when you are ready."

"Thank you, Bishop."

"Patrick. You're not my confessor any longer. Call me Patrick." Bishop O'Malley combed the fingers of his right hand back through his lank black hair. "But I know what you mean about celibacy." He hesitated but then decided to continue. This man knew all his secrets. And after all, what secrets had he? The gossip pages of the 'Springfield Republican' had put paid to those.

"I don't know when I first realized I was gay. I think I always knew I was homosexual. Gay seems so trivial a word for something so seminal. But I've always been gay. Consciously gay since those early embarrassing encounters at school, with other boys. Not that I couldn't appreciate women. I tried, when I was at college.

"There was one of those willowy, pert girls. Her name was Deborah. She was magical. She put me in mind of the Bernini sculpture of Saint Teresa in ecstasy in Rome. We had an affair, a clumsy sexual encounter, but for a while I thought myself capable of being heterosexual. I think she loved me. She took me back to meet her family; but her mother was a WASP. Anglo-Saxon to the toes. She didn't approve of Deborah's pudgy Irish-Catholic boyfriend. And Deborah wasn't one to kick against the pricks. I soon got the message, and we drifted apart. She married a salesman I believe."

Patrick O'Malley cradled his coffee in both hands and sipped at it before continuing. "Then in my last year at college, I at last became able to acknowledge in an overt sense that I was gay. There was a boy. Such a lovely boy. His name was David. And he looked like David as Michelangelo had sculpted him. Exquisite. Gentle. We had a beautiful affair. I was truly in love for the first time in my life.

"Then one day, quite out of the blue, he told me he'd decided to enter the church. I was stunned. Quite devastated. But with time I decided that was what I too must do. I quit college and entered the seminary.

"My family took it surprisingly well. They were good Catholics, after all. And I genuinely felt I was not meant to be part of this world. That God was closing all the doors. That hedonism was to be denied me as was sexual love. That I was being challenged and shown the way."

He sighed. "And all these years I was good. A good priest. A good Bishop. And then there was Sean. Sean Hartnett turned my world upside down. Such a beautiful man. And for the second time in my life, I was in love. And this time I was utterly bewildered. I was not happy but I did not want happiness. To be alive and in love was sufficient, whatever the consequences."

Seb was touched by the Bishop's honesty. In many ways he felt they had both made a similar pilgrimage. "Why does God do this?" Seb said. "Make us as we are? I mean both of us called to serve Him and both undermined by our human frailty. We were made as we are. Is it our fault? Are we weak? Or is it God's fault that we are what we are?"

The Bishop smiled his answer. "Do you think that it is our sexuality that condemns us? Do you really believe that God damns us all on that basis? If Jesus weeps, it is because he watches over a world where men kill one another—a world in which abuse and selfishness is rife—a world whose very fabric is being destroyed by our insatiable lust to exploit its resources. Perhaps God yearns for some resolution to the paradox which is man's love for both creation and destruction. You think that humankind, in some shape or form, will roam the face of this earth a million years from now?"

Seb smiled in turn. "Perhaps. We all walk a knife edge. Continue to progress as we do at present and the human race is doomed. God weeps. But not for us. Not for you and I individually. Our petty sins are not that important."

"Really? Perhaps I contradict myself here but are you so sure we are not each important in the eyes of God? And our happiness? Does that not matter?" The Bishop laughed now. His eyes twinkled. "They say that the Dalai Lama rates happiness high.

For both him and Aristotle before him, to be happy is essential, a key aspect of the purpose of life. For others, including most Christians, what matters is hope, redemptive hope in a better tomorrow in both this life and the next.

"There are so many formulas. There are those who say what matters above all else is to have no regrets. Whereas for others mere endurance is what matters."

Sebastian chuckled, "Well endurance is perhaps more important than happiness or contentment. Cows are content. But a sense of achievement, of fulfillment, that matters to me."

The Bishop sighed, "Exactly Sebastian: hope, happiness, contentment, endurance; these are all important this side of the grave—and beyond. But they are not everything. Somehow I think the essence of it all, ultimately, transcends all that. To have truly lived is everything. To have acknowledged life and grasped it with both hands. To have loved till your heart is fit to burst. That is far, far more than happiness. And more than enough."

www.ingramcontent.com/pod-product-compliance
Lightning Source LLC
Chambersburg PA
CBHW070626260626
47161CB00007B/2601